THE LAST TOP GUN©

A Story of the Last Generation of Navy Fighter Jocks

Dan Zimberoff

Fifty percent of the profits from the sale of this book are donated to charity organizations that support US active duty and veterans organizations.

This book is dedicated to

Eddie, Dinger, Furball, TC, Tuna, Tommy,

and too many other warriors who died in the prime of their lives.

You are not forgotten.

INTRODUCTION

For the first time in his life, the twenty-five-year-old pilot thought that he was about to die—not just cease being—but be blown into smoldering fragments in a fiery explosion at the stern of the steel aircraft carrier. Every neuron in his brain indicated he was flying the F-14 Tomcat directly into a watery grave below, as nothing but darkness loomed outside the windscreen.

Trying to push the thought of death out of his mind, the pilot looked down into the cockpit and struggled to keep the instrument display's needles centered. His breathing and heart rates increased exponentially. At three-quarters of a mile, his backseater keyed the mic and called the ball, "Four-two-seven, Tomcat, ball, four-point-five."

The pilot barely heard the transmission over his own labored breathing echoing in his helmet's earphones. The LSO,[1] Landing Signals Officer, responded by telling the pilot to "keep 'er coming."

Trying to settle his nerves, the pilot sucked in pure oxygen from his mask, looked up, and caught the ship's line-up lights. His nerves did anything but settle, as he still couldn't make out the silhouette of the carrier in the expansive sea of black. His RIO, radar intercept officer, coaxed subtle airspeed corrections from the rear seat like a jockey soothing a thoroughbred.

At a quarter mile, the pilot scanned line-up and angle of attack yet still only saw darkness interspersed with a handful of miniscule, flickering lights. The pitch-black night sky merged with the dark ocean, which melded into the shadowy fantail.

---

1   For help deciphering military acronyms and jargon, please see the Glossary at the end of the book.

The pilot nearly stopped breathing as every cell in his body focused exclusively on raw survival. He and his RIO were seconds away from crashing down upon the pitching, rolling deck of the *USS Constellation*, a mere sixty feet above the frigid Pacific.

Fixating on the ball, angle-of-attack indicator, and line-up lights, the pilot made one last play to the left for a line-up correction before feeling a tremendous jolt and hearing a loud clash of metal as the fighter jet thundered onto the carrier deck. Based solely on rote memorization, he rammed the throttles to military power and was thrown violently forward into his harness straps as the Tomcat's tail hook snagged the two-wire. The fighter shuddered to a stop in merely forty-five feet of flight deck.

It took a full five seconds and two yells over the radio from the LSO before the pilot exhaled and allowed his left hand to move the throttles back to idle. Instantly, his thighs began twitching. He couldn't reflect on the trap, as a yellow-shirt directed him to taxi out of the landing area. The pilot barely swept the wings back before another yellow-shirt instructed him to move them forward for launch. There wasn't even time for the pilot's legs, and now hands, to stop shaking before he taxied the jet into tension for the impending launch. The next three night launches and landings were a blur.

Later that night while reflecting on the evening's carrier quals in the ready room, LTJG Greene smiled widely, remembering that the slider he'd had for dinner before the flight had actually stayed down. After surviving his first four night carrier landings, the navy pilot would be hard-pressed to sweat doing anything else that came his way, including Top Gun training, aerial combat, or raising two teenagers.

1

Commander Greene took a swig from his beer and scanned the lounge. A shroud of dust covered the cruise plaques, photographs, and other squadron memorabilia. The billiards table and shuffleboard sat similarly neglected. The officers' club was a shadow of its former self. Even the odor was different; the lounge reeked of apathy. The recognition that he could never go back to the best times of his life hit the aging pilot square in the gut.

Gulping another mouthful of beer, Spyder could not believe how much had changed in such a short time. Surely, it had been only a handful of years since he had flown to Whidbey and shoved his way past the three-deep crowd at the bar. He could almost hear the sounds of his squadron-mates shouting blithely as they knocked one another to the floor playing crud—beer, bottles, and profanity flung recklessly around the lounge. The pilots' brashness and testosterone were intoxicating. But those days and nights were gone, long gone, and tonight the lounge was eerily subdued.

To a stranger, the Naval Air Station Whidbey Island Officers' Club probably looked like any other worn-down bar with an aged history. To civilian attorney and navy reservist Commander Eric "Spyder" Greene, the club was an icon that held personal history and fond memories in the way of an attic chest. Yet even this veteran combat fighter pilot couldn't hide the grave look of disappointment that swept across his face. The hurt pulsed when he realized fifteen years had actually elapsed since he had been in the club. *Fifteen fucking years! Where had all that time gone?* He took yet another long drink from the bottle and glanced at the bar, eyeing a lone female bartender playing aimlessly with her shoulder-length hair.

As he wondered what had happened to the place, Spyder turned to face two aviators who sat across the table from him. LTJG Grace "Drone" Miller and LT Steve "Rolls" Royce had no clue what the senior officer was thinking, as nearly a generation separated them. Both flyers were young, ready to take the world by the balls, and completely unsure of how to talk to the brooding senior officer.

Drone was surprised to see silver oak leaf clusters on the uniform lapels peeking out from underneath Spyder's brown, leather flight jacket. Spyder exuded the aura of a much younger man, and Drone would have taken the handsome, athletic-looking commander for an officer at least a rank junior. But flying in the navy was a young man's gig, and though he still looked as if he could yank and bank with the best of them, Commander Greene's cockpit expiration date had lapsed.

Spyder ignored Drone's inquisitive gaze and slammed his beer bottle down on the table with a loud *clank*. He stood up abruptly and headed toward a jukebox in the corner of the darkened lounge. He thought the right song might bring him out of his malaise. The pilot had not come to the club to reminisce morosely. Besides, it wasn't in Spyder's nature to mope, period. After a few minutes, the aviator shook his head tersely. Spyder couldn't find a song he liked; hell, he didn't even recognize half the titles in the machine.

Spyder strode back to the table. While sitting down, he made a half-hearted attempt to smile at Drone. Spyder could change moods almost as quickly as his preteen daughter. A few minutes earlier, when he had left so suddenly, Drone thought it was due to something she had said. It wouldn't have been the first time she had ticked off a senior male officer; in fact, some would call it a habit.

"Oh, hell. I've heard from you both what it's like these days for a couple of young naval aviators," said Spyder. "Let me tell you about my time as a fresh-out-of-the-RAG, F-14 driver in Miramar, San Diego."

The flyer leaned forward. "When I joined my first fighter squadron, I learned early on that I couldn't tell strangers what I did; they simply wouldn't believe me. 'Oh sure, of course you fly F-14s in the navy,' they'd say, rolling their eyes.

"Even the women in the bars knew the nomenclature of the jets, probably because of Tom Cruise and the movie. But after failing miserably to convince them I really was a fighter pilot, I relented and came up with various jobs. I was a doctor or lawyer, but those fizzled out early, so I became a teacher, construction worker, and an x-ray technician. My favorite, though, was crossing guard." Spyder flashed a crafty grin.

"Crossing guard!" exclaimed Rolls. "Naw, really?"

"Yes. Why are you laughing, Lieutenant?" Spyder replied in a deadpan tone. "Are you making fun of me and my profession? Don't you realize doting parents place unwavering confidence in me? The very lives and wellbeing of their children are entrusted to me on a daily basis—twice a day, in fact. I care for, protect, and guard with my own life these precious five-to-twelve-year-old beacons of our future. Of course I wear the yellow vest with pride and wave that big red stop sign with zeal. Wouldn't you?" Spyder finished, staring with conviction at the young aviators.

Drone stared back. "Uh, you're serious? You mean to tell me women actually bought that?"

"Yup. They wouldn't believe I was a navy fighter pilot flying off aircraft carriers, but they believed I was an elementary school crossing guard."

The female aviator shook her head in disbelief and mumbled something under her breath. Spyder merely grinned.

The commander's hazel eyes glimmered as he continued. "Wednesday nights at the club were epic. And the flying, you nuke sailors have no idea what it what like to cruise on a fossil fuel flat-top."

"Did they really put fuel in the water tanks?" asked Rolls.

Spyder responded with a hearty laugh. He wondered what this newest generation of naval aviators could possibly know about the "real navy."

"Yup. Put it this way: when the water reservoir got low, you could smell the JP-5 in everything—taste it too." Spyder took a long guzzle from his beer and continued. "You'd take a shower and be afraid to stand too close to the space heater while drying off for fear of torching yourself. And the bug juice reeked of JP-5. Hell—"

"Bug juice?" interrupted Drone.

"Yah, bug juice?" Spyder stared at her with disdain, as if to say, "You're in my navy, right, shithead?" Though the senior officer may have found her marginally attractive in a far different context—in a gym, walking along the beach, or just about anywhere out of uniform—he had zero interest in the pugnacious female sitting across from him at that moment. And with that, Spyder's affable disposition had taken another nosedive. He drained his beer.

"Excuse me." Spyder stood up and started for the head. Rolls nodded while Drone stared blankly ahead.

After a few moments, Drone broke the silence. "That guy gives me the creeps, don't you think?" She grimaced, puckering her lips as if biting into a lemon slice.

"No, not at all. Why do you say that?" Rolls was intrigued by the commander. He wanted to know more about the time that Spyder had spent flying Tomcats. Rolls had noticed the Navy Fighter Weapons School patch on the sleeve of Spyder's flight jacket. Less than one percent of naval aviators made it to Top Gun. Rolls knew that Spyder and the pilots of his era were part of aviation history; a period of absolute male camaraderie and bonding when almost everyone viewed navy fighter jocks as larger than life—combination rock 'n' roll heroes and Olympic athletes in the sky.

"I don't know. I think he's a little ancient and a lot sexist. Did you see the way he rolled his eyes at me like I was in grade school? He doesn't do that to you."

Rolls laughed. "Give the commander a break. When he flew, there were no women on carriers. He—"

"Exactly," interrupted Drone. "That's my point. He's a frickin' dinosaur."

"Well, I'm certainly not going to defend him, but I think you might be a little hard on him."

Drone gave her squadronmate one of her patented stares, as if to say, "Really?"

Rolls knew better than to push the issue. "Think I'll grab another round." He stood up and made his way to the bar. With so few people in the club, the flyer had no difficulty getting the attention of the bartender, who had moved on from twirling her hair to playing a game on her mobile phone.

Walking back from the men's head along a corridor in the back of the club, Spyder looked along walls that held numerous photos and cruise plaques. He paused to view depictions of several missions flown over the years by Whidbey-based aircraft. One photo of an Iraqi power plant destroyed on February 13, 2001, stood out in his mind. He remembered the mission well. Though unusual for an F-14 aviator to act as strike lead for a bombing run, Pop, his executive officer at the time, assumed the role for the mission. It was late enough in the war when the attack bubbas already had earned their war medals and many of the strict peacetime briefing formalities had been discarded. Spyder smiled as he remembered a gem Pop offered during the latter stages of the brief. When asked by one of the A-6 nuggets how they would know if the first bombers struck the target in all of the smoke and haze, Pop replied, "It's a power plant. This is a night strike. If the lights in the city of Basra go out, you hit the damn target—if not, you missed. Questions?" Yep, classic Pop. As dry a sense of humor as the Arabian Desert they were flying over at the time.

Spyder was still chuckling as he made his way back to the table. "Hey, we should get a game of Liar's Dice going?"

"What's that?" asked Drone.

"You're kidding, right? Don't tell me you are a navy pilot and have never played dice. Please don't tell me that."

"I'm not a pilot. I'm an NFO, and—"

Rolls interrupted, "I saw it played a few times in flight school when the instructors were waiting for the weather to clear."

"Ugggh!" Spyder sighed loudly. "OK, there is most definitely a generation gap between us," he complained as he grabbed one of the full beers on the table.

"Thank goodness!" replied Drone determinedly. She had had enough of Spyder and didn't care if he had a great smile and was three ranks her senior. It was men like him who had kept women out of combat for far too long.

Rolls had been around Drone enough to read the expression on her face. As her squadronmate, he knew that he'd better take care of his wingman—wingwoman, wingperson, whatever. Discretion really was the better part of valor, and this was one fight she did not need to take on. He quickly changed the subject.

"Commander, before we got sidetracked, you were starting to tell Drone and me about losing a couple of your squadronmates at Fallon."

Spyder eased back in his chair with a slight groan. There wasn't a need to square off with Drone. It would be pointless arguing with the ambitious officer; she wouldn't give an inch. *Forget it,* Spyder told himself.

"Yeah, we keep getting sidetracked, don't we?"

The senior officer started to recount the tragic flight when he had a sudden change of heart. With another sip of his beer, the Top Gun graduate and combat veteran decided to start from the beginning. Instead of a tragedy, Spyder began telling Rolls and Drone about his earliest days as a burgeoning navy pilot.

2

Spyder heaved the large military-issue canvas flight bag onto the passenger seat of his forest green '67 Vette hardtop. Several beads of sweat trickled off the tip of his nose, as the early morning sun already raised the South Texas temperature to a muggy eighty-two degrees. Spyder had spent the last two years in "the South" yet never acclimated to the heat, humidity, or fried food. He didn't have to try any longer, as he was leaving for California in less than an hour.

The flyer finished loading the Vette and was really beginning to sweat. Wiping his brow with the back of his hand, he walked to the condo manager's office to drop off his key with the secretary, a cute twenty-something-year-old former cheerleader who had flirted incessantly with him the past few months, as she did with all the wannabe fighter pilots. Spyder figured she'd succeed one of these days and marry herself a naval aviator.

The young officer had survived the last fifteen months in Kingsville as an eligible bachelor, confirmed countless times in bars and officers' clubs throughout the southeastern United States. He was going to make damn sure he was single for the next few years so he could experience the complete junior officer experience in the fleet unabashed, unafraid, and undeniably unattached.

Leaving Kingsville and training command with a total of two hundred forty hours in the T-34C Turbo mentor, five hundred ten combined flight hours in the T-2 Buckeye and A-4 Skyhawk, and ten carrier landings under his belt with his hair on fire, Spyder was a pinned naval aviator headed for his dream assignment: flying F-14 Tomcats at Miramar Naval Air Station, proudly known as Fightertown, USA.

The flyer made it across Texas, New Mexico, Arizona, and California with only fuel stops and one overnight in a Motel 6 in El Paso. As the mile markers clicked by on Interstate 10, Spyder became increasingly excited to reach San Diego. When he finally entered the city limits, 1,378 miles and twenty-seven hours from Kingsville, the landscape suddenly sprouted a panorama of densely packed track homes and strip malls. Ten minutes after speeding onto the I-15 freeway northbound, he saw a sign for NAS Miramar. Two F-14s in tight formation zoomed overhead at a thousand feet.

"Man, that's awesome!" Spyder yelled out loud. The pilot nearly rear-ended a pick-up truck as he struggled to keep his eyes simultaneously on the road and the receding fighters. He took the next exit and was at the entrance to the base minutes later.

At the gate a petty officer in a crisp uniform saluted smartly and motioned Spyder to drive ahead. Although a lieutenant junior grade with almost two years as an officer, it took some time for the young aviator to get used to enlisted persons saluting him, especially ones nearly old enough to be his father.

"Can you tell me how to get to the BOQ?" he asked politely. The guard gate looked down at Spyder, checked out the Vette with Texas plates, and replied, "Don't tell me, FNG pilot at VF-124?"

"Yep. How'd ya know?" replied Spyder naively.

"Lucky guess," he said, rolling his eyes. "Take a right at the first light; it'll be on your right about a quarter-mile down the road."

Thanking the petty officer, Spyder tried not to gun the 327 motor as he drove off. He found the BOQ strategically located within three blocks of McDonald's, two blocks from the base gym, and directly across the street from the Miramar O'Club. Daily maid service, a two-minute commute to the hangar, and stumbling distance from the o'club sweetened the deal. At eight bucks a night, life couldn't get any better for the twenty-four-year-old flyboy stationed in Sand Dog San Diego.

After settling into his BOQ room and unpacking his worldly possessions—which took all of twenty minutes—Spyder jumped back into his car, as he wanted to check out the flight line. He hadn't touched a navy aircraft for close to a month. Spyder parked in a small lot in front of the hangar 3, home to Fighter Squadron 124, the Gunfighters, also known as the Replacement Air Group, or RAG. The RAG trained all of the navy's F-14 pilots and RIOs.

Spyder got out of the car and stood staring at the humongous concrete hangar and flight line. *Finally!* He thought of the years and years dreaming of flying reaching back as long as he could remember. The flyer recalled the hundreds of hours building dozens of plastic airplane models as a kid and then working as a teenager at the local gas station, and washing and waxing hundreds of airplanes at the county airport on weekends to save money for flying lessons. He thought of the innumerable hours in the Sigma Chi house at Michigan hammering out calculus and physics problems with his frat brothers and watching *Top Gun* entirely too many times the previous summer. *I can't believe I'm finally here.*

Spyder was far from the type to get caught up in self-promotion, but at that moment, while standing in the morning sun looking out at a flight line full of top-of-the-line fighter aircraft mere feet away, he felt a jolt of pride. He had survived seemingly endless military entrance tests and demanding physical tests. The madness of fourteen weeks of Aviation Officer Candidate School overseen by a cadre of marine drill instructors didn't stop him, as it had for almost fifty percent of his class. Spyder had survived it all, especially two years of arduous flight training culminating in harrowing carrier qualifications. His childhood dream was literally within reach.

As he stood daydreaming in front of the flight line, Spyder remembered being back in Basic Flight Training in Pensacola when he was running near base. Alone, jogging on the sand on Perdido Key, he was thinking of what it was going to be like to actually strap into a jet and fly on and off aircraft carriers when without warning, he simultaneously heard and felt a tremendous crush of air envelop his entire body, nearly snatching the breath from his lungs. He instinctively stopped running midstride and ducked down as a large shadow swept over him. Spyder looked up at the sky just as the dazzling navy blue and gold fuselage and wings of Blue Angel #1 zoomed a hundred feet above his head.

Spyder remained crouched as the thunder from the Hornet's twin F404 engines kept him down. The young officer's mouth literally dropped open as three other Blue Angel F-18s flew by with their demonstration smoke on in perfect welded-wing diamond formation. He slowly stood, transfixed, staring at the jets as they roared down the beach so low he swore he could see sand swept up into the air behind their tails. The deep reverberations from the jet engines continued to resonate in his bones and heart long after the last aircraft disappeared from sight. At that very moment, Spyder knew he was going to make it—he was going to become a navy fighter pilot regardless of the sacrifice. Now, at Miramar eighteen months later, he was eighty percent there, with one more year to go in the RAG before joining his first fleet squadron.

As if on cue, a high-pitched roar shot down from the sky as four navy jets flew in echelon formation a thousand feet overhead. Spyder looked up and saw two Tomcats with two A-4s entering the break. The Tomcats were painted in standard navy gray, squadron markings barely visible, with the two Skyhawks painted in camouflage, one in green and one in desert brown. *How cool is that! They must be coming back from a Top Gun flight.* He did not know it at the time, but Top Gun, the Navy Fighter Weapons School, was located in Hangar 1, two hundred fifty yards to the east. It was the hangar with twenty-foot letters proclaiming "FIGHTERTOWN USA." No mistaking who were the aces of the Miramar base.

Spyder craned his neck trying to see the jets break hard and enter the landing pattern. The first Tomcat snap-rolled and turned, but the remaining jets became obstructed by Hangar 3. He followed the path of the first F-14 all the way to touchdown. The morning sun glinted brilliantly off the canopy as the jet danced gracefully onto the runway, effortlessly transitioning from flight to earthbound machine.

The excited flyer sat in the parking lot for another half hour watching four more flights of jets land and two sections take off in full afterburner. He was about to leave when three petty officers walked slowly by, admiring his car. Spyder heard one of them exclaim, "Those fucking pilots get more Southern California tail than an Eskimo gets icicles." *That's the plan,* laughed the officer to himself. *That is the plan!*

✳ ✳ ✳

Back at the Q, Spyder showered for the first time all day, shaved, and threw on a surf shirt and pair of Dockers. After dragging a comb through his military-cut brown hair, he checked out his face in the mirror. His father's eastern Mediterranean heritage blended sufficiently well with his mother's Scottish roots to produce a face that one former girlfriend had characterized as "ruggedly ethereal." Spyder wasn't sure if it was a compliment or a dig, and still wasn't after looking up the definition of "ethereal" in the dictionary. This same girlfriend also described a skirt of hers as "damask herringbone" material and his favorite light brown sweater as "sienna." But that's what he got for dating an English major in college. Spyder chuckled as he remembered her smile and inimitable vocabulary. He finished drying his hands, slipped on a pair of leather sandals, grabbed his room key and wallet, and headed out the door.

The sun was setting as Spyder approached the entrance to the officers' club. Tiki torches along with a few palm trees lined the cement walkway. About two dozen women intermixed with young navy studs stood waiting to enter the club. A civilian employee checked IDs at the door. As Spyder entered the rear of the line, he felt the slight unease of being alone. The anxiety lasted all of about eight seconds.

"Hey, don't I know ya?" asked a spunky blonde with a definitive southern drawl. Spyder could not figure out if it was genuine or imitation, as they were standing in the middle of Southern California, a million miles from the Mason-Dixon line. The gal was cute, but her friend, a brunette with silky smooth hair flowing over her bare shoulders, was a much more lucrative target for this soon-to-be fighter pilot.

"I hate to say no, but I don't think so," Spyder replied with his best Tom Cruise smile. "I just got into town today."

"Ain't that right?" The blonde turned to her friend. "He's an FNG from B'ville." Her friend gave Spyder a complete once-over from head to toe, smiled, and turned back to face the door. *Swing and a miss.*

"Whoa, do I know you?" Spyder asked the blonde incredulously. "How'd you know that?"

"Our little secret, junior." The blonde smiled broadly and turned back to her friend. She handed a piece of paper and both of the gals' licenses to the bouncer in a t-shirt two sizes too small. Barely glancing at the paper, he was much more interested in the brunette's cleavage. The man with the bulging biceps and atrophied sense of humor waved them inside while peering at their derrières as they walked by. Spyder followed after coolly waving his military ID.

The flyer had been in multiple officers' clubs, having flown to numerous airbases throughout the country while in training command. They were all pretty much the same: large bar with ample cheap booze and one or two draughts, small dining room, and outdoor pool. Inevitably, there was a golf course within a nine-iron approach. Spyder's favorite at that point of his nascent career was the revered Oceana O'Club on a Friday night. Naval Air Station Oceana, Virginia, was famous for its back room, where strippers performed to a standing ovation of aviators at the end of each workweek. While retirees and Rotary Club members ate rubbery chicken and fatty roast beef in the main dining room, a mere fifty feet away, half-naked women danced and gyrated to throngs of active duty naval aviators hooting, hollering, and spilling drinks on the women and themselves. Instructors and fleet pilots from across the country made sure to plan their flights to RON Friday at NAS Oceana.

Upon entering the Miramar club, Spyder immediately glanced upward and saw a large, one-sixth scale F-14 Tomcat model looming impressively over the foyer to the club. Miramar was home to the Pacific Fleet's F-14s, E-2 Hawkeyes, and adversary squadrons Top Gun, VF-126, and VFC-13. The latter three squadrons flew a combination of A-4 Skyhawks and F-16 Vipers. Yep, Miramar was the navy's premier jet-jock base, a true Fightertown USA.

After checking out the Tomcat model for a few seconds, Spyder walked into the main bar area, a large, rectangular room, maybe forty feet by seventy feet. Two Filipina women tended a bar spanning most of the length of an entire wall. Across the opposite wall was a row of windows that looked out over an expansive concrete courtyard. The bar was crammed with close to two hundred aviators and civilian women. A DJ at the far end of the room was mixing music next to a small dance floor. Couples danced everywhere. More aviators and women crowded around several tables playing Liar's Dice. Most every male wore an olive-green Nomex flight suit with squadron patches. The women wore shorts, skirts, and short skirts. Spyder's sandals sloshed as he walked, the soles sticking to the floor due to the mass of spilled beer. The room reeked of popcorn, beer, perfume, and perspiration. Friction between bodies spiked the mercury near ninety, making Spyder smile as he took in the entire scene. *Fucking amazing; they weren't exaggerating.* He had not seen such a large-scale mass of hormones since his college fraternity days—far better than even Oceana.

Spyder squeezed through numerous flyers and women to order a beer at the bar. Many of the gals were tens on his personal scale, and he hadn't even had a single drink yet. The club was a total meat market. After paying for the beer, he spied a door in the corner of the bar near the DJ, and made a dash around a throng of bodies gyrating on the dance floor to a heavy disco beat.

Making his way out of the club and down the five or six steps onto the outdoor courtyard, Spyder felt simultaneous drop-offs of about fifteen degrees and ten decibels. The outside area, maybe twice the size of the lounge, was filled with over a hundred more men and women. He noticed close to a fifty/fifty ratio, much better than advertised. When in flight school, the only negative thing Spyder had heard about San Diego was the terrible ratio of men to women. As a military and defense industry town, the idyllic seaside city had a hugely disproportionate number of single men. Tonight, the ratio appeared close to par and was quite promising.

Several gas tiki torches surrounded the courtyard, and a large fire flickered from a lava pit in the middle of the concrete patio. In mid-August, there was no need for the fire to warm the already balmy night air, but the flames added to the tropical ambience. A low drone of chatter hung in the air, and Spyder started to make his way around the mass of people, looking for any familiar face. Someone tapped his shoulder from behind. He turned around and saw the blonde from earlier in the night smiling mischievously. Before she opened her mouth to say anything, Spyder knew immediately she was well on her way to a booming evening.

"Haay, sailor. Knew I'd see ya again," she said with her strong southern accent, accentuated by at least one too many Sex on the Beaches.

"Hey," replied Spyder. "Good to see you too." Spyder took a step back as the blonde was rocking uncomfortably close to him. He extended his arm. "I'm Eric."

"I'm Lisa." She exhaled audibly and continued, "What's your call sign?"

"Spyder. I got it in flight school. I—"

"Huh?" Lisa interrupted him while scrunching her nose.

"Spyder," he said loudly.

Lisa took a step forward and grabbed Spyder's shoulder with her free hand, spilling her drink. "You're too far away." She smiled provocatively.

Two thoughts immediately popped into Spyder's head: *the night is young, and I can probably do better* competed directly with *she's a sure thing*. In half a second, Spyder's brain considered the size of Lisa's breasts and backside, her level of intoxication, her attractiveness, her obvious attraction to him, the time of night, and the likelihood of meeting another woman in the next ninety minutes. Synapses opened, neurons fired, and, in an instant, a decision was made.

"How about I get you another drink?" Spyder asked as he grabbed Lisa around the waist.

"Sure." She nestled close.

Spyder led Lisa through the crowd and bellied up to the outside bar, adjacent to the large o'club pool. The pool was the site of several late Wednesday night skinny dip sessions. On this night, though, the last thing

Spyder desired was to sober up Lisa or himself through an evening swim. Lisa gave every indication she didn't want to step on her buzz either.

After two more drinks and some small talk filled with liberal sexual innuendo, Lisa led him through the hoard of people to the area of the club near the back bar. The noise in the main bar rose concomitantly with the blood-alcohol levels of the patrons.

Lisa stopped suddenly and shouted in his ear that she wanted to dance. She then began rocking to the rhythm of Modern English's "I'll Stop the World." Though never completely comfortable on a dance floor, Spyder felt sufficiently lubricated to join the more-than-inebriated Lisa. After two more songs, both Lisa and Spyder were dripping with sweat. She grabbed the flyer's hand and led him out of the bar through the maze of people. As soon as they reached the foyer, there was a noticeable drop in temperature.

The petite blonde led Spyder down a hallway near the rear of the club. He noticed a sign for the main dining room and wondered where she was taking him. Lisa abruptly stopped and before he realized where they were, whispered to wait there and stepped inside the women's bathroom. Spyder glanced both ways down the hallway and did not see a soul. Though the o'club was crammed with hundreds of partiers, there was no need for any of them to come all the way down to where Lisa and Spyder were unless one of the other bathrooms became crushed with women. Obviously, Lisa was a regular and knew of the barely used restroom.

A moment later, she peeked her head out, smiled widely, and motioned Spyder inside. He darted inside without hesitation. Lisa met him with a wet, sloppy kiss. Spyder disengaged for a second and looked around. He had not been inside a women's bathroom since his coed dormitory in college. Lisa was all business, grabbed his arm, and shoved him into one of the three stalls. For the next several minutes, Spyder experienced firsthand a new meaning for the navy's definition of "head."

The couple exited the bathroom and had one more drink at the rear bar before Spyder walked Lisa to her car. He tried to convince her to stay the night in his room, but she was insistent about having to get up early to go to work. The pilot had no desire for her to stay and felt relieved when she declined. She gave him her phone number and said to call her. He pocketed it and gave her one last kiss goodnight. They both knew he would never call.

After she drove off, Spyder lingered for a moment. When he was sure she had driven out of sight, he turned and walked back in the direction of the club's entrance. It was only midnight—primetime—and he didn't need to report to the squadron the next day. Damn if he was going to bed, especially with such a target-rich environment back in the club.

3

Spyder censored his story when telling it to young flyers.

"How did all those civilians get on base?" asked Rolls. "You'd be lucky to get your sister on base in today's force protection environment."

"Yeah, ain't that the truth," replied Spyder. "Back then, terrorism wasn't on the radar screen. The squadrons got sponsor cards from base security. You were supposed to give one to your 'guest,' but truth is, the gate guards let just about anyone in. On Wednesday nights, there'd be lines of cars being waved onto the base. If you got to the club anytime after eight, you'd have to park on the grass a block away."

"Wow, different time, huh?"

"Yup. Perhaps it had to do with all of the single women in San Diego, or maybe because the movie *Top Gun* had come out. But whatever the reason, there were a lot of eligible bachelorettes hanging around Miramar week in and week out."

Drone shook her head. She did not want to sit around anymore listening to stories of bimbos who used to throw themselves at the feet of the male fighter jocks. She'd certainly never experienced any guys in bars being turned on by her line of work.

Drone looked as if she could have stepped off a college volleyball court, except for two stark differences—the desert-brown flight suit and flight boots, and the short, light-brown hair she wore in a bob style. She was the youngest of six siblings, and the only female. From a small farming community outside of Oklahoma City, she fought with her older brothers for every scrap of food from the table and attention from her parents. She possessed an intense work ethic and rarely let her guard down.

Drone received her call sign in the Growler RAG because she was one of the first female F-18 ECMOs. Though she initially bristled at the derivation of the moniker—unmanned aircraft—she wore it today more as a badge of honor.

Her squadronmate and drinking buddy Rolls fit the spitting image of the quintessential fighter pilot—blond, muscular, with a fresh-from-the-beach smile and smooth voice that could excite a librarian. In training command he was known as Hollywood—for his movie-star good looks—but his call sign changed within weeks after arriving at Whidbey to "Rolls" for its brevity and sophomoric linkage to his last name.

The perpetual bachelor took full advantage of his transient lifestyle to meet as many women as possible. Rolls had joined the navy to become a fighter pilot—what aspiring naval aviator didn't? But he was selected for EA-6B Prowlers out of flight school instead. Fortunately for him and nearly thirty of his peers, including Drone, the navy's electronic warfare community had recently transitioned from the twentieth century portly EA-6B Prowler to the twenty-first century sleek EF-18 Growler.

Drone still had a full drink to finish so she fired a shot across Spyder's bow. "So, Commander, what was it like flying Tomcats? Aren't they all in museums today?"

The senior officer ignored the dig and launched back into more memories of Miramar.

4

Spyder punched the accelerator, and the Corvette's small block roared to life, capturing the attention of several motorists and pedestrians. He and Scott "Scooter" Olsen were returning to base from Pacific Beach on their last day of leave before checking into the RAG. Scooter, an AOCS and primary flight training classmate, was a sandy-blond twenty-five-year-old from upstate Pennsylvania who lettered in four varsity sports in high school, helping him earn a full NROTC scholarship at Vanderbilt. His old man, a retired navy captain, A-4 pilot, and Vietnam veteran, pinned on Scooter's first set of navy wings for his fifth birthday. Scooter was a gifted pilot and genuine friend. He and Spyder were fiercely competitive, in everything from sports to landing grades to women. It was a friendship forged in ready rooms, golf courses, and countless bars—initially stateside and, as their careers progressed, in exotic ports spanning the globe.

Flying down Mira Mesa Boulevard, the two young flyboys didn't have a care in the world. Spyder downshifted quickly as he neared Miramar's front gate, turning as the light switched to yellow and rapidly stopping merely two feet in front of the gate. The civilian security guard was far from pleased and signaled with his left hand for Spyder to stop, which the naval officer already had done.

"Son, you can't drive that way on base. What's your hurry?"

"No hurry, Sir. The three-twenty-seven got away from me." He gave the guard a serious look, like he was attempting to appease his father, or teacher, or both—failing miserably. "I'll be more careful next time," he added in his most respectful tone, trying not to bust out laughing. The gate guard had seen enough and waved him through.

Before Spyder could drive away, Scooter coughed, "Suck-up!" loudly. Grinning, Spyder continued driving before the gate guard had a chance to say anything more. The banter did not stop there. Spyder turned to his buddy and scratched the side of his face with his middle index finger extended.

"Asshole."

"Dickweed."

"Douchebag."

"Whatever."

They drove back to the Q and agreed to meet in the parking lot at 0645 the following day. They wanted to make sure they got to the squadron at least fifteen minutes early for their "first day of school."

At precisely 0645 the next morning, Spyder drove into the lot and found a parking spot directly across the street from Hangar 3. Before locking the Vette, he made sure he had everything: orders, medical records, service record, training jacket. Scooter cruised up quickly in an adjacent spot, missing his buddy by less than a foot. He jumped out of the Nissan 300ZX with a backpack slung over his shoulder.

"Nice driving, asshole. That navy issue?" asked Spyder in jest, pointing to his buddy's backpack.

"Yeah, like my johnson," retorted Scooter smartly.

As usual, the flyers brushed aside anxiety through adolescent humor. When faced with an uncomfortable situation or emergency, naval aviators often responded with humor—the more juvenile or crude, the better. Humor was one of a pilot's best tools, along with brashness, coolness under pressure, resourcefulness, and, of course, cockiness.

Neither Spyder nor Scooter feared checking into VF-124; it was more excitement—like a first date with an attractive woman. The pilots had heard so much about the RAG that they could not wait to jump in. But Spyder and Scooter were still officially student pilots. The flyers would not be truly liberated and shake off the "cone" stigma—the pejorative used to describe flight students—until they completed the RAG and joined their fleet squadrons, a little over a year away.

The officers climbed the stairs on the outside of Hangar 3 and checked in with the duty officer in the ready room. They were told to muster in an adjacent classroom. Entering, they saw three other junior officers seated behind the first row of desks. Scooter immediately recognized one of the lieutenant junior grades from AOCS.

"Slacker, what's up, man?" Scooter thrust his hand out to the officer. Slacker could have come straight from the beach, white-blonde hair with tanned skin.

"Hey, Two-Step. I didn't know you got selected for Tomcats, too. Awesome, dude!" The two classmates shook hands vigorously.

"It's Scooter—my call sign."

"Cool. From what?" asked Slacker.

Scooter shifted uncomfortably. He disliked recounting the story, but with a burst of testosterone, smiled proudly. "After a rather eventful evening on a cross-country to Pensacola, I walked to the transient flight line and started preflighting another student's T-2. It was early in advanced and I was on autopilot after too many beers the night before. Total brain fart. Anyway, I immediately figured it out and started walking to my A-4. But it was too late; my instructor already had seen me. He said, 'It's the A-4, Scooter.'" The small group of aviators laughed. "It's been Scooter ever since," he added.

Scooter introduced Spyder to Slacker, and the remaining two officers introduced themselves. Within the next ten minutes, seven more officers entered the room. A total of twelve students were in the class, six pilots and six RIOs. VF-124 RAG Class 88-03 was assigned a class advisor, LT Tom "Spud" Riley.[2] He welcomed the class and spent the next four days shuffling them through indoc classes and squadron familiarization.

The students then entered ground school, learning the F-14's fuel, electrical, and hydraulic systems, engines, operating procedures, emergency procedures, NATOPS, flight characteristics, and crew coordination. These courses continued throughout the syllabus, but at week eight, the pilots began a rigorous curriculum of simulator flights. The RIOs

---

2   Balding prematurely, he looked like Mr. Potato Head.

commenced weapons systems training and hit the simulators two weeks later. The aircrew reunited for a one-week ejection and advanced water survival course. It was not until the eighteenth week of training that any member of the class strapped into an actual Tomcat.

✳ ✳ ✳

Spyder was the third pilot in his RAG class to make it into the air. He was scheduled for a FAM-01 flight with Mustang,[3] one of the most revered RIO instructors in VF-124. Even after four and a half months of intensive training in the RAG, Spyder stayed up until 2300 studying the prestart and poststart procedures.

Lying awake for at least another hour replaying the checks over and over in his mind, he turned on the light and checked his cheat-sheet at the nightstand one more time. The training aircraft he flew in flight school were rudimentary compared with the multi-mission, swing-wing, complex Tomcat. It was easy when he could "kick the tires and light the fires," but now he had to go through over fifteen minutes of post-start procedures just to leave the parking spot.

The young flyer awoke at 0515 and could not get back to sleep. Over two decades worth of dreaming was about to turn into reality. He was merely hours away from taking to the sky in a fighter jet. Going over his flashcards several more times prior to showering, his stomach felt like a washing machine on rinse cycle. Spyder knew he shouldn't fly on an empty stomach, so he pushed down two slices of dry toast and half a banana. Though he had yet to get sick in a navy aircraft, bananas were perfect for nerves and an upset stomach, as they tasted the same coming up as they did going down.

Spyder pulled into the squadron parking lot at 0630. He parked the Vette easily at that time of the morning and made his way up the exterior stairwell two steps at a time. As he bounded into VF-124's spaces, he nearly knocked over a petty officer standing just inside the hatch. Down

---

3   Mustang grew up on a ranch and often spoke with a Western drawl, pardner.

the passageway and entering the ready room, he looked up on the large flight status board and goose bumps rose on his arms when he saw his name stenciled in grease pencil with Mustang for the ten o'clock go. After checking in with the SDO, Spyder headed down the passageway to find a quiet classroom in which to cram in some last minute studying. Having the preflight checks down cold, Spyder reviewed his NATOPS emergency procedures several more times before gathering his gear and heading down to the ready room.

Mustang stood at the SDO desk spouting some BS story about the previous Wednesday at the club. The instructor always had at least two or three stories from each night at the club. Mustang was a great guy to have around to shoot the shit in a ready room or bar. He also had a strong reputation as a solid NFO in the cockpit.

A handful of the RIO instructors in the RAG had reputations as being frustrated backseaters who really wished they were pilots. As a result, they often overstepped their role as backseat flight crew and tried to become copilots or even voice-actuated pilots. There were no sticks or flight controls in the F-14's rear cockpit, so the best they could do was run their mouths. For various physical reasons, almost exclusively inadequate vision, these officers were not qualified to become pilots and were slated as NFOs instead. Navy pilots and NFOs had to meet the exact same physiology standards, with the single exception that NFOs could have correctable vision to 20/20, whereas pilots needed a minimum of natural 20/20 vision.

Spyder was glad to have Mustang in the rear seat for his inaugural flight. There were not many, if any, screamers at the RAG. Unfortunately, the same could not be said for the many training command squadrons. A minority of instructors believed it was in a student's best interest to increase the level of stress in the cockpit by adding a frothing, yelling idiot in the back. There was more than enough multisensory stimulation and stress while flying a navy jet; the yelling only resulted in the student tuning out the instructor, or worse.

One resultant tragedy occurred to a primary instructor and student at Whiting Field in Pensacola. This particular navy lieutenant was widely known throughout the squadron as a screamer. The entire command was aware of his personality, including the other instructors, XO, and CO. Nobody intervened, however, as the instructor's demeanor was tolerated, if not tacitly condoned. His yelling continued day after day, flight after flight, student after student. Many students felt a sudden onset of an ear infection or sinus problem the morning of their flight when assigned to LT Screamer, enabling a one-day reprieve and hopeful reassignment to another instructor.

Regrettably for one student, he remained healthy and showed up on time for his brief and flight with the infamous officer. When LT Screamer and the student were returning from a particularly bad flight, the instructor radioed ahead to the squadron and asked for the SDO to pull the student's training jacket. This in-flight request invariably meant the student had "downed" the flight and faced possible attrition from the program. The lieutenant and his student were flying in a T-34 turboprop trainer eastbound at thirty-five hundred feet above a southern Alabama soybean field when two witnesses saw the aircraft suddenly pitch down and nose-dive directly into the ground, killing both aviators instantly. The investigation team could not find anything wrong with the aircraft and determined the plane had been functioning perfectly. From a detailed medical forensic study of the bodies, a pathologist determined the student had had both hands on the stick at the time of impact. Investigators also found the rear canopy had been blown back.

The Mishap Investigation Review Board concluded the student had committed suicide and killed LT Screamer in the crash. The board surmised the student was so upset by the flight and potential down that he pushed the aircraft into a dive. LT Screamer may have tried to fight for the controls and, when he realized he could not overpower the student, unsuccessfully attempted to bail out. The student was a bachelor, but the instructor left behind a wife and two toddlers. The mishap investigation report briefly mentioned the instructor's reputation for intimidation and aggressiveness, but his style of instruction was not considered a contributing factor of the mishap.

There would be no similar experiences in the F-14 RAG, as the instructors treated the students as quasi-squadronmates. They were not quite peers but not cones either. The students lived in a gray world similar to physician interns: past residency, but not full-fledged and licensed MDs.

As he sat with Mustang in one of the small briefing rooms off the main ready room, Spyder felt a level of anxiety just below the excitement and adrenaline that now filled his veins. The brief went well, with Spyder answering correctly each of the questions posed by Mustang.

The flyers headed to the pararigger's shop to gear up. After so many months without flying, it felt great to put on his speed jeans, SV-2, and harness again. He and Mustang reviewed the maintenance book. After signing for the jet, the aircrew exited Maintenance Control and stepped out of the hangar into the burgeoning morning.

As he stepped out onto the tarmac, the flyer was awed by the beauty of the day. The scattered layer from earlier in the morning had burned off, and there was a crystal cobalt sky filled with the early morning sunshine. The hangar faced south across the dual runways with a panoramic view of sagebrush and San Gabriel foothills. The city dump was on the other side of Runway 24, but an onshore breeze kept the stench away from Miramar. As he took several more steps toward the first line of jets parked parallel on the apron, Spyder's nostrils filled with the combined smell of JP-5, oil, and hydraulic fluid. His stomach immediately tightened.

Spyder tensed whenever he neared a navy jet. Sure, he had a set of genuine naval aviator wings—aka Golden Leg Spreaders—pinned to his chest, but he was not really a navy pilot until he had made it to his first fleet squadron. Something about the smell of JP-5 and other aircraft fluids livened his senses, boxed up his mind, and left all ordinary thoughts on the ground. He ignored the fact that his car payment was late, the stock market was down, or his desk was overflowing with paperwork. The navy shrinks called it compartmentalization. It was a mind tool every flyer needed to master or else they could be distracted and lose the concentration required when their life and the lives of their shipmates were on the line. *I'm about to strap on two TF-30 afterburner engines and a sixty-million-dollar jet and ride it to the heavens!*

Airman Rodriguez, plane captain for aircraft 424, walked nonchalantly up to Spyder and Mustang as the aircrew approached the jet.

"How's it going, Sir?" he asked sincerely. Most plane captains felt a professional bond with "their" pilots. Rodriguez was an eighteen-year-old kid from the barrio of Los Angeles who'd joined the navy to escape the grip of Latino gangs. He was a hardworking young man whose goal was to become an officer and fly navy jets one day.

"Pretty good, thanks," lied Spyder. He was far from feeling calm and collected, and when he spotted Rodriguez, his mind shifted into high gear, trying to remember all of the preflight checks he had been up half the night attempting to memorize.

"Understand we're gonna pop your cherry," remarked Rodriguez with a smirk. "If you get hung up on the checks, no problem. I'll work with you, Sir."

"Thanks, but I think I got it," Spyder lied once more.

Mustang and Spyder, assisted by Airman Rodriguez, spent almost a half hour on the preflight before strapping into their respective cockpits. Finally, after pulling the three ejection firing device pins and arming the seat, Spyder climbed into the cockpit. He sat down and adjusted his seat with electronic switches similar to a car. The mighty F-14 Tomcat featured air conditioning, hydraulically powered steering, and electronically adjusted Martin-Baker MK GRU-7A rocket-assisted ejection seats. He then clasped the two shoulder harnesses and cinched the two lap belts. Though uncomfortable, it was best to tighten the lap belts across the hips to minimize seat slap and the possibility of shattering his femurs in the event of ejection.

Next, Spyder began confirming the hundred or so switches and fuses were in their proper places. Rodriguez had done an excellent job and had set all of them properly. The nervous pilot then closed his eyes, took a deep breath, trying to relax for a second, hoping he hadn't forgotten anything.

When it appeared, Spyder was ready. Rodriguez inserted the index finger of his right hand into his outstretched left hand, signaling he was ready to hook up electrical power. Spyder gave a thumbs-up, and the plane captain repeated the signal below his waist to another airman near the jet. A few seconds later, many of the cockpit switches and annunciator lights lit up. Spyder did not hear the usual electrical connection sounds he had in other navy jets he had flown.

Boy, the Tomcat sure is quiet. Continuing to prep for engine start, the fledgling pilot was in his own little world. A minute later, he thought he could hear Mustang yelling. Spyder looked down and turned up the volume on his ICS set, but it still sounded as if his RIO was a mile away. Then, in an alarming instant, it dawned on him, so he reached down and connected the jet's communication cords to his helmet's jack.

"Spyder, how ya hear me?" sprang into Spyder's ears as if Mustang had a bullhorn inches from his head. The pilot jerked his hand back to the ICS knob and quickly turned down the volume.

"Uh, lima charlie, how me?" replied Spyder.

"Same. Have some trouble hooking up, pardner?" chided Mustang.

"Yeah, setting up the cockpit, you know?"

Spyder gathered his composure and performed the engine start and control checks without any further hiccups. Mustang received a good INS alignment from the jet's navigation system. A troubleshooter dressed in white coveralls gave Spyder a final thumbs-up. *We're going flying!*

Spyder returned Rodriguez's salute and taxied the jet forward. Following Rodriguez's precise hand movements, the pilot dutifully started a left turn. In the navy, ensigns up through admirals in charge of multimillion-dollar aircraft loaded with lethal bombs and missiles took direction from eighteen-year-old kids, some of whom barely had their GEDs.

Upon reaching the end of VF-124's parking ramp, Spyder stopped and allowed two A-4 Skyhawks from VFC-13's aggressor squadron to taxi by. He swallowed hard but was having difficulty relaxing. Following the jets to the hold-short for the parallel runways, Spyder listened as Mustang began the pretakeoff checklist. When parked alongside the A-4s, a young airman in coveralls and a "cranial" helmet walked up to the jet and performed a final check before takeoff. After two minutes, the sailor reappeared on the left side of the aircraft, gave a thumbs-up to both Spyder and Mustang, and then saluted the aircrew smartly. Returning the salute, the flyers looked over their cockpit gauges one final time.

"You all set to light 'em up, Spyder?" asked Mustang over the ICS.

"You bet," replied the young pilot anxiously. *Holy shit, this is it!*

"Tower, Gunslinger fur-two-fur, takeoff, in order," radioed Mustang in his deepest southern drawl.

"Gunslinger 424, good morning. Hold short runway two-four right, number two following a flight of two A-4s," replied a petty officer in the control tower.

"Fur-two-fur."

Parked alongside the active runway, Spyder adjusted the A/C, mirrors, and nav aids for the umpteenth time. Looking to his left, he saw the Skyhawk pilot gazing at the Tomcat. Spyder wondered if the A-4 pilot was longing to be back in a fleet Tomcat squadron. Or maybe he was a reservist weekend warrior who flew 737s for a living and had never flown Hornets or Tomcats and eyed Spyder with envy. Or perhaps he had two thousand hours in the dual-seat F-14 fighter and loved flying the simple single-pilot A-4 jet. Whatever the case, the thought kept Spyder from dwelling on his nervous energy and his first-ever flight in his prized Tomcat.

The tower finally cleared the two Skyhawks for takeoff and the pilot waved adios to Spyder. The RAG pilot nodded back as the two A-4s taxied onto the runway and took off simultaneously in a section takeoff. A minute later, the tower cleared the Tomcat to position and hold on the runway.

Spyder could feel his heart pounding beneath the layers of flight gear, harness, and survival vest as he strapped on his oxygen mask and taxied the forty-million-dollar jet forward. He turned the Tomcat to the right and deftly aligned the jet's nose with the runway centerline. *Looks just like the simulator.*

Mustang ran through the most important emergency procedure on the ICS prior to launch. "We snuff a motor, and we're flyin'. You set ten-degree pitch attitude not to exceed fourteen units AOA, stomp rudder on the good tapes, stay in burner or go to mil, gear up, we don't got nothin' to jettison."

"Got it," replied Spyder confidently. Gripping the throttles in his left hand brought a reassuring familiarity. He felt a distinct dryness in his mouth, but the promising fighter pilot was ready.

"Gunslinger 424, cleared for takeoff runway two-four right," a voice from the tower crackled in Spyder's headset. The pilot was so excited he barely comprehended the words. *I'm cleared for takeoff!*

"Fur-two-fur rollin' on the right," replied Mustang.

"Remember, easy with the throttles," Mustang reminded Spyder over the ICS. "Kick in the afterburner in smooth stages."

Spyder's training kicked in. He stayed on the brakes and methodically moved both throttles with his left hand to mil power and checked his engine gauges quickly. The tapes and dials showed normal. The roar of the motors shuddered through the cockpit, and the jet lurched forward like a cat about to pounce. He let off the brakes and moved the throttle around to the first left detent, stage one of afterburner. Systematically shifting the throttles through all five stages, Spyder felt a kick in his ass when each stage fired.

The afterburner nozzles introduced raw fuel into the exhaust of the last section of the TF-30 motors, allowing for enhanced acceleration as flames shot out almost forty feet behind the jet. At night, the effervescent glow made for one hell of a light show, whether off the catapult at sea level or reflecting off a cloud at thirty thousand feet. Today, the afterburners lurched Spyder and Mustang forward incrementally as the Tomcat rumbled down the runway. Gunslinger 424 reached one hundred thirty knots in less than eight seconds. Spyder glanced at the airspeed indicator one more time and heard Mustang call one hundred forty knots—flying speed.

Spyder eased back on the stick, and the Tomcat leaped into the air. Without external tanks or ordnance, the jet was light and nimble. Spyder nudged the stick forward and leveled the jet at approximately fifty feet, momentarily allowing the aircraft to fly in ground effect and accelerate. Hangars and taxiways rushed by his peripheral vision in a blur. He could hear the sucking sound of excited breathing over the ICS—his own.

Rather than perform a low transition on his first flight in the RAG and gain a new call sign, Spyder routinely raised the gear handle and started a rapid climb to twelve hundred feet. The Tomcat responded instantly, soaring upward. He banked sharply right thirty degrees and then a moment later turned left to fly out the two hundred eighty degree radial over La Jolla on the published VFR departure from Miramar.

"Departure, Gunslinger fur-two-fur with you at one-point-two," radioed Mustang.

Seconds later the San Diego Approach controller replied. "Good morning, Gunslinger 424. Positive radar contact. Climb and maintain two thousand feet. Fly the tango-zero-two departure."

"Fur-two-fur," responded Mustang succinctly.

The oxygen mask barely contained the broad smile plastered on Spyder's face. His heart must have slowed to its regular rhythm because he could no longer feel it pounding in his chest. Even after almost two and a half years in the navy and over three hundred flight hours, Spyder could not believe he was actually piloting an F-14 Tomcat—at fucking Fightertown USA, no less!

"Keep your scan outside the cockpit," cautioned Mustang in his western drawl. "Ya get a lot of helicopter and bugsmasher activity along the beach checkin' out the bikinis. I know I would if I could," he added.

The landscape zipping underneath him brought a whole new perspective of the city that Spyder had been getting to know over the past six months. He prized the opportunity to view earth from the vantage of sky and heaven; it made life on the ground seem so simple, almost trivial. In the span of one shoulder to the next, the flyer could see the Mexican border to the south, Los Angeles city limits to the north, and every mile, peak, and highway in between. When at altitude, Spyder often looked down upon thousands of schools, churches, synagogues, businesses, and millions of people and thought how small the planet could be, how the mass of activity of an entire city could be swallowed by the singular image of ground, sea, and sky. Sometimes, when looking out the expansive Plexiglas canopy of a navy jet, Spyder felt as if he were sitting in a pew in direct contact with a higher being.

"Can you believe they pay us for this, pardner?" asked Mustang.

"I was thinking the exact same thing," exclaimed Spyder. "If my harness and flight gear weren't so tight, I'd be sportin' wood!"

"Aww, keep that one to yourself," replied Mustang.

Spyder watched the ocean waves form as the jet skimmed along the coastline above Torrey Pines, where he often surfed in his downtime. At seven miles off the coast, the aircraft was cleared to climb to eleven thousand feet. At three hundred twenty knots, Spyder pulled hard on the stick and reefed the jet upward. His g-suit inflated and began wrapping tightly around his thighs and abdomen as four positive g's pushed down on his entire body, about the same as a twisting rollercoaster, and the aircraft broke through four thousand feet in a heartbeat. *God, I love this!* His smile widened.

In the warning area a hundred miles off the coast, Spyder performed basic aerobatic maneuvers that included loops, Immelmans, inverted flight, and even an impromptu air show alongside a cruise ship likely en route to Ensenada, Mexico. After twenty-five minutes of burning holes in the sky and turning cold air into hot gas, Spyder wanted to go supersonic. Mustang performed a quick calculation in his head and determined if they cut their time in the warning area by several minutes, they would be OK.

With a whoop of excitement, Spyder kicked 424 into zone-five afterburner and instantly turned raw fuel into fireball rings of power and speed. He glanced down and saw the Mach indicator moved rapidly from 0.7 toward 1.0. While passing 0.95 Mach, a strange refraction of light— waves looking like bubbles of water about two feet wide—surrounded the canopy, distorting sunlight, and moved slowly from the rear of the canopy forward. Spyder blinked twice to make sure he wasn't seeing things.

"Mustang, can you see that?"

"That's the shockwave. Happens when the atmospheric conditions are right and there's humidity in the air."

The Tomcat's wings were swept completely back with the glove vanes extended on the leading edge of the scissor wings. Spyder felt as if the jet itself wanted to jump right through the sound barrier.

"Keep the stick steady. You'll likely feel a slight burble as we pass through the number."

Half expecting to hear a sonic boom, Spyder looked back at the airspeed indicator and saw the needle pass through 1.0 and continue to rise. Sure enough, he felt a slight vibration on the stick that only lasted a second. The shockwave along the canopy disappeared as the Tomcat shot past the sound barrier.

Zorching along at Mach 1.2 and thirty-three thousand feet, Spyder became a member of the elite club of supersonic aviators. After a few brief moments of beating the sound barrier, he slowly pulled back on the throttles to save fuel. As soon as the throttles hit the afterburner detents, he was pushed forward in his harness almost as violently as a carrier landing. The force of the deceleration surprised the pilot.

"Oh, man," Spyder exclaimed excitedly. "That was cool!"

"It's even better at five hundred feet whipping up sand over the desert," replied Mustang. "Why don't you coast down to sixteen thousand feet and head to North Island."

Spyder turned toward the coastline. The supersonic sprint had lasted less than two minutes but sucked up over twenty-two hundred pounds of fuel. They would have to fly the remainder of the route at a conservative altitude and airspeed; but it had been more than worth it. The flyers headed out of the warning area and picked up their flight clearance to Yuma via Ramona and Calexico.

Spyder shot a simulated instrument low approach at MCAS Yuma and then climbed out for the twenty-five minute return flight to Miramar. He wanted to fly into the break at five hundred knots with his hair on fire, but the syllabus called for a routine instrument landing. The student flew a flawless TACAN approach to full stop at Fightertown. There would be ample opportunity to scare himself and his RIOs in the break on future flights. Today, he was satisfied with flying the numbers and needles at one hundred thirty-five knots with the wings swept forward all the way to touchdown.

While taxiing to the octagon fuel pit, images of the flight continued to replay in Spyder's mind. A shot of adrenaline could not have raised the budding fighter pilot any higher than his present state—pure euphoria. Spyder could now go to the club and walk the walk, even with only a single F-14 flight in his logbook. It was still more than ninety percent of military pilots. This thrilling experience would forever be forged in his memory. He could not wait to call his parents and tell them about his big day.

Not every flight for Class 88-03 went as smoothly as Spyder's first hop. A month from graduation, something went terribly wrong for one of his classmates. The pilots were undergoing an abbreviated curriculum on unusual attitudes and recoveries that included a flight in the rear seat with an instructor pilot at the controls. The F-14 rear cockpit lacked flight controls, but the student pilots could experience the abnormal flight regimes first-hand with an experienced pilot guiding the aircraft to recovery.

On a typically promising sunny San Diego fall morning, LT Glen "Bucket" Lystrom[4] was scheduled for a 0840 launch with LCDR Tim "Willy" Wilson in the front seat for the unusual attitudes flight. Bucket, a natural stick who had harbored a deep passion for flying since adolescence, was married with a toddler. He excelled at balancing his young family with the rigors and stresses of flight school and now the RAG. He was liked among his classmates, most who overlooked his inclination for looking out for Number One. Not as bad a diode as some, but highly competitive all the same.

Willy and Bucket briefed and suited up normally. They both reviewed the maintenance book for NJ430, and Willy signed for the jet. With CAVU

---

4   His head was as large as a bucket.

weather, both aviators felt pumped to fly on such a glorious day. Preflight and pretakeoff checks went smoothly, with the singular exception of Bucket experiencing some trouble with the highly temperamental AWG-9's inertial navigation system. Willy heard the student pilot mumbling before the jet's nav system finally stabilized and oriented itself properly.

Gunslinger 430 garnered a thumbs-up from the final checker and received immediate takeoff clearance. With a pilot in the rear seat, Willy wanted to show Bucket how the pros did it. In zone-five at one hundred thirty-five knots, he pulled back on the stick and immediately flipped up the gear handle. The weight-on-wheels sensor functioned properly, so the gear did not move until the jet actually lifted from the runway. As soon as the jet climbed, Willy could feel the gear begin to rise, and he ever so slightly bumped the stick forward. From the cockpit, it appeared as if the jet was still on the ground. In about six seconds, Willy and Bucket accelerated to three hundred fifty knots, with the runway rushing by fifteen feet below.

When they were approximately a thousand feet from the end of the runway, Willy yanked back on the stick and instantaneously snapped five g's on the jet, causing Bucket to groan. As the Tomcat shot upward, Willy immediately rolled thirty degrees to the right and manually swept back the wings. *Got to look good!* He immediately rolled the jet back wings level and leveled off at twelve hundred feet.

"God I love this!" Willy exclaimed happily from the front seat.

Bucket was trying to adjust to the discomfort and unfamiliarity of flying in the back seat and barely managed a weak, "Yeah."

Willy was a solid stick—not too conservative yet far from flashy. Occasionally, however, he did something completely out of context, like the sierra-hotel, textbook Fightertown low-transition takeoff just performed for Bucket.

Departing Miramar, the flyers headed to the usual warning area west of San Diego to begin their flight syllabus. Willy first described what he was going to do and quizzed Bucket on the proper recovery technique. The instructor pilot then demonstrated the maneuver. They were through their first series of maneuvers and beginning their second when they heard a slight *pop* followed by illumination of the "Master Caution" light.

Willy leveled the wings and looked down to see the annunciator panel lit up like a Christmas tree. The "YAW STAB OP," "YAW STAB OUT," ROLL STAB 1," "ROLL STAB 2," "HYD PRESS," and a half-dozen other lights shone bright amber. He immediately checked his hydraulic gauges and saw that the combined side was at 2400 psi, or 600 psi below normal.

"We got a problem, Bucket," stated Willy calmly. "Break out your pocket EPs for hydraulics and back me up. I'm showing twenty-four hundred pounds on the combined system. Flight side is fine for now."

Willy began a gentle turn northeast toward San Diego. He could barely make out the coastline in the early morning haze. He reached down and pulled out his own copy of the F-14's NATOPS Emergency Procedures. He had this particular procedure committed to memory but followed his military training and waited for his copilot to back him up.

"Uh…got it," replied Bucket.

"Go ahead."

Bucket and Willy followed the checklist by rote.

"Hydraulic isolate switch to flight," stated Bucket.

"Switching to flight," responded Willy.

"Skipping inflight refueling probe step."

"Right."

"Wing sweep set to twenty degrees," said the temporary backseater.

"Sweep set at twenty degrees."

Willy's voice remained calm, as he had automatically shifted to emergency problem-solving mode. The experienced Tomcat driver and RAG instructor had lost part of his hydraulic system before without major incident. This would be yet another similar occurrence barely registering enough concern to mention over a beer at the o'club later that night. The flyers were ninety miles from San Diego with nothing but the deep Pacific Ocean below.

As a combat aircraft, most of the Tomcat's systems were duplicated in the event of battle damage. The jet's hydraulics were run off the left motor but could also be powered by a backup flight side driven by the right motor, if necessary. At that moment, that's exactly what NJ 430 was doing, as the aircrew shifted the hydraulic load from the bad combined system to the apparently good flight side. Willy minimized hydraulic demand by maintaining a gentle hand on the stick and hardly touching the rudders. He and Bucket would deal with the landing gear later.

"Left inlet ramp switch, uh, to stow," stated Bucket.

"Left inlet to stow," repeated Willy.

"DLC, do not engage."

"Got it."

"We'll want to go to emergency flight hydraulic to high right before dirtying up."

"Yep," replied Willy.

"Land as soon as possible."

"We're headed back to Miramar."

Willy glanced back at the hydraulic gauge and saw the pressure had not moved any lower. He was not sure if the stick felt mushy and did not want to make any extraneous deflections to check. To get to Miramar as quickly as possible, Willy set the throttles to mil but did not want to stage afterburner, as increased speed of the jet would quickly overspeed the wings that were set manually forward. Bucket read the remaining warning and caution segments of the hydraulic system malfunction emergency procedure and asked what else he could do.

"Give me Miramar on the INS," requested Willy matter-of-factly.

Willy then radioed VF-124's SDO on the front radio, reported their problem, and inquired if the maintenance officer was around. A few minutes later, the MO radioed back and they discussed the situation. After quickly reviewing the maintenance logbooks for NJ 430, the MO determined there had been two recent gripes regarding the hydraulic system, but nothing that led either aviator to believe this was going to be a catastrophic failure.

Both instructors agreed to bring the jet back to Miramar, unless the situation worsened, in which case they could take an arrested gear landing at NAS North Island.

The decision was made not to declare an emergency outright but to advise San Diego Approach of their situation and request priority handling. Although the NATOPS manual's emergency procedure stated that under these conditions the aircrew should land "as soon as possible," Willy and the MO decided to overfly the closest navy airfield, North Island, in favor of returning home to Miramar where the squadron and maintenance infrastructure was located. It was a decision that would be second-guessed for a painfully long time.

At sixteen thousand feet and three hundred fifteen knots, the F-14's navigation system showed that they were sixty-five miles from Miramar. Point Loma and the vague outline of San Diego Harbor were in sight. Other than the slight haze, it was a chamber of commerce day. The flyers were optimistic that they would be on deck in less than twenty minutes.

As they crossed the coastline north of Mission Bay, the backup system was performing. The aviators didn't want to say anything to jinx their current stable situation. Among other things, pilots were ardently superstitious. Whatever the cause of the hydraulic system malfunction, the shift to the flight side seemed to have mitigated the damage. In less than twelve or thirteen minutes, they would be on deck with another story to tell about the Tomcat's "fucked-up hydraulic system."

Over Mission Bay with Miramar in sight and their nerves settling, all hell broke loose. Willy noticed the stick had become heavier. He looked down and saw the hydraulic gauge fall below 1,000 psi. The "Master Caution" light flashed again.

"Shit, we lost the combined side!" he declared to Bucket. "I'm turning off the hydraulic transfer pump switch. Hydraulic isolate switch is already at flight, and wings are already at twenty."

"Approach, Gunslinger 403. We're declaring an emergency." A hint of apprehension suddenly appeared in the pilot's voice. Willy was not aware of a single pilot who had successfully landed a Tomcat after losing all hydraulic pressure. He slowly and ever so gently started to put the nose in the center of the hangars.

"Gunslinger 403, San Diego Approach, roger. I understand you are declaring an emergency. State nature of the emergency, souls on board, and fuel."

"We've completely lost our hydraulic system, with two souls and about an hour and a half of fuel onboard." The previous rise in inflection disappeared as quickly as it had emerged. Anyone listening would have thought it was a common occurrence for an F-14 to lose total hydraulic pressure.

"Bucket, we're gonna have to blow the gear down," he stated over the ICS. "Let me know when we reach one hundred ninety knots."

"Wilco."

Bucket had never felt so helpless in his entire life. He was used to being in control, in the front seat, with stick and throttle in his hands. In this instant, he was in the back without any controls, feeling completely vulnerable. At least now he had something to do. He fixated on the airspeed indicator, watching the needle slide below two hundred fifty knots as Willy pulled the throttles back to their stops.

"You may want to tighten your straps and roll down your sleeves," cautioned Willy, as coolly as he could.

"Gunslinger 403, San Diego Approach, you still trying to get back to Miramar? You've got clearance anywhere you want to go."

"Yes, Sir," responded Willy. "I've got Miramar on the nose."

"You're cleared direct Miramar three-five-two degrees at one-seven miles at any altitude below ten thousand feet. The tower's on the line. They're expecting you. They're rolling equipment now."

There was no response from Willy, as he was wrestling snakes in the cockpit. The Tomcat slowed below two hundred ten knots and began rolling back and forth longitudinally and porpoising up and down. In seconds, the jet began an uncommanded constant roll to the right. Willy corrected with the stick and tried to trim the aircraft for level flight. He wanted to thank approach control for their help but continued fighting the controls just to keep the jet somewhat level. Without hydraulic fluid, the flight controls in the cockpit were essentially worthless. The stricken Tomcat wanted to keep rolling on its back. Whatever had caused the initial failure was worsening and having catastrophic effects on everything Willy was trying to do to save the doomed aircraft. The flyers were rapidly running out of time.

The jet performed a complete three-hundred-sixty-degree roll and pitched significantly downward.

"I'm losing it!" stammered Willy over the ICS.

Bucket's stomach knotted; he instinctively knew ejection was imminent.

Without hydraulic fluid or pressure to control them, the large stabilators in the tail of the Tomcat whipped around the airstream like barn doors in a tornado. As hard as he was battling, Willy simply could not overcome rudimentary aerodynamics and physics. The experienced pilot looked for an open field, airport, or any unoccupied land to try to coax the jet to. Tragically, they were over downtown El Cajon and he could only see block after block filled with homes, apartments, and businesses. Gillespie Field sat a mile to the south, so Willy stomped on the right rudder in a desperate attempt to guide the Tomcat to the civilian airport.

NJ 430 performed a last uncommanded roll. This time Willy could not right the jet. He and Bucket were partially inverted and sideways, nose down passing six thousand feet when Willy called for ejection. Bucket was not fully prepared and had been hanging upside down in his straps. His head was turned to the side as he reached down and pulled the lower ejection loop located between his legs. A bright flash burst from below him, which was actually above, since he and Willy were now inverted. As he traveled up the ejection seat rails, all seemed surreal, and time virtually stood still. Bucket's mind focused on minute details: the glove of his right hand unrolled below the edge of his flight suit sleeve, his unfastened kneeboard falling away from his right leg. And then everything went black.

Willy was still fighting for control of the aircraft when he heard a deafening *whoosh* and saw a bright flash below him. He was not prepared for the violent ejection. With both hands gripping the stick tightly when ejection occurred, Willy's arms flailed wildly as he was shot like a cannon ball from the cockpit into the three-hundred-knot wind stream. His helmet ripped off his head and the rush of air instantly became earsplitting. Before he could consciously comprehend what was happening, the pilot felt a sharp pull on his back and shoulders followed immediately by an intense pain that tore through the length of his right arm. He had never felt such excruciating pain in his life.

As the pain became unbearable, the deafening noise ceased, and the world around him suddenly turned serene and quiet. Now floating underneath a parachute toward the ground, Willy glanced to his right and saw the pilotless Tomcat plummet to earth and crash in an enormous fireball a mile away.

Miraculously, it looked as though the crippled jet had missed any neighborhoods. For a few moments, he wondered if Bucket had gotten out, but then was greatly relieved to see a large, orange chute a thousand feet below him and several football fields to his left.

Willy estimated he was three or four thousand feet above the ground. The pain in his right side was debilitating. He looked down and saw a major roadway directly beneath him. With his injured arm and shoulder, there was no way to reach the woven risers designed to steer the parachute. As he continued descending, he saw he was still headed directly for the middle of the road.

Great, I survived an airplane crash only to die by getting hit by a truck! Adding to the danger, there was a large power line that ran parallel to the roadway. The wind was pushing Willy slightly north of the road and directly toward the power line.

OK, electrocuted instead of flattened by a bus.

Willy tried one last time to reach a riser, but the pain was too great. His attempt to steer the parachute by grabbing the left riser with his left hand only resulted in a spinning circle that made him immediately nauseous. Without the ability to slow his descent, Willy dropped to the road like a rock in a sock. He whispered aloud a short prayer, which must have been answered, because an El Cajon police car, with lights flashing and siren blaring, skidded to a stop in the middle of the road to block traffic. As Willy hit the ground not more than ten feet from the cruiser, the officer ran to him and immediately began administering aid.

Bucket was not nearly as lucky. Although he had landed on a patch of grass adjacent to the roadway, the pilot lay crumpled and unconscious on the ground.

Both Willy and Bucket were rushed to Sharpe Memorial Hospital in Claremont, located between San Diego and Miramar. Willy suffered two broken heels, a broken right clavicle, and numerous cuts and contusions. But his prognosis was good. With any luck, he might even be able to return to flying status within six months. Other victims of the mishap were not nearly as fortunate. Two mechanics were seriously injured when the unmanned jet seemingly came out of nowhere and crashed into a hangar at Gillespie Airport in El Cajon.

Bucket lay in ICU with grave injuries. He had a broken spine with significant swelling and trauma. He would be lucky to live—certainly would never fly again—and probably not be able to walk. The ER physicians and neurosurgeons hoped he would survive the golden twenty-four hours.

Within minutes of the crash, the navy's mishap teams sprang into action. Security personnel from Miramar and North Island hurried to the crash scene to guard against anyone trying to remove pieces of the aircraft. A public affairs officer held an abbreviated press conference at the scene. Casualty assistance and crisis officers were dispatched to pick up both Bucket's and Willy's families and rush them to the hospital. VF-124 ceased flying, and a JAGMAN investigation was initiated within an hour of the news reaching the squadron.

While the aircraft crash was playing out, Spyder was returning home from a run. The local news interrupted daytime programming to report live from the crash scene. Turning up the volume, Spyder tried in vain to see what type of jet the reporter was talking about. The television correspondent simply reported that a navy jet had gone down near Gillespie Field in El Cajon. Spyder immediately dialed several classmates. His stomach sank with a sickening feeling.

Twenty minutes later, the PAO officer spoke on television and confirmed it was an F-14 Tomcat from Miramar that had crashed on a routine training mission. She stated that both aircrew had ejected successfully and were taken to Sharpe Hospital.

Spyder jumped in and out of the shower in less than two minutes. He threw on his flight suit and raced to the squadron, leaving a bunch of rubber on the road. He knew VF-124 would be a hive of activity and the staff would not want extra bodies lurking about, but he had to find out who was in the airplane. As he dashed into the squadron spaces, Spyder had flashbacks to a similar scene of a year ago when a flight instructor in his intermediate T-2 Buckeye training squadron died following a midair collision during an ubiquitous peacetime "training mission." Memories of that day and the subsequent investigations and memorial service flooded Spyder's mind as he entered the Gunfighter's ready room.

It took Spyder less than a minute to hear that it was Willy and Bucket who had crashed. The fact that Bucket was married with a young daughter only worsened the sickening feeling in his stomach. No one at the squadron knew how bad Bucket was injured, but everyone agreed it was best if the class didn't rush over to the hospital. A feeling of despair draped over the squadron, affecting officers and enlisted. Class 88-03 headed out of the building to regroup at the hospital at 1900.

Spyder hung out all afternoon and early evening with Scooter speculating on what could have caused the crash. Neither was hungry, so when it was time to go, they drove straight to the hospital. Spyder knew the route as he had been there many times as a monthly volunteer at the adjoining Children's Hospital. When they got to the ICU, class advisor LT Riley, several classmates, and a handful of instructors were milling about outside a separate waiting room. The group sat, paced, and tried to comfort Bucket's wife, Stephanie. A neighbor was taking care of Bucket and Stephanie's daughter back at home.

The class was given permission to see Bucket for a short visit. They walked cautiously into the sterile room and observed a startling scene. Their classmate, lying lifeless on a gurney, was hooked up to a metal halo contraption with steel pins running into his skull, his body leaning at a bizarre upward angle. Several intravenous lines ran into the fighter pilot's arms, and monitors flicked on and off, spitting out electronic data on his vital signs. The eerie silence of the room—broken only by the rhythmic mechanical sounds of a respirator filling Bucket's lungs every few seconds—brought tears to the eyes of most of the military men.

As he stared at his classmate, Spyder thought that just the day before the two aviators had spent the afternoon studying and reviewing recovery procedures. Now his friend, this young man with so much energy, drive, and passion, was lying before him, motionless, needing a machine to breathe.

Bucket died twelve hours later.

Though the navy trained the young officers to march in tight military formations, fly sophisticated combat aircraft, and land on aircraft carriers, the flyers were wholly unprepared to bury a squadronmate. Over the next week, they received on-the-job training that Spyder prayed he would never have to use again. LT Riley was assigned as the CACO, Casualty Assistance Calls Officer, for Bucket's family. Class 88-03 was taken off the training schedule and given seven days special assignment to assist in planning the memorial service and funeral, as well as providing emotional support to Bucket's family.

Six days later, over four hundred officers and sailors filled the Miramar base chapel for Bucket's memorial. The service contained several poignant and memorable comments from classmates and navy dignitaries. Local news channels covered the ceremony and deeply moving missing-man flyover formation by four VF-124 Tomcats.

Spyder and the remainder of the class didn't have much time to mourn following the ceremony, as they left the next day for San Jose, Bucket's hometown, to begin planning the funeral and interment. The pilot was buried with full military honors at a national cemetery eight days after his death. Following the service, his parents held a final reception at their home. Bucket's family and friends bonded with Class 88-03 in the short, but highly emotional, time they were together. Tears slid down several officers' cheeks as they made their final farewells and left for the airport for the return flight to Miramar.

On the plane back to San Diego, Spyder let his guard down and truly felt the impact of Bucket's death. Until then he had felt a responsibility to remain strong and composed for Stephanie and the other members of Bucket's family. At thirty-one thousand feet, while staring up at the heavens from his window seat, Spyder allowed himself to feel the full weight of the grief that filled his soul. He had not been especially close to Bucket, but the young flyer's death was a true tragedy and hit a lot closer than the T-2 instructor's death back in flight school. Spyder knew Bucket quite well and had trained with him every day.

But for the grace of God, I could have been in that back seat. For the first time in his short flying career, Spyder felt pings of doubt and anxiety cloud his lifelong dream. Up to that point, he had felt that if things ever got that bad, he could always pull the handle, give the jet back to the taxpayers, and ride a parachute to safety. Now he wasn't so sure. Sadly, this haunting feeling would be repeated too many times throughout his flying career.

5

Spyder eased back in his chair and sighed heavily. He hadn't told the story of Bucket's death for at least a decade. The former aviator began reflecting on other friends and shipmates who had died in navy jets, when Drone interrupted his somber thoughts.

"That's really sad," she said lacking her usual edge. "Do ya know what happened to Stephanie?"

"I heard a couple of years later that she married another pilot. I lost touch with her after that. I'm sure she moved on. She was intelligent and resourceful, like most navy wives." As soon as it was out of his mouth, Spyder regretted adding his last comment. He meant it as a compliment but was sure Drone would somehow misconstrue the statement.

"What do ya mean by that, Sir?" In an instant, Drone's demeanor changed. Her brow furled and teeth clenched. "What? Only women who marry male military members are intelligent and resourceful? Is that what you're saying?"

"That's not what I meant at all. I said Stephanie and many other navy wives are independent by nature—they have to be with their husbands away so much of the time. Now that there are many more females in the active duty forces, I guess that includes male spouses as well."

Though she was seething inside, Drone merely stared blankly at Spyder. She wanted to do more—glare at him or say something more inciting in response—but instead, the officer demonstrated a modicum of deference. Rolls had watched his squadronmate nearly tee off against the senior commander for the better part of an hour. As a good wingman, he was doing his damnedest to keep her out of trouble, but it was proving increasingly difficult. She was going to blow up at any moment.

Rolls quickly jumped into the conversation. "I've never really thought a whole lot about dying either. I mean, of course, flying a navy jet is dangerous, but I've always felt if you are disciplined and strictly follow NATOPS and regulations, you pretty much minimize that risk, right?"

"Yup. That's the way I saw it," replied Spyder, The senior officer was reluctant to square off with Drone and allowed the conversation to flow back to the RAG. "But Bucket's death gave me a new perspective. No matter how prepared or disciplined you are, sometimes it's simply out of your hands." Rolls nodded.

"At least Bucket died doing what he loved most. He was only a twenty-four- or twenty-five-year-old kid, probably your age, lieutenants, but he died living his dream. How many people live like that?"

Neither aviator replied. The mood of the table had turned somber and contentious. Spyder decided to shift it back upbeat. "Hey, let me get another round and tell you a bit about my first squadron—if you care to hear about it, that is."

"Actually," replied Drone, "I've got to get up pretty early to go hiking with some friends tomorrow morning." She had been looking for the right time to excuse herself. "But it's been, uh, interesting hearing your stories, Commander," she added with an emphasis on "interesting."

"The pleasure's been all mine," replied Spyder with as much mockery as he could muster. "We'll have to do it again sometime." He smiled widely at the young officer.

Though Spyder's sarcasm hit a nerve in the combative aviator, his smile hit equally as hard. Drone didn't want to acknowledge within herself that he had a great smile. Instead, she dismissed the feeling as awkwardly as his derisive comment and merely stood up to shake Spyder's hand. Swallowing hard, she gripped the senior officer's fingers firmly and looked him square in the eye as she politely said good-bye. Spyder shook back equally as hard and continued smiling. *Does this woman ever let her guard down?*

Drone waved casually good-bye to Rolls and wished him a good weekend. She didn't look back as she strode out of the club.

After Drone left the bar, Spyder remained standing. He offered to buy Rolls another beer and headed toward the bartender, who put down her nail file as soon as she saw him approaching. She asked how his evening was going. The flyer told her it was better than expected but quite calmer than he had remembered. The two exchanged smiles, and Spyder returned to the table with a second wind of energy.

"OK, Rolls, I just met you." He paused. "But what the hell. You asked earlier how it used to be in the navy, and I'm gonna tell you. You good with that?"

"Of course," Rolls replied eagerly.

Spyder grinned and began talking in earnest.

6

Class 88-08 was invited to its first boat party to help celebrate Class 87-04's completion of carrier qualifications, or CQ. The timing of CQ was dependent upon the local aircraft carrier's schedule but usually occurred in the last quarter of training for each RAG class. CQ was by far the most gut-wrenching and difficult phase of the RAG. Advanced ACM and aerial gunnery pushed the needle, but the gauge blew past the redline from the arduous training and daunting time behind the boat.

On average, approximately eighty percent of RAG students CQ'd on their first attempt in a Tomcat. By the time the aviators got to the carrier, it was actually their third time at sea, as they had CQ'd in Intermediate in T-2s and again in advanced flight training in A-4s. In training command, it was strictly day traps. But the F-14 RAG included the highly dreaded night carrier landings. In a class of six to eight pilots, usually one or two did not make it on their first attempt. However, the flyers almost always got another try. Washouts for CQ in VF-124 were rare, but happened a few times each year. By the time they reached that point, the navy had invested close to a million dollars on each pilot. Class 87-04 didn't worry about those statistics, as they busted the curve when each of their pilots passed the six day landings and four night traps without concern. Tonight, they were more than ready to party hard in celebration.

LT Harry "Slum" Liddy[5], a member of class 87-04 who had CQ'd earlier in the week, was hosting the party along with his two housemates. By the time Spyder, Scooter, and classmate Bill "Flash" Akins[6] arrived at

5   Kept his living space and office cluttered.
6   Put too much gasoline on a bonfire at a class beach party, singing his eyelashes and eyebrows.

Slum's rambler, the flyers were locked and loaded. They had unknowingly timed their arrival perfectly because as soon as they entered the house, Slum's unmistakable brash New Jersey accent exclaimed it was time for the entertainment to begin. "Yo, dudes!" Slum yelled as he stood on the staircase leading to the second floor. A mix of about fifty RAG students and instructors quieted down. "Bring it on for tonight's entertainment—" He was interrupted by a chorus of catcalls and whistles. "The Banana sisters, Melanie and Marny!"

Slum walked down the remainder of the stairs followed by a large, muscular man in a tight-fitting black t-shirt looking and acting like a nightclub bouncer. The large man stopped near the center of the living room, crossed his arms, bulged his biceps, and looked first to his left and then to his right with clenched jaw and narrowed eyes. Spyder swore he heard the man growl.

The crowd of aviators groaned in anticipation. Finally, two blonde bombshells emerged from the top of the stairs. Both women were in their early twenties and were wearing dolphin-type shorts with very tight white t-shirts. Neither gal wore a bra. Their large, artificially enhanced breasts stood out prominently. It was obvious there would be no teasing during this show—these gals were all business. Marny grasped a bunch of bananas in one hand and a can of whipped cream in the other, while Melanie clapped her hands together riling up the crowd. As if on cue, the entire room of men lurched forward and began yelping.

"Step back!" growled Big Bouncer. He didn't have to yell; his voice was as deep as a Memphis soul singer. "Give the girls some space!" The fellas in front inched backward but were met with push back from the ones behind who were clamoring for a better view.

Melanie and Marny stepped into the center of the room. Even with the sliding glass door and every downstairs window wide open, the temperature in the room was spiking along with the anticipation. The heat didn't seem to matter to a single soul, as the officers waited impatiently for the show to commence. Dance music from a boom box was turned up, which prompted the girls to finally begin.

Marny threw the bananas to Jonesy, a RAG instructor in the front row who howled at his good luck. Melanie walked over, ripped a banana from the bunch, unpeeled it with her teeth, and showed Pie exactly what to do with it. She sprayed Marny's now naked body with several squirts of whipped cream. Throughout the show, the aviators chanted, "Go...go... go...go!" in unison.

With a hundred set of eyes fixated on the two undulating women, Marny and Melanie proceeded to make their way through the five bananas and the complete can of whipped cream. The gals didn't get their nickname for nothin', and Slum and the rest of the RAG officers certainly got their money's worth.

The show ended abruptly as the ladies had a bachelor party in La Jolla to get to. Within minutes following their departure, the flyers quickly rearranged the living room furniture and cleaned all remnants of whipped cream or banana peels. To guests arriving for the party at 2030, there was no evidence of any prefunc activity, other than a barely perceptible sweet smell that lingered downstairs. Obviously, no one mentioned the strippers to the wives or girlfriends who showed up to join their partners later in the evening, having told their significant others that they needed "to help Slum set up for the party" as a way to explain having to arrive ninety minutes early.

At a squadron picnic the next month, Spyder saw Jonesy clowning around with his wife and two small children. From all appearances, it looked like he and his wife were truly happy with a beautiful family. This dichotomy——recalling Pie weeks earlier fondling naked college students in front of a group of peers compared to watching the instructor tussle with his wife and kids at the picnic——was the first of many such instances Spyder observed over his navy career. He figured it was part of the package, similar to cops and professional athletes, the fighter pilot Type-A personality that thrived on excitement, adrenaline, risk, and ego.

The navy emphasized compartmentalization heavily in flight training. Be singularly focused and think of nothing else other than the task at hand while dealing with a fire light at twenty-five thousand feet or trying to locate a target while screaming along at a thousand feet and four hundred twenty knots, inverted and pulling seven g's. Some aviators extended this training beyond the cockpit, like popping your nut with a nameless stranger without giving your loving wife a second thought, or sharing intimacy with your girlfriend and not thinking of that one-night stand in Las Vegas the previous weekend during Red Flag. Spyder wondered if that attitude was a consequence of the career choice or predilection of the type of person who chose the fighter pilot career. Chicken or the egg?

Spyder knew not every naval aviator joined the infidelity club. Plenty of faithful husbands and boyfriends partied hard but never crossed the betrayal line. Some guys had reputations for playing the field, while others remained faithful. Infidelity was neither rare nor common, but lay somewhere in between the moral continuum.

✳ ✳ ✳

Other than the traumatic events associated with Bucket's death, RAG Class 88-03's remaining months in VF-124 passed routinely. As graduation neared, the aviators became increasingly excited. Unlike the military pomp and circumstance surrounding graduation from flight school, completion of the RAG was marked by an informal meeting in the VF-124 ready room. After rudimentary opening remarks by the commanding officer, the Ops O and Spud briefed the class. Spyder and Flash were assigned to the VF-1 Wolfpack, while Scooter received orders to the VF-2 Bounty Hunters; both squadrons part of Carrier Air Wing TWO.

Each officer gave obligatory kudos and thanks for a job well done to their RAG instructors. They toasted Bucket, and then the class dismissed for the last time as a group.

Class 88-03 had spent the last fifteen months joined at the hip, working, playing, and partying together. They'd experienced intense joy, sorrow, and excitement and had worked incredibly hard as a singular unit.

Abruptly, they were now being sent to "the Fleet"; some in the same air wing, while others across the Pacific to squadrons already deployed. Most of the friendships would not endure the test of time, yet the memories of the period spent together as fledgling fighter pilots and RIOs in the RAG would remain with them for the rest of their lives.

7

"Wow, Commander, your time in the RAG was a whole lot different than mine. We had some pretty crazy parties, but the Whidbey Island experience isn't anywhere near the same league as San Diego," said Rolls with a hint of envy. He simply shook his head and smirked. "I think what you experienced must have been the end of an era."

"No, Rolls, just a different experience. No different than comparing college fraternity stories."

"Yeah, I guess."

Rolls wanted to say something to Spyder since Drone had left twenty minutes earlier. "Commander, I know Drone seems a bit overstrung, but she's really a solid officer and good squadronmate. She's probably the best ECMO in the squadron, too."

"I'm sure she is," responded Spyder sincerely. "I think I press a couple of her buttons, huh?"

"Probably. Plus, things have changed some since you were on active duty."

"Ya think?" Spyder replied sarcastically. "Most days I have trouble reconciling today's navy with the one I grew up in. I used to push back and fight the inevitable change but got tired of banging my head against the wall. Now, I simply throw up my hands and commiserate with my buds."

"Hmph," sighed Rolls. He didn't know what to say. Part of him wanted to agree with the senior officer, as he fully understood what it meant to be a member of a fraternity, yet he also had trained with women since his first day in the navy and experienced first-hand the value they brought to the mission. Though the young officer remained somewhat conflicted, he realized the decision had been made, and there was no turning back.

"It seems to work out okay."

There was a long pause as both aviators reflected. After a few moments, Rolls broke the silence. "How'd you get your call sign?"

"Nothing outrageous or infamous. An instructor in advanced blurted out at an AOM that I better focus more—I was like a spider spinning plates. That's all it took."

Rolls chuckled. "I've heard some good ones in my day. How about Clang—clueless arrogant new guy. Or Slaw—shops like a woman."

Both Rolls and Spyder laughed.

"One of my RAG mates know-it-alls was anointed Sage—self-appointed guru of everything," added Rolls.

"I knew a guy who slept constantly on cruise and became Mantress—half-man, half-mattress."

Spyder and Rolls exchanged several more call signs before the senior officer launched back into more stories from his first fleet squadron.

8

The first thought that flashed through Spyder's mind was the ignominy of earning a new call sign. He and Flash were in VF-1 less than a month when they were directed to report to the Ops O. As he sat in front of LCDR Bob "Bourbon" Miller[7] and was told he and Flash were scheduled for a missile shot in a week, instead of undergoing a rush of excitement, the FNG pilot felt pure dread. Sure, not many nuggets were lucky enough to participate in a live-fire missile exercise, let alone an AIM-54 Phoenix shot, but the young aviator's mind immediately went to the many ways he could foul up the shot and become Blanks, Jettison, or Buoy Killer.

Later in the week, after he and Flash had talked about the mission, Spyder relaxed and actually looked forward to the flight with enthusiasm. Jim "Drum" Johnson,[8] VF-1's Executive Officer, and Chris "Pill" Rodgers,[9] a first-tour nugget pilot from Tennessee, were designated back up in the event Spyder and Flash's aircraft suffered mechanical problems or their missile failed. The zero-dark mission brief headed by the XO went smoothly once the aviators cleared the haze in their heads from the early morning wakeup. In addition to standard briefing items, every possible detail was reviewed, including a wide array of comm frequencies and range procedures. As they neared the end of the brief, Flash was on his third cup of navy standard issue sludge and needed to hit the head, quickly. Spyder despised coffee, so instead he sipped a Coke to grab the much-needed caffeine at that God-awful time of the morning. When Drum got to the

---

7 His drink of choice.

8 As a JO, followed the beat of his own drum.

9 Cool, calm and collected, often told squadronmates to take a "chill pill."

section in the brief discussing firing of the missile, both Spyder and Flash looked quizzically at one another. Over the past couple of days, the friends had discussed many elements of the flight but neglected to designate who would press the button. In the Tomcat, either the pilot or RIO could fire an AIM-54. Neither flyer said anything, but they both assumed they would depress the trigger. Now Drum's query left them dumbfounded.

Spyder was never much of a gun guy, but he wanted to take the missile shot. Not surprisingly, the aviators who liked to shoot and blow things up were the flyers who chose air-to-mud aircraft such as the A-6Es or F/A-18s. There was a reason Spyder selected Tomcats—he was a fighter pilot through and through. Notwithstanding his lack of interest in things that go "boom," it would still be a kick in the ass to depress the trigger and watch the million-dollar AIM-54A Phoenix fly off the rail of his Tomcat toward the target.

"Well, er, I guess…," stammered Spyder.

"I guess since I was senior, I was thinking I would," answered Flash.

"Why don't you do rock, paper, scissors for it?" joked Pill.

The XO agreed and refereed the impromptu roshambo challenge. Spyder won with a rock beating Flash's scissors in a heated two-out-of-three match. The RIO capitulated, as long as Spyder bought him lunch after the flight if the shot was successful.

Palpable energy flowed throughout the squadron as the flyers entered Maintenance Control to review the aircraft books. Spyder saw that the ordnance night-checkers had stayed on to assist with the aircraft load-out. Additional personnel from COMFITWINGPAC and VX-4 were also milling about smartly with clipboards in hand to observe the exercise.

After reviewing the logbooks and signing for the jets, Spyder, Flash, Pill, and Drum grabbed the remainder of their flight gear and headed outside. Another perfect day in paradise welcomed them—unlimited visibility with a thin scattered cloud layer and a light and variable breeze from the west. At that time of the morning, sunbursts beamed down onto the tarmac. Long shadows from the hangar spilled over the ground. No aircraft were turning or flying during the 0700 FOD walkdown, so the usually bustling and noisy base sat eerily quiet. Sunking 602, the E-2C Hawkeye designated as in-flight mission commander, had launched forty-five minutes earlier and was likely north of LAX scanning the range area with its powerful APS-145 air-to-air and air-to-surface radar.

Since both Tomcats for the mission were loaded with live missiles—though warheads removed—the fighters were parked and prepped in an entirely different location than VF-1's flight line. Whenever a missile shoot was planned, the aircraft were loaded and taxied to a highly secure section of the base southeast of the runway and adjacent to Miramar's weapons storage area. Spyder and Pill had never been there before and did not realize they had to be driven to the area, about two miles from Hangar One.

"You shittin' me?" exclaimed Pill when a 1977 Chevrolet Impala station wagon approached the hangar. He and the three other aviators were standing around looking like they were waiting for a city bus when Master Chief Horatio Rollins, the most grizzled, raunchy, and feared enlisted member of the squadron, skidded to a stop directly in front of the warriors and yelled from the driver's seat, "Sorry, Sirs, the limo was already booked." The salty master chief jumped out of the car and opened a passenger door for the XO. "It's the missus's, and she said not to dirty the seats," he added in a huff.

Pill turned to Drum. "He's serious? This is our ride?"

"Shut up, Pill," replied Drum curtly. It's what executive officers did—sounded and acted pissed off all the time. "Would ya rather walk?"

"No, Sir." Pill shook his head and then dutifully followed his XO's lead. The four aviators dumped their gear into the back of the station wagon, and then Pill, Spyder, and Flash clambered into the backseat of the vehicle as best they could. It was difficult enough to walk upright in a cinched parachute harness and SV-2 vest, but being wedged in the backseat of a passenger car with two other aviators made the feat downright cumbersome.

After leaving a film of rubber on the paved road at the end of the threshold to Runway 24-Left, the master chief started down a dirt path filled with ruts. The station wagon had over one hundred sixty thousand miles, and the flyers felt each and every one as the car bounced along, flinging them off their seats like a roller coaster each time the vehicle hit another bump in the road.

Spyder's mind wandered to what he had seen and heard about the air force. Unlike the navy, the air force treated its pilots like rock stars. The air force was all about airplanes and the men who flew them. Flying was the primary duty for its pilots and weapons systems officers. The air force paid separate officers to maintain the airplanes and administer the squadrons. Pilots in the air force, at least until they rose to field-grade officer, O-4 and above, focused the majority of their time on becoming more proficient in the cockpit. There were some collateral duties for air force junior pilots, if you could call Charts Officer or Social Coordinator a job. Then again, it was the air force.

Conversely, flying in the navy was a collateral duty. Because every squadron in the navy deployed, to either ships or forward-based airfields, the navy could not afford the space to bring along separate maintenance or support officers. As the US military's sea service, the navy prioritized its spending on ships. Aircraft and aviation personnel were important, but funding did not approach the amount spent on the big grey warships and submarines. The primary duty for an officer in the United States Navy was related to operations, maintenance, or administration. A line officer in the navy was a branch officer, division officer, department head, executive officer, or commanding officer. Flying was done in concert with, and sometimes subordinate to, the officer's primary leadership and management job.

In this vein, Spyder wondered aloud how his air force brethren would handle their current mode of transportation. "No offense, Master Chief, but I can't help thinking about how the air force would be doing this. Right now, there's a flight of F-16 pilots being driven to their aircraft on the Nellis flight line in an air-conditioned crew van. When they get to the aircraft, a tech sergeant will prepare the cockpit for them, help them strap in, hand them their helmet, and wax their dick prior to engine start."

The officers chuckled. "Don't go there, Sir," replied the Master Chief. "You don't wanna know what my ordies might polish if you ask." Even the XO huffed at that comment.

"No problem. I was just comparing the differences between our fine services, and I'm very appreciative of your transportation, Master Chief." The master chief was the most senior enlisted person in the squadron and about the same age as Spyder's father.

Just then, Rollins punched the accelerator as his wife's car rounded a turn at the top of a hill. The Chevy fishtailed in the dirt with the master chief overcorrecting, but he caught the wheel and straightened the car as the road ended onto a paved area. He slammed on the brakes and the wagon skidded to a stop fifty feet from two Tomcats glistening in the early morning sun. Two pickup trucks, a Chevy Nova, and a huffer sat parked near the aircraft.

Notwithstanding the eventful ride to the jets and the fact that each Tomcat was loaded with a live AIM-54A missile strapped under its fuselage, the preflight and pretaxi checks proceeded routinely. The fighters had good navigation and weapons systems, with the missiles and cooling systems indicating up and running. Both aircraft taxied right on schedule.

Due to their location on the field, the flyers had to back taxi across Runway 24-Left and ended up on the opposite side of the hold short for 24-Right. The final checker scooted across the runway in his Nissan pickup truck and after looking over both aircraft, gave the aircrew a thumbs-up. Two VF-1 ordies had driven their civilian pickups alongside and performed the final arming of the AIM-54s. Master Chief Rollins sat in one of the vehicles like a proud mother hen watching his enlisted troops ready and OK the aircraft for launch.

Even though Spyder and Flash were the primary missile shooters, Pill and Drum were flight lead because rank has its privileges. Spyder looked over and gave Pill a thumbs-up, indicating he and Flash were ready for takeoff and everything looked good on Pill's jet. Drum called for takeoff, and the flight of two was cleared to "rock 'n' roll on the right." That's not exactly what the tower controller stated, but that is what Spyder heard. *This never gets old!* The pilot watched and felt the deep vibration of Pill's and Drum's jet blowing down the runway in full afterburner. Ticking off six seconds in his mind, Spyder moved the Tomcat's throttles forward and felt the now familiar five-stage kick in the ass as Wolf 104 lit it up. Eleven seconds later Spyder and Flash were airborne, rising through the crystal clear Southern California sky.

The departure and flight along the standard airways north to Los Angeles went smoothly. *Just another walk in the park.* Spyder flew about five hundred feet in loose trail off Pill. Air traffic control called out numerous traffic, as LAX was busy at 0900 in the morning. Spyder loved hearing Center call the fighters as traffic to the mundane litany of commercial aircraft sharing the sky.

"United 711-heavy, traffic at eleven o'clock, eight miles, one-seven thousand is a flight of two navy F-14 fighters."

That's right, Mr. United bus driver, you've got two shit-hot navy fighters with a couple of Phoeny-bombs on their way to deliver one ton of hate and discontent. Blow that up your one-hundred-fifty-thousand-dollar-a-year Greyhound salary, Boss!

As if he were reading Spyder's mind, Flash commented over the ICS, "Kinda weird, huh, Spyder?"

"What's that?" asked the young pilot as he looked down at the ground, searching for the Hollywood sign—a favorite pastime of his whenever he flew over LA in the daytime.

"Here we are a couple of twenty-four-year-old knuckleheads flying over Los Angeles in an F-14 with a million-dollar missile capable of taking out any aircraft in the world. If the taxpayers only knew!"

"Yeah, Flash, I tell myself that all the time. Now if the young ladies of San Diego would treat us with the same respect, I could die a lucky man." Flash double-clicked on the ICS foot switch, rogering Spyder's comment.

Center vectored the section northwest direct to Whiskey 289. Twenty miles over the ocean, the fighters were switched from LA Center to PLEAD control. PLEAD immediately cleared the flight into the warning area, where Spyder and Flash began performing their precombat or prefiring checklist. Pill switched Spyder the lead as soon as the section entered the warning area. The young pilot was surprised at how nervous he felt. *It's only a stinkin' missile shoot.*

As Flash worked furiously to locate the A-6E and coordinate with range safety, Spyder flew a north-northwest heading waiting for further steering guidance. His mouth was dry and his g-suit felt particularly tight over his abdomen. The old naval aviator axiom rang in his mind, "Better to die than look bad." *Don't fuck this up, Spyder!* Even if the flyers did everything right—flew the perfect profile, performed all the correct cockpit switchology, acquired the target track, made subtle flight corrections during and after launch, and maintained the target all the way to intercept—and the missile malfunctioned, back at the bar or ready room, it would still be Spyder's and Flash's fault.

"Got him!" reported Flash excitedly from the rear seat. Spyder's HUD snapped to life with the target designator jumping to the center left of the aircraft's windscreen. Flash transmitted on PLEAD control, "Wolf two, contact, two-niner-three at one hundred five miles, angels three-zero. Heading one-six-zero at three hundred ten knots."

"That's your bogey," replied Sunking.

"Master arm on," stated Spyder to his backseater. He looked and saw the target designator drop to the bottom of the HUD. *Oh shit!*

Flash had dropped lock and switched to TWS. The missile shot was planned for track-while-scan mode, so Flash was preparing the AWG-9 for the launch. Spyder fixated on the HUD and had forgotten which radar mode would be used for the tracking. In his high-anxiety state, he thought the radar had dumped the target. Within a couple of seconds, the target reappeared on the pilot's MFD as a bogey at a range of eighty-eight nautical miles and the pilot breathed a sigh of relief.

Spyder pushed the throttles forward to increase the Tomcat's airspeed to four hundred knots, giving the Phoenix ample inertia at launch. The AIM-54, also known as the "buffalo" due to its large size, needed as much smack as possible at launch.

"Vampire's away," affirmed the A-6E pilot as he launched the BQM-74E target drone.

Almost immediately, Flash picked up the streaking drone on radar as it accelerated and climbed. The AWG-9 continued tracking the drone as it leveled at forty-five thousand feet and five hundred fifty knots. Within a couple of breaths, the distance already had decreased to sixty-four nautical miles and continued to close at an impressive fifteen miles per minute. Spyder and Flash had less than thirty seconds to maneuver and then stabilize the aircraft and radar system to optimize the shot.

"Confirm green range?" queried Drum from the rear seat of the wing aircraft.

"Green range, green range," replied PLEAD control.

"Sunking confirms."

"Spyder, you got a hot trigger. Your shot," reminded Flash from the backseat.

Spyder didn't reply, as he was laser focused on flying the jet. He gently steadied the target on the nose of the Tomcat, took a deep breath, made sure he had AIM-54 selected on the stick for the tenth time, and pulled the trigger. Before he saw anything, Spyder felt the aircraft shudder. The Phoenix dropped from the aircraft, and four-tenths of a second later, the motor fired. The missile roared from under the Tomcat and left a smoke trail high in the sky. The missile was designed to climb at over Mach 2 to well above sixty thousand feet where the air was less dense, allowing for much greater range, and then dive almost straight down onto its target at over fifteen hundred miles per hour—telegram from Popeye!

In barely more than a flash, the missile was out of sight. The flyers merely observed its exhaust trail make a twenty-degree jog to the left and streak almost straight up in the sky. Within twenty seconds, the line of smoke was gone. The AIM-54A was miles away.

"Twenty-three seconds time of flight," reported Flash from the backseat. Both he and Spyder stared at the target designated on the AWG-9's radar displays. Spyder made sure he kept the Tomcat steady without any abrupt maneuvering. The Phoenix was not truly independent until the last few seconds of the flight, after its seeker-head acquired the target internally. Neither Spyder nor Flash breathed. They remained fixated on the target image flashing across their respective cockpit displays. The time of flight ran down to fifteen seconds. Suddenly, without warning, the target disappeared from the radar display.

"Oh, shit. Lost the target!" exclaimed Flash from the rear seat.

"Fuck!" declared Spyder.

"Come on, baby, come on. Come back," coaxed Flash as he thumbed the radar elevation dial on his radar toggle.

But the target failed to return. The time of flight froze at twelve seconds. Both Spyder and Flash were sure they had screwed something up and would be blamed for the failed exercise. They both had the same simultaneous thought of gaining new call signs. The last thing Flash wanted to report for all to hear over PLEAD control was that he had dropped lock on the target. He stayed silent, sucking up his seat cushion.

"Target has cut and run, missile still tracking," reported Sunking.

Then it hit Flash like a splash across his face. He exhaled loudly. "Hey numbnuts, remember this is a non-warhead shot?" he declared to Spyder over the ICS.

"So it means the missile doesn't go boom. They'll still know we didn't get a hit," replied Spyder from the front seat.

"No, stupid. They turned the drone."

Spyder then realized what Flash had concluded seconds earlier. The flyers had been so focused on the setting up and maintaining the shot that they had forgotten about the recoverable target. "Oh, yeah, duh!"

A wave of relief swept over Spyder. He didn't muck up the shot after all. The missile tracked the target, maybe too well. "It's not going to shoot down the drone, is it?" he asked Flash.

"Hope not. If it does, guess we'll get new call signs all the same."

The XO let Spyder maintain the lead for the remainder of the flight all the way to touchdown. Spyder wanted to request a carrier break on their return to Miramar, but Drum nixed the idea.

Neither Spyder nor Flash received new call signs as a result of the missile shoot—which was a good thing. VF-1's mission was deemed a success, as VX-4 received accurate telemetry data and the AIM-54A guided all the way until ten seconds from intercept, after the drone had turned from the streaking missile. Both aviators received "Boola-Boola" AIM-54 Phoenix patches and plaques from Hughes Aerospace Division, manufacturer of the Phoenix. During his three-year tenure in VF-1, Spyder was lucky enough to participate in two additional missile exercises, both AIM-9L Sidewinder shots, with similar bull's-eye results.

9

Nobody missed the Tomcat Ball, and nobody went without a date. No one. Spyder's squadronmate, Mike "Tank" Rogers,[10] had a plan for getting a date to the ball. It wasn't a great plan but it was better than Flash, who had no plan at all. Tank had been in the RAG class ahead of Spyder and Flash and joined VF-1 about two months before they had. The three aviators were becoming good friends in and away from the squadron. Tank had a reputation as a genuine "great" guy with one significantly deficient character flaw—he couldn't resist psycho women. If asked, Tank wouldn't admit to choosing high-drama/high-maintenance women; they just seemed to gravitate to him.

Two months before the ball, Tank called an old girlfriend out of the blue. He hadn't spoken with Mandy for some time but asked her if she wanted to come out to San Diego for the weekend. The fact that Mandy was engaged at the time wasn't an impediment to either of them. She was thinking of calling off the wedding and agreed to take Tank up on his offer as long as she could bring along her best friend. Being the penultimate "nice guy," Tank yielded happily and paid for both girls' airline tickets. Based on past experience, he figured a weekend with Mandy would be well worth it, and a friend could only add to the fun.

As for Flash, he still hadn't found a date weeks before the ball and started contemplating alternative modes of acquiring one. The idea of hiring a "date" from an escort service was short-lived because he knew if discovered, he'd be ribbed for the remainder of his natural life. And it wasn't only his squadronmates he had to worry about. Growing up in a household where even the pets were female meant Flash always heard what his

---

10   Played fullback at the Academy and ran through the line like a tank.

three older sisters and domineering mother had to say. It was no wonder Flash had joined the navy. The same swagger and confidence he displayed in the cockpit and ready room were conspicuously absent at bars and parties. The young RIO blamed his shyness on the overflow of estrogen in his childhood home.

Short of bringing one of his sisters—a nonstarter—Flash did the next best thing and acquiesced to taking the sister of one of his squadronmate's girlfriend's sister. It was a blind date, as she lived in Indiana. "She's not one of those Midwestern heifers, right?" Flash must have asked Travis "Trapper" Brice[11] a dozen times in the week leading up to the ball. Trapper finally calmed down the flyer by showing him photos of his girlfriend, a slim and attractive twenty-three-year-old medical student. "Her sister's not adopted, right?" badgered Flash after looking at the photos.

The ball was part of a weeklong celebration at Miramar known as Tomcat Follies. As if naval aviation didn't have enough traditions or excuses to party, each community of aircraft celebrated their own individualized festivities. The revelry included flying and simulator competitions, a golf tournament and sporting matches, usual Friday evening fracas at the o'club, and Saturday evening ball at a local hotel. Other than those deployed at sea, the entire West Coast F-14 community would be at the Saturday night formal affair.

A few hundred aviators and their dates packed the San Diego Marriott. Nearly everyone had reserved a room for the night, with each squadron reserving blocks of suites to continue socializing, drinking, and dancing into the early morning hours. The ball always created a great source of entertainment; one never knew where the liveliest of the entertainment would come from. In years past, wives and girlfriends usually tamed the party-hearty aviators, but on occasion it might be the young wife cooped up with toddlers for several months who needed to let loose, or the new girlfriend who drank her nervousness away, losing articles of clothing along with her balance as she stumbled off the dance floor, knocking over

11   Caught a No. 3 wire with his left foot and planted his face on *USS Constellation* during CQ—OK 3 wire.

the admiral's wife while simultaneously sending her date into Tomcat Ball lore.

The evening presented the perfect opportunity for the aviators at Miramar to show off their wives and girlfriends. Spyder invited his current casual—a pretty yet vapid waitress he had been dating for the past three months. Although Pam had a tendency to drone on, she looked great in a dress, and that was more than worth putting up with for her slight quirk. When he saw her slip into her gown in the hotel room before they headed downstairs, Spyder knew he had made the right choice.

The two made it to the ballroom as the last minutes of the formal cocktail hour ticked off. The band started off with top-forty hits, giving the impression of a high-school prom. Once inside the grand ballroom, however, that perception quickly faded with the sight of smartly dressed officers in their choker white uniforms. The walls of the large room were covered with each squadron's drinking banners, along with various naval aviation and F-14 Tomcat posters, adding to the military decor. A small table with place setting, bible, and officer cover sat near the entrance representing the fallen sailors and aviators who would never attend another event. It was a navy tradition to include such a memorial at each formal military dinner. At the end of the evening during the toasting period, glasses would be raised to these fallen heroes. As they walked by the solemn table, Spyder started to explain the significance of the setting to Pam, but she stared blankly ahead, so he stopped midsentence.

As the band continued to play, the couple looked around for the Wolfpack tables. They made their way through the throngs of partygoers, chairs, and tables looking for the red and grey balloons signifying the squadron's colors. Spyder finally spied the balloons and quickly recognized his Skipper and XO. They walked over to the lead table and after the obligatory introductions of Pam to Pole[12] and Drum, and their wives, Spyder led her to the adjacent table where Trapper and Flash sat with their dates. Flash looked like a kid on Christmas morning—Trapper hadn't lied.

---

12 Early in his career was tall and skinny as a bean pole.

Susie was as pretty as her sister. Spyder shared a look with Flash that said, "Dude, you scored big time."

The evening was looking as promising as the dates. After further introductions, conversation flowed easily. Two chairs sat conspicuously empty, as Tank and his date had yet to arrive. After hearing so many stories from Tank, the officers around the table looked forward with great anticipation to finally meeting Mandy. Her reputation most definitely preceded her.

As if on cue, a woman's loud cry of "Fuck!" emanated loudly throughout the ballroom. The band had suddenly stopped playing, and the large room quieted instantly. Over five hundred heads turned in unison to the dance floor and saw two women and a junior officer in the midst of a struggle to keep standing. The scene that ensued was a comedy of errors. The first young woman in a dress one size too small clutched the officer in an attempt to regain her balance. It didn't work. She was short, but by no means petite, so when she grabbed hold of his arm as she started to fall, he lost his balance as well. The silenced crowd gasped and then laughed as both the woman and officer plumped onto the ground. The second woman then tugged at the officer's waist and yanked him upright. Startled, he let go of the first woman, who promptly went down on her backside with a very loud *thump*.

"Fuck!" she cried out again.

Her second expletive garnered further laughter from dozens of partygoers. Someone from the Wolfpack section yelled "Tank!" proudly. The band quickly resumed playing, and the three guests gathered themselves sufficiently to stagger toward the Wolfpack den.

"Guess that would be Mandy," said Flash.

"Guess so," responded Trapper.

Tank and his dates quickly bypassed the Skipper's table and made their way directly to the two empty settings alongside Pill's wife.

"Hey, guys. Guess we're a little late, huh?" announced Tank sheepishly. "Mandy dislocated her arm getting out of the shower, and then it took both girls a while getting ready," he continued as if it were the most perfectly normal explanation for their inauspicious entrance.

Hearing her name, Mandy staggered forward and stuck her hand out to no one in particular. "Hi. I'm Mandy, and thish ish my friend Barb. We're from Baltimore." The two girls plopped down onto the two empty chairs, leaving Tank standing awkwardly alone.

"It washn't that bad. Happens all the time, and Barb popped it back into place in no time," added Mandy.

No one knew quite what to say, so Pill took over and suggested that Tank ask a waitress to bring another place setting. He moved closer to his wife to make room and put distance between himself and the two inebriated guests. Karen, Pill's wife, was not as fortunate. Her seat, next to Mandy's, was going nowhere. Tank ended up squeezing in next to Pill while everyone else adjusted to having the evening's opening entertainment sitting with them. Pam took the opportunity to excuse herself as she headed to the restroom.

The Wolfpack officers' fund had purchased four bottles of wine for each table, so the alcohol flowed freely. Conversation at the table started up again as if nothing peculiar had happened. Just another day in the life of Tank and the junior officers of VF-1.

Mandy and Barb quickly monopolized the conversation. Mandy, with her drunken Maryland accent, told humorous stories, including how she and Barb had flunked out of cosmetology school together. Gretchen, trying to get a word in, interrupted and told a story about an anatomy class at Indiana med school. It was an amusing anecdote about a missing cadaver's especially sensitive body part that was found the next weekend in a fraternity's punch bowl during rush week.

When Pam finally returned to the table, everyone was laughing, but she didn't seem to notice. Whispering in Spyder's ear, Pam told him that she needed to talk. Spyder reluctantly walked out into the hallway with her. Pam told him her old boyfriend had been in a motorcycle accident earlier in the afternoon and was in the hospital.

Spyder was incredulous. He could not believe what he was hearing. Pam might have been acting odd since the pool earlier that afternoon, but this ex-boyfriend thing came completely out of left field. Here he was at the Tomcat Ball, in front of his peers and superiors, and his date was blowing him off before the salmon was even cold. The flyer suggested he drive Pam to the hospital, but she declined, saying they both had already had too much to drink. Spyder conceded, as he didn't see any alternative short of forcing her to stay, and he would never do that. He felt miserable as he walked her through the lobby. Pam gave him a peck on the cheek as she climbed into the waiting taxi. She sat down in the back seat and in a moment was gone. Spyder knew he would not be hearing from her later that night.

He turned and quickly walked away, too embarrassed to even look at the hotel doorman. *Three hours ago, we're shagging in the hotel room, and now I get dumped before dinner with a fuckin' kiss on the cheek. Seriously?*

Spyder flirted with the idea of returning to his room to watch TV but opted to rejoin his squadronmates and continue drinking. By the time he made it back to the table, the entrée had been removed and was being replaced with dessert. As he stood wondering if the evening could get any stranger, he noticed a commotion a few feet from the table. Pill, Barb, and Tank were bending over something on the ground. As he walked closer, he saw Mandy writhing on the floor. Dumbfounded, Spyder stopped and watched the surreal events play out before him.

Barb and Tank were arguing over who would help Mandy. Tank tried comforting Mandy, who sat upright, apparently in some degree of pain. Spyder peered closer and saw Mandy's left arm hanging grotesquely out of its shoulder joint. Her open-shouldered green dress offered a full view of her obviously dislocated shoulder. The band, oblivious to the scene unfolding before it, continued to play loudly. Half the dinner guests in the vicinity of Mandy stared at the developing scene, while the other half were unaware, or too drunk to care.

Finally, Barb knelt down and grabbed Mandy's drooping arm. Scampering behind her friend, she put a knee along Mandy's back. The two women struggled against one another. Whatever Barb was trying to do wasn't working, as Mandy grunted several times. By now, most guests at the nearby tables were staring. Barb laid Mandy on her back, slipped off a high-heel shoe, and stuck her bare foot in Mandy's armpit. She grabbed Mandy's dislocated arm with both hands. Anticipating what was about to occur, several women watching from the adjacent tables looked away. Barb gained the needed leverage and quickly jerked Mandy's arm. A loud *pop* could be heard over the live music. An audible moan followed from numerous onlookers. Mandy immediately jumped up, straightened her dress, and plopped back down at the table. Barb stood up, dusted herself off, readjusted her strapless bra, and sat next to her friend.

"See? It happens all the time," stated Barb triumphantly to the group. "You just have to know what to do."

The two women continued talking as if nothing unusual had happened. Tank looked around at the others and shrugged, as if to say, "Yeah, that's my girlfriend."

"Guess I missed some excitement, huh?" said Spyder as he finally sat down at his chair.

Pill filled Spyder in on the details and told him that on the way back from the bathroom, Mandy had fallen yet again and dislocated her chronic shoulder.

"Isn't that special," commented Spyder dryly. He didn't have it in him to be interested.

When Flash asked about Pam, Spyder explained that she had a family emergency and had to leave. Flash knew better, but left it alone. The group returned to their half-eaten desserts and continued chatting idly. Spyder barely picked at the piece of chocolate cheesecake in front of him.

The band picked up the pace, and Barb seized the opportunity to ask Spyder to dance. He had absolutely no interest in her but gave in and was led onto the dance floor. After just two songs, Spyder had had enough and took Barb back to the table. He arrived as Flash was walking up without Susie.

"Dude, really, she is hot!" exclaimed Spyder, not giving a damn whether Barb heard.

"Yeah, no kidding." He paused. "But she's acting strange. I think she's hitting on Trapper." Flash went on to tell Spyder how his date had been paying a lot of attention to her sister's boyfriend and was out dancing with him and her sister now.

"She totally blew me off the last dance."

"Wow, weird night," commented Spyder. "You and me both." He started to tell his friend about Pam, but decided to get another beer instead.

Spyder got up and started making his way to the bar when he realized that he hadn't asked Barb if she wanted anything. He turned back around and arrived at the table in time to see Gretchen dragging her sister off the dance floor.

"You bitch! I can't believe you did that!" yelled Gretchen. She clenched both fists hard at her side.

"Oh, back off Gretch, I didn't do anything," responded Susie as she turned away from her sister.

Before Susie could take a step, Gretchen grabbed her sister's arm and swung her around. Susie pulled away and gave Gretchen a *don't-fuck-with-me* look. Flash, always the gentleman, stepped in between the two and asked Susie if she wanted to get some fresh air. He looked around for Trapper, who was nowhere in sight, and guided his date toward the hallway and away from the still fuming Gretchen.

Spyder followed his buddy to the hallway bar and stood behind as Susie tried to rationalize her actions. Flash turned around to Spyder and rolled his eyes. The aviator was held hostage in line listening to too many details about Trapper, when out of nowhere, Gretchen appeared and grabbed her sister, swung her around and got back in her face.

"Don't you run away from me!" Gretchen shrieked.

Flash tried to step back in between the sisters, but Susie already had started to take a swing at her sister that hit him flush in the face instead. The two siblings were in an all-out catfight with Flash stuck in the middle. Managing to avoid a flurry of fists and fingernails, Spyder moved in hot to assist his wingman and adroitly grabbed Gretchen around the waist, pulling her back, while Flash took Susie and forcefully guided her away. Susie's dress hung in a way that revealed one of her bare breasts. Before Flash could say anything, Susie adjusted her top and turned back toward

Gretchen to start in again. Two other officers stepped in to help Flash and Spyder keep the women apart.

Without asking, Spyder escorted the still-fired-up Gretchen back to their table, the whole time listening to her berate her sister. Spyder didn't say a word and was relieved to see Trapper sitting at the table talking to Karen, completely oblivious to the entire scene that had just played out in front of dozens of his peers.

"Hey, babe. What's up?" he asked innocently. *Oh, dude! If you only knew.*

Once Gretchen was reunited with Trapper, Spyder started back to the bar for the third time in ten minutes. From two tables away, he could still hear Gretchen's angry voice now aimed at Trapper. Spyder shook his head for what seemed like the hundredth time that evening. *What's next? The Skipper's wife doing a striptease on stage?* Nope. Only Flash, standing in a corner of the hallway trying to console Susie. When Spyder got within a few feet of him, he could see a gnarly scratch with a good amount of blood on his buddy's neck. One of the girls must have accidentally clawed him. Susie didn't seem to notice because she continued her own sibling rant.

After hearing more than enough, Spyder decided to assist his wingman and took him aside.

"Dude, this is a totally insane night. Why don't you blow her off, and let's hit the admin upstairs?"

Glancing over his shoulder and seeing Susie's distraught face, Flash confirmed there was no way he was going to get any that night. For the first time, he also felt the sting of pain as he dabbed his neck with a finger. He gladly turned and walked away with Spyder, missing the quizzical expression on Susie's face. She stood in the now empty hallway, mouth agape in midsentence with no one left to hear her complain.

Before leaving, Spyder finally made it up to the bar and ordered that round. The two flyers started to make their way out of the crazy scene when they ran into Tank, who had Mandy on one arm and Barb on the other.

"Guys, want to join Barb, Mandy and me for some drinks in our room?"

Flash and Spyder politely declined, not knowing if their squadronmate was serious, and afraid to find out for sure.

The two flyers continued toward the lobby and room elevators. Spyder chuckled and put his arm around his good friend; "Hey, the way this night's going, we probably should have joined Tank and his two-woman traveling circus, eh?"

"Yah, no," replied Flash. "Let's skip the admin and head down to the Jacuzzi. Maybe there are a couple of lonely swimsuit models from LA looking for two single naval aviators."

"Yeah, counting on it," commented Flash.

The squadronmates stopped off at the admin to grab a handful of beers and headed down to the pool. Shockingly, no swimsuit models awaited them. Instead, the two friends sat at the side of the pool with their feet in the water, bemusedly rehashing the entire evening. It certainly was a Tomcat Ball to forget—more infamous than epic.

10

"Whoa!" exclaimed Rolls. "That sounds like one helluva night. I've had my share of dates gone bad myself, but that was righteously bad."

"Yup, righteous," Spyder mimicked while laughing to himself.

After both officers paused to drink from their beers, Rolls asked Spyder if he always wanted to be a pilot.

"Absolutely." The question brought another smile to Spyder's softening face. "My parents told a story about me as a three year-old boy constantly running around flapping my arms like a bird. Running and flapping at a playground. Running and flapping down the sidewalk. Running and flapping down the supermarket aisle. And any time a plane flew overhead, I looked up and stared, enthralled at the sight and sound of an aircraft—any aircraft. Still do. Guess I was born with flying in my blood."

"Yeah, me too." replied Rolls. "My dad worked as a flight instructor for a second job. I had my first flight as a three-month-old when my mom was away and my dad couldn't find a babysitter. She still glares at him to this day when he tells the story."

Spyder laughed. "I've never met your mom, but I know that glare; seen it myself from my ex on more than a few occasions. Remind me to tell you later about my then three-year-old daughter and the Mike's hard lemonade. Who knew hard lemonade meant alcohol? And who drinks that crap anyway?" He shifted slightly and continued explaining that no one in Spyder's family flew or was in the military; not even a distant cousin or uncle.

He wasn't sure how or why he got the bug, but it sure bit hard. A young Spyder worked two jobs in high school saving money for a car and then flight lessons. He could be found at the local airport most every weekend washing airplanes and helping load small cargo planes in exchange for rides. On his seventeenth birthday, Spyder took the FAA check ride and received his single-engine rating the first day he was eligible. He flew as much as he could in high school before he woke up one day to find sports and girls had suddenly become a higher priority. But his true mistress, flying, took him back with a vengeance in college when he worked at an FBO at Ann Arbor Airport.

"What about your family, Commander? You mentioned kids."

"Twelve year-old daughter, Erin, and fourteen year-old son, Andrew—Drew for short. They're doing reasonably well, considering the divorce."

He started to say more but stopped. A pang of guilt persisted. Spyder knew he hadn't done anything wrong but still had trouble acknowledging he couldn't salvage his marriage. He wasn't used to failure and dissolving a marriage after fourteen years felt as bad as it gets.

"Sorry to hear that," said Rolls. "I've heard way too many stories of navy divorces already."

"Yeah, seen my share as well. Deployments are hell on marriages," added Spyder.

Before becoming more melancholy, the senior officer resumed telling the young aviator about his JO experiences in VF-1.

11

At the conclusion of Carrier Air Wing TWO's Fallon det, VA-145's "Poker" was anointed a new call sign: "FUSBAAC," a nickname well earned in naval aviation's tradition of mucking things up. The Ops Officer hated the call sign, which made the moniker stick indelibly.

Along with the squadron's NAS El Centro det completed six months earlier, the three-week Advanced Integrated Air Wing Readiness Training det, shortened to simply "Fallon," was the highlight of the eighteen-month turn-around cycle for almost every naval aviator. Navy Strike Warfare Center, or Strike U, was located at NAS Fallon in central Nevada fifty-five miles east of Lake Tahoe. Strike U's full-time instructors were the most proficient and highly trained strike aviators in the navy, comparable to the better-known Navy Fighter Weapons School, or Top Gun, instructors.

FNGs to CAGs looked forward to the balls-to-the-wall flying and superior liberty around Fallon. Short of yanking and banking over Beijing or Tehran, aircrews could not experience more realistic combat flying anywhere. The det included twenty days of flying hard and partying harder. The majority of missions were flown during the day, which left many evenings free for personal time. Aircrew flew daily, and except for a handful of missions or the last week's comprehensive final exams, there was sufficient time to prepare for the next day's flight without cutting into the all-important liberty calls.

The aviators flew over expansive sections of desolate and inhospitable terrain. When the weather cooperated, Fallon rivaled the most satisfying flying anywhere. Rugged, snow-capped mountains jutted out from a backdrop of crystal clear blue skies. Flyers scooted around and through numerous low-lying valleys and over jagged mountain peaks. The area was sparsely populated, so aircrew could bust the number in designated areas without worrying their sonic booms would damage property or livestock. Flying over and near Fallon made a pilot feel like the luckiest chap in the world. Yet when the weather turned inclement or the clouds thickened—which occurred often in the fall and winter months—the exact same terrain turned menacing and sometimes deadly.

The flying mirrored the liberty around Fallon—paradoxical. The women in proximity of Fallon were as ragged as the hills and almost as large as the cattle. Fortunately, the bright lights and cool casinos of Reno were only thirty miles down Interstate 80, and the ski slopes of Lake Tahoe were less than a three-hour drive away. Equally alluring for some sat the legendary Chicken Ranch, a mere forty-minute drive from Fallon's front gate.

Almost all of the missions were flown in the Fallon Range Training Complex, a sprawling ten-thousand-square-mile military operating area located in and above the desert, far from dense populations and FAA air traffic control. Once wheels-in-the-well, pilots had extraordinary freedom to zorch and scorch. For Spyder and the rest of the VF-1 and VF-2 fighter guys, missions varied in complexity from 1v1 ACM hops, to 4v2 Mig Sweep flights, to comprehensive Alpha strikes incorporating fifty or more aircraft in a single coordinated mission.

Several of the training missions proceeded through the Fallon electronic warfare range in GABBS Central. The EW range was a 30 nm-by-10 nm rectangle area filled with threat jammers and acquisition and fire control radars designed to closely simulate the bad guy's electronic weapons systems. Aircrew started at the border of the range and flew through it, while maneuvering dynamically in an effort to avoid getting "shot down" by simulated missiles or bullets. Aircraft were lit up by a myriad radars and jammers and had to yank, bank, dive, climb, roll, pull, and fly as close to the ground as possible—commonly known as "nap of the earth" flying—without auguring in. Qualified navy pilots were allowed in peacetime to fly within two hundred feet of the ground.

Flying at two hundred feet and five hundred knots, rolling upside down and right side up several times while pulling six and a half g's, left little margin for error. As if this environment were not challenging enough, radar warning sensors and receivers whined and warbled loudly, snuffing out aircrew radio calls between flight leads and wingmen. Simultaneously, the flyers visually scanned for bogeys, avoided clouds, maintained sight of the strike package and wingmen, continued to navigate through jagged terrain, located and acquired multiple targets, ensured proper weapons system switchology and then maneuvered the aircraft for precise weapons release—all without crashing into the rocks or getting shot down by enemy AAA, SAMs, or fighters. Upon successfully completing his mission and following egress from the target area, a pilot or NFO could literally wring his flight suit of perspiration, even in the heart of winter.

The FAA and navy shared a strict policy of no alcohol eight hours prior to flight, more commonly referred to as the "bottle to throttle" rule. The tenet was mostly followed by navy aircrew, as no sane person would risk life or career, or the lives of his shipmates or civilians, by being intoxicated while strapped to a sixty-million-dollar jet; though many an aviator strayed into the proverbial gray area. Briefs were ordinarily scheduled two hours before takeoff. At Fallon, for some of the more complex missions, the briefs began three hours early. That meant an aviator could hit the bar at 1900 and drink straight through until 0100, be driven one hour back to Fallon, sleep for three hours, and awaken at 0500 for a 0600 brief and 0900 takeoff—not a wise or recommended practice, but one that occurred on occasion during El Centro and Fallon dets.

* * *

The first night in Fallon, Spyder and Flash were awakened at one in the morning by a loud ruckus next door that included banging and muffled shouts. Not wanting to miss out on the fracas, the roommates rushed into the BOQ's passageway in time to see Mauler[13] in a headlock from Trapper,

---

13 Had large hands which he liked to use to put his squadronmates into headlocks.

with both flyers falling to the floor. The squadronmates were locked in a heated wrestling match and continued grappling for several more minutes before Mauler finally got the best of Trapper, forcing the larger but less adroit squadronmate to call "uncle." Apparently, Trapper had tired of Mauler's propensity for expelling gas and had flung the room window open. Mauler didn't appreciate the cold and took offense. The squabble started as a pillow fight and quickly degenerated into WWF grappling out in the p-way.

The det featured many similar squadron juvenile escapades and incidents. The Q was more akin to a college fraternity house than a military barracks, especially considering the copious amount of beer jammed into the mini-refrigerators in many of the rooms. Large-scale food raids, wrestling matches, hallway basketball tournaments, and other testosterone-laden competitive antics sprung up throughout the det. Surprisingly, there was minimal inter-squadron sniping. The air wing extracurricular activity consisted primarily of beer calls at the club and a few evening or weekend road trips. Because Fallon consisted primarily of strike or attack-centric training, the fighter jocks took a back seat to their attack brethren, which was fine, as it allowed for maximum nonflying "training" opportunities.

✳ ✳ ✳

Near the end of the three-week evolution, Spyder and LT Steve "Austin" Reynolds[14] were crewed together for a major strike. The comprehensive mission brief was conducted by Poker, a department head from VA-145, one of two A-6 Intruder squadrons in CVW-2. Bucking for an XO tour, Poker was the consummate professional and well liked throughout the air wing. He knew the primary portions of the mission cold. Clearly, he had not gone skiing over the weekend, as the VF-1 JOs had done.

Following the main strike brief, the F-14 aircrews broke off to conduct smaller element briefs focusing in greater detail on the air-to-air

---

14 Was a huge fan of WWF and "Stone Cold" Steve Austin.

fighter mission and tactics. After the briefings and reviewing the maintenance book for Wolf 105, Spyder headed out to the flight line while Austin grabbed a candy bar from the geedunk machine. Spyder heard the whine of two huffers starting a flight of A-6s in the adjacent row of parked jets. There must have been a hundred ground crew scrambling over and around twenty jets within a stone's throw of Wolf 105. The flyer could almost reach out and touch the energy and excitement that filled the air preceding the large air wing simulated strike.

As he climbed the boarding ladder on 105, Spyder paused to look around. He saw sunrays dancing off the majestic snowcapped peaks of the Stillwater Mountains. Inhaling heartily, the pilot took in the splendid crisp mountain air. Looking back onto the fuselage and wings of the mighty Tomcat shimmering in the early morning sun, the young flyer felt grateful to have an opportunity to fly this marvelous fighter aircraft across two states, through the EW range, and then cap off the mission by dogfighting F-5s from the aggressor squadron.

After reflecting on his good fortune, Spyder manned up, started up, and fired up without a hitch. He and Austin were dash-three behind the Skipper and Slum and in front of Trapper. After watching the first two jets rumble down the runway and ticking off six seconds in his head, Spyder released the breaks and roared down the right side of the centerline in full zone-five afterburner. Austin was hollering from the backseat like a cowboy on a bull—the RIO loved flying more than many of the pilots in the squadron. The Tomcat broke free from the runway, and Spyder bunted the nose forward in low transition. He flipped up the gear handle to avoid overspeeding the landing gear and as the jet accelerated through three hundred knots, reefed back on the stick. The F-14 streaked upward like a raped ape and Spyder banked the jet hard on its right wingtip. Austin grunted from the backseat as the g-meter passed 5.0.

"Hey, Austin," remarked Spyder over the ICS. "What d'ya think, we shoulda gone to grad school, huh?"

"Yeah," Austin played along after catching his breath. "Wish I were on Wall Street right now."

Spyder eased the throttles out of burner but kept them at the mil stops to expedite joining on Pole and Slum. He wanted to impress his skipper and anyone watching the join-up from the ground. Within forty-five more seconds, he was welded to Slum's wing awaiting the signal from Pole to kick both wingmen out to cruise formation.

The flight began impressively and proceeded as planned until a minor navigation SNAFU occurred. A planner transposed two numbers and inadvertently set a low-level waypoint twelve miles west of its intended location. Such a mistake could prove disastrous, as twelve miles could place an airplane into a mountain or through a tower. But in this particular part of the desert, twelve miles would not have mattered much except for a top-secret air force airfield, which sat four miles west of the incorrect low-level waypoint Foxtrot.

When CVW-2 was at Fallon, the existence of Tonopah Airfield remained a well-guarded secret. Part of Area 51, the airfield was a top-secret section of the Nevada desert not acknowledged officially by the air force or US government. As disclosed publicly later that year, Tonopah was home to the 4450th Tactical Group and 37th Tactical Fighter Wing, evaluators of the F-117A Stealth Fighter. Lockheed's Advanced Development Projects, known as the Skunk Works out of Burbank, California, developed the top-secret fighter/attack aircraft in the desert. The defense contractor flew transport planes in the middle of the night from southern California directly to Tonopah. To keep the footprint as small as possible, the air force shuttled close to a thousand personnel on transport airplanes to and from their homes on Nellis Air Force Base just outside of Las Vegas to the top-secret base. The personnel had to sign confidentiality agreements stating they could not disclose what they were doing, not even to their own families.

Saying the air force was anal about keeping Tonopah below the radar screen was like saying the former Soviet Union kept a lid on their press corp. During the indoctrination briefs on the first day at Fallon, CVW-2's aviators were briefed to stay well clear of Area 51. If an aircraft inadvertently strayed into the prohibited area, the crew was to land ASAP, remain in their cockpit, and await further orders. Batteries of I-Hawk SAMs were rumored to ring the prohibited airspace with orders to shoot down unidentified aircraft. A navy A-7 Corsair allegedly flew into Area 51 in the early '90s and was immediately intercepted by two F-16s and escorted to Nellis. The A-7 pilot was rumored to have been debriefed for two days before the air force finally released him—and he was a US Navy attack pilot!

It was in this context all nineteen navy aircraft of Poker's strike package violated the 10 nm no-fly zone around Tonopah when they mistakenly overflew the erroneous waypoint Foxtrot. Though no air force fighters scrambled to intercept the wayward navy aircraft, as soon as he landed, Poker was laid into by the base commander. The formal mission debrief was delayed twenty minutes as CAG was fully briefed on how the screwup occurred.

A three-star air force general had called the Vice Chief of Naval Operations within minutes of the incursion, thinking the navy was conducting a mock strike on Tonopah. The proverbial "shit" quickly rolled downhill and before the first strike aircraft had even landed back at Fallon, the phone rang and the base CO was on his feet at attention on the phone with the navy's top aviator, a three-star admiral at the Pentagon. General Quarters finally downgraded when the brass determined none of the strike package aviators saw anything out of the ordinary—or so they said.

The remaining five days of the det flew by, as Spyder and his VF-1 squadronmates participated in three more complex Alpha strikes. The last two days of Fallon consisted of a graduate-level final exercise that included a forty-eight-hour consolidated simulated war. There was little free time away from the cockpit or planning rooms for any aircrew during the last days of the det. Suffice to say Poker's strike was the highlight of CVW-2's Fallon det and provided ample ammunition at Kangaroo Court the last evening of the exercise. It was during the festivities that Poker became FUSBAAC, short for Fucked Up So Bad An Admiral Called.

12

"You know, an instructor of mine back in Meridian told some crazy stories of weird things the air force was doing in the desert near Las Vegas," stated Rolls. "Later on when the government finally acknowledged Tonopah, he let it slip that he had been assigned there as a navy rep working on the F-117 project. He was originally working on the A-12, and when the navy cut the program, the air force used his expertise on the one-seventeen."

"Yeah, it was a real shame when the navy axed the A-12. That was a turning point in naval aviation's history. From that point forward, we relinquished the heavy bombing mission to the air force," said Spyder. Though a quintessential fighter pilot, even Spyder had been disappointed when the navy cancelled the A-12 and yielded all heavy bombing missions to the air force. A decade later, the navy got rid of the A-6. The all-F-18 Hornet navy meant a significantly reduced power projection role for the sea service from the mid-1990s forward. The admiral ring knockers who led the navy conceded naval aviation no longer constituted a power projection force. Instead, the lighter, more limited air assets could act only as a contingency element, a sort of 9-1-1 reactionary force until the air force or army arrived in theater to conduct the heavy lifting.

"Tell me about it," added Rolls. "But at least us electronic warfare aviators started getting EF-18 Growlers last year. Nice to get out of the ugly and slow Prowler."

Spyder nodded in agreement.

There was a pause in the conversation that was finally broken by Rolls. "So why did you get out, Commander?"

"Hmm. My original plan was to serve my minimum obligation and then punch out and go to law school. But I was having so much fun I signed up for an additional tour. I got to about the ten-year mark, make-it-or-break-it time, and it coincided with President Clinton taking office and the transfer of power to the Democrats. I saw the writing on the wall regarding major defense cutbacks. Realize, Rolls, I joined the navy in the mid-'80s during the Reagan era when money was flowing into the military like a prostitute on payday. Flight hours and weapons proliferation were at high points.

"I already had participated in the first Gulf War. Most military men of my period trained and trained and trained for combat but never actually got to the show. I got there. But unlike professional sports, where athletes train and dream about making it to the World Series or Super Bowl and then want to repeat or three-peat, no one I know who has experienced combat wants to relive the experience. Having already flown in the real deal, I didn't want to go back to training, training, and more training. Turns out, I was mobilized for Iraq Two as a reservist. I saw that war from a computer terminal eight thousand miles from theater."

Rolls nodded his head. "Yeah, I caught the very tail end of that fight. Just mopping up on my first cruise."

"Be thankful," commented Spyder.

"I guess," replied Rolls reluctantly. "Ever regret getting out?"

Spyder sighed heavily. He paused before continuing and thought immediately of his two children. No, he didn't regret leaving the navy, but he'd always miss the flying and the camaraderie. When he thought back on his ten years of active duty, the flyer didn't recall the monotonous days steaming circles in the North Arabian Sea in a hundred ten degrees and ninety percent humidity. He didn't relive studying for hours and hours and sweating each and every flight in flight school. He certainly did not miss standing alerts in the middle of the night in the middle of the Pacific for no reason and zero chance of launching. No, when Spyder recalled his days in VF-124, VF-1 and VF-213, what came to mind were memories of exhilarating flying, partying in ports across the globe, and innumerable experiences bonding with his squadronmates.

"No, no regrets." The commander paused. "Hey, I still get to put on the uniform and hang out with my contemporaries and the likes of you, Rolls."

"What about the boat? Ever miss cruise?"

"Ha," Spyder laughed. "Now we're getting somewhere." Spyder grabbed his beer and grinned smugly. "Remember the song 'Funkytown?' Wait, never mind. Anyway, we used to call CV-61 *Rangertown*."

13

Spyder's first fleet cruise began consistent with over two hundred years of navy tradition that preceded him. The young aviator clung to Flash as the two junior officers staggered across the brow drunk as skunks at 0230 in the morning. The flyers had met with several squadronmates at Haciendas, a dive Mexican restaurant on Coronado Island, for a send-off meal of greasy food and humongous margaritas. What better way to spend their last evening Stateside than to get ripped on cheap tequila and stumble to their stateroom, only to sleep through the pomp and military pageantry of the ship's departure from San Diego the next morning?

While hundreds of sailors manned the rails at parade rest in their dress white uniforms during the laborious line releases and tugboat push-off, Spyder, Flash, and a handful of other Wolfies and air wing aviators slept off their hangovers deep in the recesses of the super carrier. While the Officer of the Deck, Senior Watch Officer, and a half-dozen junior SWOs sweated shoving off the pier and getting underway in a stiff breeze and swift tide witnessed by several hundred onlookers, family members, dignitaries, and well-wishers, the flyers snored in their warm racks dreaming of far-off ports and intriguing women of the upcoming cruise. Oh, the life of an aviator in the US Navy!

Spyder's parents had flown down from Sausalito for the weekend to send him off on his maiden voyage. They shuttled back and forth from his condo and *Rangertown* several times to get the last of his personal items and flight gear aboard ship and then spent a leisurely Sunday morning walking along Mission Bay before having brunch at the Admiral Kidd Club. The restaurant lounge overlooked San Diego Bay, with stunning views of the water, palm trees, and expensive yachts and sailboats that sailed by.

After taking one final stroll along the waterfront, Spyder's parents drove him to the carrier. Seven years earlier, his parents had enacted a similar scene when they had dropped him off at Ann Arbor with instructions to call home weekly. This time a sense of danger crept into their minds; their only son was leaving to fly a fighter jet off an aircraft carrier in the middle of the ocean ten thousand miles from home. His mother shed the predictable tears while his father gave him a handshake and heartfelt hug.

Spyder felt his eyes moisten as he said good-bye. He had no doubt he would survive his first deployment unharmed but also knew he would have only sporadic opportunities to speak with his mother and father, or any family member, over the next half year. The young pilot had no idea what lay ahead for him and his squadronmates, other than multiple adventures of one type or another in and over foreign lands and seas. He began walking up the steel brow of the behemoth ship.

As Spyder crossed the brow, he witnessed firsthand organized chaos. Scores of sailors and civilian contractors streamed aboard the ship like worker ants to a nest. Large and small cranes moved crates, and multiple forklifts scurried back and forth across the pier. *I'm going on WestPac tomorrow!* Thoughts of the Philippines, Hong Kong, Thailand, Singapore, and Australia filled his mind. He stopped before stepping onto the quarterdeck, pausing long enough to look across the expansive breadth and height of the warship. *How can something be so mammoth staring up at it pier-side yet look like a postage stamp while flying over it at three thousand feet waiting to land?* Spyder took one last look toward shore and saw his mother waving earnestly from the pier. He waved back and stepped aboard *USS Ranger*, his home for the next six months.

When Spyder finally woke up the next morning, the ship had cleared the harbor and already steamed halfway to San Clemente Island. He slipped out of his rack with a soft *thud* as his feet hit the deck. He surveyed the tiny space. A junior officer stateroom on a navy combatant, whether guided missile cruiser, frigate or aircraft carrier, is a lesson in efficiency. Spyder, Tank, and Flash's room, as with the other three-man staterooms on *Ranger*, stretched a whopping nine feet by five feet. The hatch opened to a bank of steel cabinets along the opposite bulkhead. Three small metal desks folded into the steel recessed cabinet wall, separated by two floor-length wall lockers. On the opposite bulkhead stood a third wall locker on one side of the hatch, and on the other was a freestanding sink and medicine cabinet. The third bulkhead was bare, with a television attached to a shelf dropped from the ceiling. Three racks sat on top of one another along the fourth bulkhead, the lowest one attached to the deck and the top one approximately four feet from the ceiling. The racks were stacked upon twelve-inch horizontal lockers stretching the length of the mattress. Each officer had only the rack locker and a three-by-six wall locker to store uniforms and personal items for the six-month global voyage. Three small steel chairs clogged the last remaining floor space. Unless at least one of the officers was in his rack, all three roommates could not fit or work comfortably in the room at the same time. Texas death-row prison cells had more living space.

The racks had sliding curtains that provided the only privacy on the entire one-thousand-ten-foot ship. Among the cavernous hangar bays, flight deck, ready room, wardrooms, gym, library, chapel, or aircraft, the six-by-three-by-three foot rack was the only true personal space each sailor possessed while at sea. Even the back third of the headstalls was removed for maintenance reasons, which minimized privacy during the most personal moments of a sailor's day. Most officers and sailors personalized their racks with photos, perfumed envelopes, religious pendants, or other mementos taped to the inside bulkheads of racks, allowing a touch of home while across the globe.

When the curtains were closed, the racks closely resembled steel coffins. During a previous two-week work-up period, one of the VF-2 JOs experienced several nightmares where he woke up in a panic in the middle of the night thinking he had been buried alive. The first few nights his roommates turned on the light and calmed him. After the third consecutive night, the tired roommates played into his fears and shouted that he was buried underground in a coffin and they couldn't help him. Spyder was not nearly as claustrophobic, but it even took him a few nights to feel reasonably comfortable sleeping in the blackened steel box.

As if the cramped living and tight sleeping conditions were not enough, *Ranger* emanated almost continuous noise of one type or another. Since it was constructed of steel, sound radiated throughout the ship's decks, bulkheads, and passageways like echoes in a cave. Maintenance was conducted on every piece of equipment. Hundreds of hydraulic, fuel, oil, water, and jet fuel pumps whirred, spun, or clanked constantly. The ship's various weapons systems also required routine maintenance and repair. Similarly, the air wing's ninety aircraft were constantly being worked on in both hangar bays, as well as the flight deck. Jet motors were fired up at all hours of the day and night. Steel doors slammed, hammers pounded, wrenches clanked, fluids flushed, boots kicked, and sailors cussed loudly day-in and day-out.

There was no break in the routine, as both day and night check shifts kept the ship abuzz twenty-four hours per day with indefatigable activity. Announcements on the ship's 1-MC intercom system rang out routinely throughout the day. A homeless person on the corner of Forty-Second Street at midnight had a better chance at falling asleep than a new sailor on the O-3 level of *Ranger*.

Once a crewman finally acclimated to the plethora of ship-borne sounds, there were two additional noises associated with carrier operations that increased discomfort to an entirely new level. The first time Spyder had stayed overnight aboard a navy aircraft carrier was during RAG CQ on the *Constellation* off the coast of San Diego. He was sitting in the ready room talking to the SDO when without warning he heard and felt a very loud *boom* that violently shook the entire space. The clamor was followed immediately by a screeching whine and vibration as if a sea monster was dragging its steel fingertips along the deck of the carrier like a teacher's fingernails across an enormous blackboard. The nascent aviator was sure something had just exploded on the ship and jumped to his feet. "What was that?" he exclaimed wide-eyed to the SDO. The salty RAG instructor laughed at Spyder.

"I think it was an A-6. Check out the PLAT," he added calmly.

From within the massive steel ship, Spyder had experienced his first landing of a navy jet onto the aircraft carrier. The loud *boom* had been the jet slamming onto the deck. No wonder they called a carrier landing a "controlled crash." The screeching sound was the steel cable being pulled out of the arresting gear and dragged piercingly along the flight deck. For the uninitiated, witnessing a navy recovery for the first time could be an alarming experience. For the salty sailor, it was another aspect of carrier life to get used to.

Spyder, Flash, and Tank's stateroom was below and forward of where the four-wire stretched across the flight deck. Located on the O-3 level, the stateroom's ceiling was connected to the flight deck, so fewer than eighteen inches separated the top of the flight deck from the bottom of their ceiling. After recovery and roll out of each aircraft that landed upon *Ranger*, the arresting gear pulled the plane backward away from the edge of the flight deck. Depending upon which wire it caught, an airplane was pulled to the approximate location above Spyder's stateroom. At that point, the pilot lowered the landing gear, which spit out the arresting cable. This action resulted in a loud *bang* as the steel hook dropped onto the steel deck and sounded as if Iron John was driving a steel shank directly through the stateroom's ceiling.

The entire recovery—controlled crash onto flight deck, full power of engine thrust, catching and unwinding of the arresting cables, hook dropping onto the deck, and recoiling of the steel cable dragged along the deck—occurred within a few feet of Spyder's and the other VF-1 officers' heads as they lay in their racks. They sequence repeated itself every thirty to forty-five seconds for an entire aircraft recovery cycle consisting of a dozen or more aircraft. The cacophony of sound and vibration took some time to get used to, but amazingly, after a week of cruise, the flyers' brains adjusted to the environment, and the officers could sleep through an entire fifteen-plane recovery. But that was only half of carrier airborne operations.

The sailors living in the forward half of the ship had to adjust to catapult launches. VF-2's officer berthing was located on the second deck of

Ranger near the bow. The officers did not hear much of the recovery, but these crewmen were subjected to a unique set of sounds and vibrations associated with the launch of a navy aircraft via steam catapult. The sensational vibration resulting from a catapult launch and dull thud of its rapid termination, though not as loud or disconcerting as an aircraft recovery, took considerable time getting used to. Not exactly the promenade deck on a Princess cruise liner.

✳ ✳ ✳

The first week of cruise was, predictably, the most difficult as each crewmember acclimated to life at sea. Sure, there had been multiweek work-up periods throughout the previous year that provided glimpses of seaborne life, but each of these training cycles had ended after a few weeks. During those evolutions, time was measured by a few missed episodes of a favorite television show or a handful of sons' or daughters' little league games. A six-month deployment was measured by absences of entire seasons, hit songs, movies, and short-lived fads. Navy officers and sailors were plucked from society and plopped back down six or more months later, not having any idea of the latest Hollywood celebrity crisis, Washington political fray, or local news trend. This isolation may seem impossible in the current age of Internet, Skype, and instant e-mail, but it was reality for a sailor on cruise through the 1990s and earlier.

Even with the intermittent contact through snail mail or in-port phone calls, sailors with families routinely missed a child's growth spurt, new teeth, birthdays, school projects, sports seasons, and a hundred eighty bedtime stories. The isolation and missed intimacies from a spouse were too varied and numerous to detail.

As a single guy with no current girlfriend, Spyder had little anxiety about leaving on deployment. Other than missing his parents and sister, his only real concern was his car. He arranged to store his Vette in a friend's garage with strict instructions to drive it only once a month.

Following the two traps during night CQ, Spyder only flew twice during the first week of cruise. The flight schedule for the entire air wing was fairly abbreviated, affording an opportunity for the flight deck crews and ship's company to ease into the groove. There would be plenty of opportunities over the next few months to ramp up and push the limits of man and machine. In the interim, Spyder and the other VF-1 aviators adjusted slowly to their cruise routines.

After the first week of cruise, Spyder averaged a flight or spare about four times per week. "Spare" was the term for a back-up flight crew and aircraft readied for every mission in the event a primary aircraft experienced a mechanical problem and could not launch. On cruise, Spyder sometimes flew several consecutive days but rarely missed more than two days in a row, unless he was unlucky and his plane broke down or he pissed off Bourbon, the Ops O, or Oxford,[15] the schedules writer.

To make the time pass quicker, Spyder tried to stay busy even when he wasn't flying. The worst part of cruise was the monotony when not airborne. Geek, a BN from VA-155, followed the premise that if he slept twelve hours a day, cruise was only three months long. Not a bad concept, except when the time came for his fitrep.

The first morning after four days of idyllic Pearl Harbor liberty, Spyder was walking through Maintenance Control on his way to the ready room following morning FOD walkdown. As he walked past the counter and opened the hatch to the ready room, he noticed Master Chief Rollins with the entire day-check assembled in a small group in front of him. The six junior enlisted and three senior petty officers stood in a semicircle around the menacing sailor. Master Chief Rollins' back was to the counter so Spyder couldn't see what he was doing, but the shocked looks on the faces of the enlisted revealed something serious was occurring. With his curiosity piqued, the officer paused long enough to see Rollins turn with his penis in his hand. Spyder immediately looked away and walked out of the office without saying a word. *I don't want to know!*

---

15 Possessed a vocabulary like an Oxford dictionary.

Two days later while on the flight deck performing FOD walkdown, Spyder ran into the master chief. "All right, Master Chief, I gotta ask. What was going on the other day in Maintenance Control with your pecker out of your pants?"

A former high-school offensive lineman tipping the scales at 260 pounds, the master chief smirked. "Oh, you saw that, did you, Lieutenant?" said Rollins sheepishly. "Well, I got sick and tired of somebody using my coffee mug. I tried taping my name to it; keeping it in my desk. Tried everything. Dammit, Sir, they can get their own from the ship's store for three bucks and a quarter." The embarrassment was gone from the master chief's voice as he now spoke in his usual bellow. "I was tired of it, Sir, so I pulled the entire day-check together and grabbed my coffee mug for 'em to see. I then whipped out my johnson and rubbed it all around the inside of the empty mug. Told 'em the next time someone uses my mug, it'll be like they were sucking my dick!"

The chief stopped walking on the flight deck and stood smiling defiantly, proudly crossing his arms across his chest. Everyone within earshot broke out laughing. It took almost a minute before the flyer gained enough composure to congratulate the master chief for his fine leadership skills.

Spyder witnessed first-hand another humorous incident less than a week later. The Air Boss, another demonstrative figure, sipped coffee eighteen hours a day and spit nails the remaining six. Every sailor and aviator feared him—for good reason—especially the aircrew who flew in his airspace and the enlisted and officers who worked on his flight deck. The "Boss" owned the flight deck and the five miles of airspace that surrounded the ship. One morning Spyder was manning a jet prior to commencement of flight ops. All personnel were in full flight ops gear, including full-length deck uniforms, float coats, and cranial.

As Spyder got to his aircraft to begin preflight, he thought he heard a whisper from one of the 5-MC speakers attached at various points on the flight deck. Ordinarily loud orders and commands were shouted over the 5-MC. On this occasion, he heard a faint voice, almost as if he were imagining it. "Hey you," whispered someone over the 5-MC. No, Spyder was not imagining it.

He looked up at Pri-Fly but could not see whether the Air Boss was on his throne. "Yeah, you," the whispering continued, "in the port, bow cat walk." Spyder went to the front of the Tomcat and peered out toward the bow, trying to catch a glimpse at whomever the whisperer was talking to. "Yeah, that's right...you," continued the whisper. "See that speaker a few feet to the left of you? Bend down and look real closely at it."

Spyder could barely make out what looked like a sailor in running gear in the port bow catwalk. The shipmate bent down toward the flight deck. "Lower, just a bit lower," urged the whisperer. The sailor looked around, as if thinking to himself, *Who is talking to me?* But he did as he was told and bent down and put his head directly next to the speaker. "Now get off my fucking flight deck and never come back during flight ops without the proper uniform!" The whispering had suddenly turned into ear-splitting shouting that bounced around Spyder's ears—and he was ten yards from the closest 5-MC speaker. He saw the sailor spring three feet in the air like a startled cat and scamper out of sight down the catwalk. The sailor's head must have been ringing for hours. Just another day on *Rangertown*.

Prior to joining VF-1 and beginning his sea tour aboard *Ranger*, Spyder had not thought much about being assigned to a ship. He knew he would spend a considerable amount of time aboard an aircraft carrier and that it would be his home for months at a time, but he had never spent much time really thinking about it. He'd joined the navy to fly and dreamed for hours and hours about streaking through the sky turning-and-burning among the clouds. He had no desire to fly during a war, yet on an intellectual level, he knew combat could be part of the deal he struck with the government. Spending months at sea on a ship, however, escaped his imagination until he actually was onboard *Ranger* for his first fleet cruise.

At least once per day, Spyder made a point to escape the bowels of the massive ship in favor of breathing the fresh, salty air and staring at the ocean swells as they passed endlessly underneath the catwalks and sponsons of the mighty warship. One of his favorite places to escape to was the hangar bay, where he could walk out onto the edge of a hangar elevator and stand mere feet above the wave tops with sea spray rising up and stinging his face. He also enjoyed being in the foc'sle, lying down on the steel deck with his head in the eye of a large anchor chain hole, perched fifty feet above the sea and looking straight down onto the rushing water below.

Spyder also found the fantail below the flight deck peaceful when flight ops were suspended. Looking down at the churning whitewater awed him, as he could see firsthand the remarkable effect that the four oil-boiler turbines churning out two hundred eighty thousand horsepower and four twenty-one-foot diameter screws had upon the sea. Thinking of the weight of the ship and power necessary to move it along at twenty to thirty knots was difficult to grasp for his liberal arts brain. To think explorers once traversed the seas by sail further boggled Spyder's mind.

Whatever the vantage—on a catwalk, on the flight deck, or in one of his favorite meditative spots—the flyer could stare for long periods at the sea methodically rolling by, knowing the ship was moving at fifteen or eighteen or twenty-plus knots, making its way nautical mile by nautical mile across the vast ocean. Over several weeks, the ship transited great seas and slowly made its way across the globe.

There was a calm, sanguine peacefulness that moved through Spyder's body and mind as he stared out into the emptiness of the endless Pacific Ocean. He lived to fly and felt physically uneasy if he spent more than two consecutive days saddled to a desk onboard *Ranger* without getting airborne. But the naval officer also treasured those moments alone, meditating on the ocean and basking in the gloriousness of the sea. Spyder had grown up near the ocean in Northern California, learned to swim as a toddler, and sailed a Laser at summer camp as a ten-year-old. While at Miramar, he surfed most weekends and often before or after work in the summer. He discovered that being at sea, even onboard a military combatant, could at times be almost tranquil. He even enjoyed the storms.

During the fiercest squalls, when the battle group's small boys were tossed about like bathtub toys, *Ranger* was able to maintain at least some semblance of stability. The floating steel island slammed repeatedly against forty-foot swells, with each punch reverberating throughout the eighteen decks and sixty-five passageways of the super carrier. To avoid sliding onto the deck, condiments were removed from all of the mess deck tables. Hatches were dog-eared, racks strapped, and planes double-chained. In sustained elevated sea states, almost half the crew got sick. Spyder didn't mind the storms—that is, until it was time to midair refuel or land on the rolling, pitching deck. Then he would feel a controlled terror.

The transit from eastern Pacific past Hawaii rarely turned foul. The sea did not usually become volatile until nearing Southeast Asia. And it wasn't only the ocean that heated up in that part of the world.

14

When *Ranger* pulled into Republic of Philippines, Spyder and his shipmates knew the significance of the hallowed ground upon which they were about to walk. The battle hymns of Bataan, Leyte Gulf, Corregidor, and Guadalcanal were etched in blood in the annals of US Marine Corps history. The ghosts of the fallen marines wandered the islands fifty years after the last battle.

In contemporary times, Subic Bay's storied history as a liberty port superseded its military and historical significance. Images of Olongapo brothels, Magsaysay Boulevard, and Cubi Point O'Club triggered tremors of excitement in the bodies of US Navy sailors worldwide. A ten-year-old kid walking through the turnstile to Disneyland did not have as much adrenaline pumping through his veins as an eighteen-year-old sailor stepping off the brow of *USS Boat* pier-side Subic Bay. Spyder and his six thousand buds in Battle Group Echo were almost drooling at the mouth for the wondrous experience awaiting them on their six-day port call to the PI.

Rangertown was barely tied to the pier when the brow lowered and sailors streamed off the ship like students on summer break. Spyder and the rest of the Wolfies headed straight for the legendary Cubi Point O'Club. The club sat on a hilltop overlooking the airfield with sweeping views of Olongapo Bay with the carrier docks and outskirts of Olongapo City. The club patio was approximately eight hundred feet above sea level, which meant patrons could look down at aircraft in the break landing at Cubi Point and nearly throw a shot glass at the streaking jets.

During the Vietnam War, the Cubi Point O'Club was legendary, downright biblical. Carriers pulled into Subic or Cubi Point between combat line periods for a week or two to give sailors and officers well-deserved R&R while weapons and systems maintenance was performed and ordnance reloaded. Stories of combat aviators blowing off steam within the confines of the o'club reached nearly epic proportions.

One of the sea stories dating back to Vietnam involved the "Dilbert Dunker," a rudimentary aircraft arresting gear apparatus that slid into the pool, complete with boltering device. The "aircraft" chair slid on a track from a height of about eight feet that extended into the water. If a pilot lowered the tailhook prematurely, the hook skipped over a metal bracket, sending the pilot and aircraft into the pool. If the hook was lowered too late, it missed the wire altogether, with similar wet results.

It might surprise some that grown men—combat proven fighter pilots—found so much satisfaction in such simple amusement. Yet that paradox played out repeatedly in naval aviation. Men who flew jets at twice the speed of sound and landed on pitching, rolling, four-hundred-foot runways in the middle of the night in stormy weather also loved video-games, sophomoric movies, and juvenile antics. Add alcohol, and the sanity bar dropped to boot level.

In addition to the Dilbert Dunker, the club was known for its "Cubi Specials"—fruit punch laden with generous amounts of rum. These frou-frou drinks tasted like Hawaiian Punch going down, but three or four, especially after a month at sea without alcohol, knocked many an aviator off his barstool. When spiked with a shot of Bacardi 151, the seemingly innocuous cocktails were instantly transformed into Thermonuclear Cubi Point Specials, or "Thermonukes," for short.

The first night of liberty, VF-1's skipper led the charge out of the club and into town. As soon as the Jeepnies crammed with aviators slowed and stopped at the base fence outside Olongapo City, the odor hit Spyder like a left hook. He had been abroad several times in high school and college and recognized that unmistakable Third-World stench. The outskirts of Olongapo reeked of the universal open-sewage odor. Filipino civilians and American sailors flurried about as everyone vied to get off base— the locals to their homes after a long workday and the GIs to the bars for nighttime liberty—as soon as possible. Within five minutes, fifteen Wolfies headed out the gate and into the belly of the beast, led by their fearless leader, Pole.

Before entering Olongapo, the group had to transit a no-man's-land of approximately one hundred yards through a field and then over what was reverently referred to over the years as the adeptly named "Shit River." It served as the primary sewer for much of Olongapo. The river was dark brown and had long ago lost much semblance to water. In daytime feces could be seen floating on the surface along with animal parts, refuse, and just about any other type of garbage a town of two hundred thousand persons could heave or wash into the tributary. For as long as any US sailor could remember, local kids dove into the river after pesos thrown in by transiting military members. For the value of less than a penny, seven- to fifteen-year-old youths fought each other for the opportunity to retrieve a few pesos from the flowing cesspool.

When they neared the small bridge spanning the Shit River, Spyder and the rest of the Wolfies gagged from the noxious odor. They tried pulling their shirts up over their noses, but it didn't stop the smell from infiltrating every fiber of their lungs. A tin fence approximately six feet high had been erected along the side of the bridge. The aviators were told later the Filipino government had forced the city to construct the barrier in an effort to curtail the peso diving. Unfortunately, the quality of construction was sorely deficient, with several gaps in the metal sheathing. The voids had been pulled apart to create large openings where Spyder and anyone else on the bridge could look down onto the river flowing eight feet below. There, several young boys treaded water and clamored for attention, yelling for the group of Americans to throw them money. Spyder pitied the boys and figured he should not encourage such desperate conduct but also felt hard-pressed not to give them something. He and a couple other Wolfies threw handfuls of paper pesos into the water. The youths scrambled to grab the money, kicking and splashing water everywhere, which only increased the pungent odor. Spyder gagged, barely stifling the upward surge of his dinner, and picked up his pace to get across the bridge.

Thankfully, the bright lights and numerous bodies of Olongapo lay merely thirty yards ahead.

Spyder had been to Times Square for New Year's, Las Vegas for Tailhook, and New Orleans for Mardi Gras. He'd lived through a hundred college frat parties and a handful of RAG boat parties where he'd consumed dozens of kegs of beer and witnessed obscene and rowdy displays of female and male debauchery. But nothing in his young adult life had prepared him for what he was about to witness during the next three hours along two hundred yards of Magsaysay Boulevard, Olongapo City, Republic of Philippines.

As soon as he stepped off the bridge spanning the Shit River, the flyer and his squadronmates were deluged by school-aged girls selling sodas, a few crippled adults begging for pesos, food vendors hawking barbecued mystery meat—rumored to be monkey—and the first wave of prostitutes—female, male, male pretending to be female, and female looking way too male. *Dorothy, we're not in Kansas anymore.*

"Keep your hands in your pockets, grab your wallets, and keep together," shouted Pole. "We're going to the second bar on the left."

Spyder looked around and was amazed by what he saw. Based on the stories he'd heard back on the boat and earlier that night at the o'club, he'd fully expected a surge of activity but was overwhelmed by the aggressive swarm of locals. The kids wore tattered and torn clothes. The prostitutes wore skimpy shorts that rode obscenely high into crevices that should never see the likes of Lycra, and white, braless, form-fitting halter tops that left nothing to the imagination. Sunburned sailors in various stages of public drunkenness piled in and out of bars. Loud bass-enriched music blared out onto the street from competing dance clubs located merely yards from one another. Brightly colored neon lights flickered from the bars, discothèques, and restaurants. It was past 2300, yet every business was open, and Magsaysay Boulevard teemed with drunkards, peasants, dogs, and dozens of feral chickens.

The Skipper never paused and marched directly to Marilyn's a Go-Go. Five dancers in scant bathing suits loitered outside beckoning potential customers into the bar. As the aviators approached, the gals started pulling on the shirts of the first Wolfies.

"You so strong. You US sailor. You come in. We love you long time," one seemingly fifteen-year-old gal proclaimed to Pill with a smile wider than the gap between her two front teeth.

The Wolfies tightened the formation around their commanding officer as they entered the dance bar.

Spyder and Flash managed to make it into the club without being badgered by any of the salacious greeters. The only illumination in the darkened bar consisted of black lights, which highlighted the skimpy white bikinis worn by most of the dancers and waitresses. The room was split into two separate stages, each with two fully naked female dancers. Most of the tables and chairs were filled with US servicemen and female "escorts." Numerous dancers walked around in various stages of undress, flirting with any man exhibiting a pulse. Madonna's "Holiday" thumped loudly from oversized speakers throughout the club. Nicotine and stage smoke permeated every inch of the club. It took a minute for their eyes to adjust to the darkness before Spyder and Flash could make out the unmistakable profile of their CO. The roommates made their way to the end of the bar where the Wolfies grouped together.

Before Spyder and Flash had even stopped walking, two bar girls appeared out of nowhere and draped themselves over the aviators. The first girl nudged closely next to Spyder and whispered into his ear, "You want to take me to bed?" The flyer looked down at her and smiled. The young woman fit the precise physical profile of ninety-nine percent of the Olongapo females he had seen thus far in country: five foot three inches tall, petite frame, B-cup breasts, smooth olive-skin, straight black hair just past her neck, brown eyes, and crooked teeth. Spyder discovered over the next few days there was a definite bell curve to the women of Olongapo. Eighty percent could barely be picked out of a lineup, as they were so similar—attractive, yet not beautiful. Ten percent were unattractive, with the last ten percent being stunningly gorgeous. After enough San Miguels or Thermonukes, any or all could become evening company for the average sailor.

Since the night was young and he didn't want to get tied down within the first five minutes of the first bar in the Philippines, Spyder whispered into the girl's ear that he didn't like women. She took a step back, gave him the once over, said something to her friend in Tagalog, and moved on to Trapper. A bar full of American sailors on their first night of liberty awaited, and she was not about to let Spyder slow her down.

Trapper, Tank, and a few other Wolfies had bar girls draped on them, trying to communicate in their pidgin English. The rest of the aviators stood around the bar drinking San Miguels and watching the go-go dancers. Marilyn's was a full strip bar, but the gals did not perform lurid sex acts or other anatomically challenging tricks Spyder had heard transpired further down the Boulevard. Mauler and the Skipper explained to the first-cruise Wolfies how prostitution worked in Olongapo.

Each bar had a mamasan who acted as the bar girls' pimp. She was usually a former bar girl who was well beyond her best years and had turned from the selling of her body into upper management. The rules were quite basic. If a customer wanted sex from one of the bar girls, he had to pay a bar fine to the mamasan. An hour trick was fifteen dollars and all night cost forty dollars. Clients were expected to pay the girl an additional tip, depending on the extent of the job performed. In Olongapo, several of the bars had small rooms exclusively for prostitution; alternatively, some of the girls turned tricks in the back alleyways. A few of the ladies rented tiny apartments or a room in a house where they took their johns. The police turned their backs, as they knew how much cash was infused into the local economy through prostitution. The Philippine culture was based on service dating back centuries. What better definition of service than the world's oldest profession?

The Skipper made good on his promise and paid the bar fine for two girls who were hanging onto Tank. He smiled from one end of bliss to the other. Pole pre-tipped the gals, exuding almost as much excitement as the young JO.

"Think he's gonna join 'em?" nudged Flash to Spyder. But Pole stayed at the bar with the other Wolfies as Tank left to go upstairs with his female escorts. As he got to the top of the stairs at the back of the bar, he turned back, grinned widely, and gave a thumbs-up.

"That's my boy!" exclaimed Mauler.

After an hour of drinking and dancing with the bar girls, the Wolfies grew restless as the lure of the legendary sex shows persisted. The Skipper agreed to stay at the club to wait for Tank. Pole exercised the buddy system and wanted to hear all about Tank's exploits the instant the junior officer came back from his "date." Mauler agreed to steer the group of ten remaining squadronmates further along Magsaysay.

To the chagrin of the bar gals, the aviators spilled out of Marilyn's and began walking down Magsaysay. Even at 0130 in the morning, the boulevard streamed with activity, primarily sailors and hookers. The shops were closed, but several small restaurants remained open to serve bar clients who tried to sober up before heading back to the ship.

Mauler stopped at a corner to get his bearings and recall the name of one of the dance clubs where the dancers performed the infamous sex shows. As he stood gazing along Magsaysay, a petite prostitute approached and began flirting provocatively. A fairly large man who did not get a lot of attention from females back in the States, Mauler welcomed the attention. She put her arm around his waist and began whispering in his ear.

The remaining Wolfies, quite drunk, at first didn't pay much attention to Mauler or the hooker. But after standing around for two minutes watching the large aviator flirt with the diminutive prostitute dressed in short hot pants and a cutoff t-shirt, Pill looked closer. Something didn't look right. The hooker was wearing sandals, and it took a minute for Pill to notice her huge feet. The aviator could not stop laughing. Even Mauler's attention was diverted. Finally, Pill caught his breath. "I, uh," he sputtered out, laughing. "I think Mauler's with a Benny Boy."

Mauler took a step back from the prostitute and took a good look at her. He paused at the feet and then glanced back up to the neck, where he noticed for the first time a pronounced Adams apple. "Oh, shit!" he shouted incredulously.

The transvestite smiled sweetly. "Is OK. I treat you nice."

"Shit!" exclaimed Mauler again. He turned away from the Benny Boy without uttering another word and dashed into the closest bar in sight. The Wolfies laughed and shook their heads as they strode past the greeting hostesses directly into the Florida Club. Before the group made it to the bar, a waitress intercepted them and pushed a pitcher of dark brown liquid their way with a handful of empty glasses.

"You like MoJo?" she asked cheerfully.

Spyder turned to Flash with a serious look, as serious as his face muscles and eyes could manipulate considering he was half-baked. "Shhhit," he slurred. "I don't shink MoJo is such a good idear right now. I've heard all about thish stuff. It's supposed ta make the…th…ther-mo-nu-cle-ars seem like lemonade." Flash swayed back and forth to the music, smiled, clanked Spyder's glass, and downed his drink in two large gulps.

"Ohh, dude," responded Spyder. "We're gonna be hurtin' tomorrow."

Spyder raised his glass toward Flash and chugged away. The flyer was surprised how easily the shooter went down. Like the Cubi Specials, MoJo had a fruity, benign taste. The cocktail, however, was anything but benign. Another waitress quickly filled both Spyder's and Flash's glasses.

Spyder's second glass of MoJo went down easier than the first and the third easier than the second. Plopping down at an adjacent table, the young aviator closed his eyes. Even with eyes closed, the room began to rotate slowly and then quickened. The flyer felt someone sit down next to him and move closer, but his eyes would not open. Though he recognized Depeche Mode's "The Kiss" playing loudly from the speakers, Spyder could only see bright colors erupt on the back of his eyelids. The beat of the music droned on. Somebody mumbled something next to him.

✳ ✳ ✳

Spyder awakened with a start. Although it was pitch dark and he couldn't see two feet in front of him, he knew it was morning. Clambering noises ricocheted down the passageway. A few more seconds elapsed before he realized he was in a rack back on *Ranger*. Fumbling for the light switch, the flyer finally was able to flip it on. The fluorescent bulb flickered on and off and on again. The bright flashes singed his retinas all the way to his frontal lobe. The flyer looked down and saw that his clothes and shoes remained on, and that he was lying on top of the covers. Familiar photos of his parents and sister were taped to the side of the steel confines, thus confirming: one, he was alive; and two, actually in his own rack. *How the hell did I get here?* Spyder had absolutely no memory after drinking the first shots of Mojo at the Florida Club. *Was I drugged?* Spyder's head pounded from the inside out. It was the worst hangover he had ever experienced, and the pilot had just woken up.

He closed his eyes and tried to go back to sleep. More banging down the passageway. A machinery pump whirred on and off. Somewhere, a sailor clanked a steel hammer onto a piece of metal and the sound pierced Spyder's skull to the core of his brain, echoing behind his eyes. The officer grabbed his pillow and gently placed it over his head—not that it provided the least bit of insulation from the noise and rising nausea. He tried to go back to sleep.

One of the best aspects of liberty was the freedom from work. Unless he had to assume a watch, Spyder did not have to do a lick of work the entire time he was in port. It was like a weekend away from the office, except he slept and sometimes ate onboard *Ranger,* at least in-port PI. Later, when the ship pulled into Singapore, Hong Kong, or Thailand, the officers doubled up on hotel rooms and were completely free from the ship. Port call Subic Bay was different in that the ship was almost at the epicenter of many liberty attractions; plus, the officers weren't passing up luxurious hotels or other accommodations in Olongapo—since there were none. As long as the routine sounds of shipboard life did not awaken him, Spyder and his shipmates could sleep in as long as they desired. He didn't have to assume SDO until the third day of liberty, so he planned to sleep and nurse his hangover until the nausea and pain ceased.

That evening, the Wolfies had dinner at the club, reliving tales from the first twenty-four hours of liberty. Tank's 1v2 was the highlight, followed closely by the MoJo-induced blackout. Mauler recollected that soon after the second round of MoJo pitchers, several of the Wolfies faded, and others passed out. The remaining officers took their squadronmates by the scruffs of their necks and literally pushed and pulled them back over the Shit River and into Jeepnies back to the ship. The OOD almost sent the entire gaggle to medical for BACs, but Slum sweet-talked the officer into letting them back onboard without restriction. Upon reliving the experience, several officers moaned, having passed through the piercing headaches and dreadful hangovers left by the MoJo madness only in the last few hours.

After dinner, the Wolfies, along with most of the diners, retired to the bar for after-dinner drinks and prefunc activity prior to another night out on the town. The Cubi Point O'Club was unique in that it displayed scores of plaques from squadrons that had cruised the Pacific on carriers and amphibs and shore-based dets out of Cubi. The mementos ranged in size from basic three-feet-by-two-feet wooden inscriptions with squadron logos to huge replicas of a variety of military hardware. Spyder's favorite was a six-foot long Russian submarine that hung over the shuffleboard table. The submarine was split in half by a large thunderbolt extending from the arms of a two-foot tall Mauler, the mascot for VS-32.

Spyder grabbed a beer, and while the majority of the flyers gravitated around the shuffleboard table or the bar doing shots, he strolled back to the entrance and began reading the plaques. The entry to the o'club bar consisted of a short hallway with standard plaques and base commendations attached to the walls. He finished perusing the dozen or so plaques and entered the main section of the bar. The hallway spilled out to a room with an L-shaped bar along two walls. A dozen tables filled the remainder of the room. Intricate wood inscribed plaques splattered the walls, and replicas hung from the ceiling. Colorful squadron paraphernalia covered most every foot of each wall, and most of the ceiling.

Spyder had seen a few of the squadron plaques back in flight school when he visited Trader John's in Pensacola or back at the Miramar O'Club. But viewing a handful of the plaques paled in comparison to the breadth and size of the collection amassed in the Cubi O'Club. Cubi was the true "promised land" for navy aviators—like viewing a Monet or Renoir collection in the Louvre. As he read line after line of aviator names, and saw squadron after squadron listed with WestPac years and cruises, Spyder was struck by the enormity of it all. Every aviator listed on each plaque had numerous stories to tell about his particular cruise. Each squadron history was filled with achievement and accomplishment, danger and sacrifice, whether or not a combat cruise. Deployments included multiple events that made global headlines or at least impacted the region in some meaningful way. Spyder reached out and reverently touched several of the plaques in the way veterans touched the Vietnam Memorial. Odds were high some of the aviators whose names he touched were now dead.

As his peers partied at the bar, Spyder nursed his beer and became more morose by the minute. He stepped back from one of the plaques and looked around. He realized he and the other flyers were in the primes of their lives—young, athletic, intelligent, confident naval aviators who had life by the balls. They flew jet airplanes on and off ships for a living and rarely thought much about it. He estimated close to two hundred aviators were enjoying their evening and liberty at the club without a care in the world, except for the occasional pang of missing family and friends. Chances were good that four or five would die in a navy airplane sometime over the next half-decade. Spyder paused for a moment and said a prayer for Bucket and other aviators he knew who had died in navy aircraft.

After a few minutes, Spyder walked down to the lower section of the lounge, He heard a loud roar from the corner of the bar. The flyer saw Slum and Austin on one side of a table with CAG and the captain of *Ranger* on the other. Four pitchers of beer sat between the VF-1 JOs and the navy captains. Aviators stood around chanting loudly, "Chug, chug, chug!" It was a classic drinking contest right out of "Animal House" or "Old School."

Hoser, a BN from VA-155, stood next to the table and raised his hand. The officers grabbed their pitchers. The shouting increased. Hoser dropped his arm and yelled, "Go!" The four officers raised their pitchers, tilted their heads back, and began chugging. Foam and beer spilled from their mouths. Slum was the first to finish, a full five seconds ahead of CAG. Austin and the CO finished simultaneously a few seconds later. It was impressive that the senior officers could hold their own.

What Spyder did not know but found out the next morning at breakfast was that Slum and Austin had preceded the beer chugging with a shot contest. The two Wolfies had challenged the captains to several rounds of shots to see who could last the longest after CAG had been talking trash about how back in the day he could've drank any of the JOs under the table. The officers squared off to multiple rounds of Jack Daniels. Youth bested age in that Slum had previously arranged with the bartender who was delivering the drinks to serve them Coca Cola in shot glasses while serving CAG and the ship's captain genuine bourbon. The senior officers never caught on and remarked with worsening speech and reddening cheeks how quickly Austin and Slum kept ordering the shots. Five rounds later, CAG suggested a final beer chug off. After losing to Slum, CAG stood up to go to the head, took one step forward, and fell flat on his face. The ship's captain rose slowly and stumbled trying to assist his friend.

By the time *Ranger* pulled out of Cubi Point after a full six-day port call, its crewmembers' livers had raised white flags. Sunburned skin and drooping eyes filled each level of the ship. Mercifully, there was no flying the first twenty-four hours out of port, allowing time for the crew time to detox. Except for the dozen or so seventeen- and eighteen-year-old sailors who had fallen in love for the first time in their young lives with local Olongapo girls, almost every crewmember of *Ranger* was ready to get underway and continue the adventure known as WestPac.

15

"The PI is something I'll never get to experience in my career," commented Rolls. "I've heard stories similar to yours."

"It's a different world today, a different navy," replied Spyder. "You can hear about it and read about it, but you don't need to experience it first-hand—other than the Cubi Point O'Club. That was a unique experience laden with amazing tradition."

"I still can," Rolls replied enthusiastically.

"Ha?"

"The navy shipped all of the cruise plaques stateside and recreated the entire bar it in the Pensacola Air Museum. You can go there and eat lunch or drink beer and Cubi Specials."

"Really? Huh, I haven't been to P-Cola in years," replied Spyder. "Hey Rolls, let me ask you something, Rolls." Spyder looked around the club. Other than themselves, at most fifteen aviators stood around drinking beer. "What's with the club? Don't people come here anymore?"

"You know the deal. The navy consolidated its clubs. Kind'a tough to get large or party hard when petty officers from your division are at the next table. Plus, from what I heard how the navy used to be, there's a heckuva lot less reason to drink on base. Today, DUIs are a career killer."

Spyder shook his head. "Yeah, I can understand the DUI part, but there's a time and a place to let your hair down."

Rolls continued, "Well, the other factor is emphasis on family. I don't know what it was like when you were on active duty, but nowadays guys like to spend off-duty time with their families. The navy rides us hard enough with extended cruises and work hours. The Iraqi and Afghanistan deployments were tough. The last thing a guy wants to do is spend more time away from his wife and kids to sit around the club and drink with squadronmates he's just spent the last eight months with."

"Yeah, but look around," Spyder stressed. "Even this club has its share of cruise and squadron plaques and history. There's a certain tradition an officers' club maintains in naval aviation lore that is now gone—poof, downright gone. I think we're losing the warrior spirit."

"Maybe. But we still have the occasional dining out. Prowler—now Growler—Week was cut back dramatically a couple of years ago, but we still have a golf tournament. Everything hasn't gone by the wayside."

Spyder continued to look at the rapidly emptying club. *Wow, a fucking golf tournament!"*

"If you say so, Rolls. But back in the day. . ."

16

When *Ranger* pulled out of Cubi Point Harbor, Spyder and 5,499 of his shipmates looked forward to drying out after six consecutive days and nights of near alcohol poisoning. The pilot was anxious to get back into the air. He didn't have to wait long. Before the ship cleared the last channel buoy, a rumor began circulating throughout the 03-level of an impending alert posture being set.

The air wing's younger aviators had heard stories of the high amount of Soviet Bear and Badger activity in the mid-'80s in that region of the world. Many of the intercepts involved aggressive Soviet bombers with aircrew who antagonized the American pilots and tried to provoke them. Only a handful of these aerial events rose to the level of international incident. By the time Spyder made his first WestPac, Mikhail Gorbachev's Glasnost had gained traction, and the Soviet Union was making overtures to the West. Even so, *Ranger*'s battle group remained vigilant and would not be overflown by a Soviet, Chinese, or any other country's aircraft without proper escort by a Tomcat or two from the Wolfpack or Bounty Hunters.

On the fourth day out of Subic, the weather deteriorated, and several flight cycles were scrubbed. The next day, flight ops were cancelled altogether, yet the alert schedule remained. A one hundred-foot ceiling with fog and embedded thunderstorms continued to keep all aircraft on deck. The schedule ticked off CAG, as now all air wing pilots had to night qual following the upcoming six-day port call in Hong Kong. Ordinarily a port call, especially to such rich and diverse liberty as Hong Kong, elicited smiles and warm feelings throughout the O-3 level. But the recent weather put a serious damper on the anticipation in the ready rooms, not to mention the proliferation of green faces in the passageways.

Twenty-four hours prior to pulling into port, VA-145 had Alert Bravo tanker duty and VF-1 was the alert fighter squadron for the day and night. Pill, assigned with Oxford for the 0200 to 0600 alert, didn't care, as it gave him an opportunity to write a letter to his wife and catch up on some much-needed paperwork. As Div O for the Line Shack, Pill had a constant stream of evals, special request chits, page thirteen counseling forms, and award write-ups to keep him busy. Thankfully, they were at sea or he would have a stack of leave and school requests stuffing his inbox as well.

Most civilians thought being a pilot in the navy was pure glamour. Unfortunately, naval aviation had its share of administrative duties. If the flyers had kept track of all the time spent on administrative duties and their ground job, the hours would outnumber the hours spent in the air ten to one. The aviators hated the paperwork and gladly would trade one hour of flying if it meant ten hours less paperwork. Pill despised it as much as every other aviator but knew the work needed to get done. He grabbed several eval folders from his inbox and dropped them onto a chair before heading to the PR shack.

Oxford, on the other hand, did not feel like strapping on his flight gear for the middle of the night alert with little chance of launching. Ordinarily, the RIO aggressively sought out every opportunity to bag a trap, even the slim chance related to alerts. He regularly volunteered for PMCFs or CQ hops if it meant more traps in his logbook. Traps were not nearly as important for RIOs as they were for pilots. Perhaps Oxford wanted to maximize his navy carrier aviation experience. Perhaps he really enjoyed strapping on the Tomcat and catapulting off the flight deck. Or perhaps he simply sought any opportunity to get off the goddamn ship. Whatever the reason, any time there was a remote chance of getting a hop, Oxford could be found hanging around the ready room. Oxford was not a "lifer" by any stretch. An Academy grad with brains and political acumen, his squadronmates knew the officer had aspirations greater than flying in the US Navy.

They teased him by saying his call sign should have been "Gov'ner," as they would not be surprised to find him one day sitting in the governor's mansion in Alabama, his home state.

Oxford and Pill met in the PR shack, a space slightly larger than a broom closet. On aircraft carriers in general, and fossil-fuel flattops particularly, space was a precious commodity. The PR shack on *Ranger* was stuffed with flight gear for each of the thirty VF-1 pilots and RIOs. SV-2 survival vests, speed jeans, harnesses, and helmets hung from tightly spaced metal pegs. These pegs hugged the bulkheads and a lone steel desk for the parachute rigger enlisted petty officer filled the space. There hardly was enough room in the PR shack for two aircrew to gear-up simultaneously. The junior pilots and NFOs had their gear doubled up in the far reaches of the closet. A pilot had to pull off two or three sets of gear to reach his own. With each set topping out at thirty to forty pounds, this was no easy task, especially in the heat of the summer in the middle of the North Arabian Sea. In early evening, after the first or second cycle was complete, the PR shack reeked worse than an NFL locker room at halftime. Fortunately, tonight off the coast of southern China, the temperate weather kept the flight gear dry.

Rather than use the PR shop, Oxford took advantage of the capacious ready room to dress. Well, if capacious could be used to describe any portion of a navy ship. Efficient, tidy, and compact were more common adjectives. But compared to the PR shop, the ready room was roomy, spacious, and yes, even capacious.

At precisely 0145, Pill and Oxford relieved Paul "Otter" Ottman and Mustang as the Alert Bravo fighter aircrew. Unlike about any other navy watchstander turnover, there was no substantive information to pass from the offgoing to the oncoming alert crew. The flyers merely passed pleasantries, which at 0146 in the morning, did not amount to much.

Mustang and Otter stepped out of the ready room and into Maintenance Control. They reviewed the maintenance logs and gripe sheet for Wolf 106, the Alert Alpha bird poised on Cat 4. No significant discrepancies were noted, so Otter signed for the jet. Both aviators made their way slowly onto the deck to relieve Bourbon and Austin, currently the Alert Alpha crew—for six more minutes, anyway.

As Bourbon and Austin unstrapped and eased their sore butts out of 106 and Mustang and Otter replaced them, Pill and Oxford settled into their recliners. The ready room was filled with thirty-three metal-framed recliner chairs cushioned with foam and covered with thick Naugahyde cushions. There was a small metal drawer to store a small number of personal items, similar to the old desks grade-schoolers used to keep their pencils, writing paper, and chewing gum. The navy's version held objects such as Sony Walkmans, GQ hoods, gloves, and maybe a novel or two. Today it would more likely hold an iPad, Kindle, or Nook.

Each officer had his own chair, with location determined—as everything else in the military—by seniority. The CO and XO had front-row center, with the department heads in the field level, and JOs in the bleachers—not necessarily a bad thing, as it allowed the young officers to catch a wink or two during boring lectures or GQ. The Air Intelligence Officer and Maintenance Admin Officer also had their own ready room chairs, as they were official members of the squadron's officers' mess.

At 0200 in the empty ready room, both Pill and Oxford had their pick of recliners to watch the alert aircrew brief. The brief essentially repeated the exact same information for the past forty-eight hours, as *Ranger* was steaming in small circles approximately three hundred miles south of Hong Kong, waiting out a typhoon raging off the coast of Vietnam and South China. The storm clouded the skies and churned the seas, resulting in a ten- to fifteen-foot pitching deck. The young ensign briefer noted the lack of change in METOC, ship posit, sea state, or location of foreign aircraft and vessels. The entire brief could have been summed up in a single statement: NSTR, or nothing significant to report. The ensign added the usual mention of no-fly areas in the proximity of the Spratlys and Hainan Island and concluded his brief in the same manner as every flight brief on *Ranger*, with the Babe of the Day.

The Babe of the Day was a pinup shot from *Playboy* or *Penthouse*. At the conclusion of the briefer's comments, the cameraman panned from the briefer to the photo and zoomed in on a particularly provocative body part or parts. Before shoving off for deployment, CVIC compiled hundreds of such photos. Preceding each brief, the designated briefer would leaf through the file and select one that caught his eye. If the audience slept through the substantive brief, they most certainly perked up at the end for the BOTD. Tonight was no exception, as Pill and Oxford were both wide-eyed for Miss August.

"Damn, would you look at that," yawned Pill. "And I've got three more weeks before I see Karen in Singapore. I knew we should have met in Hong Kong."

"At least Karen's coming to Singapore. Laura won't be out until Thailand." Oxford let out a deep sigh and looked fretfully away from the television.

The roommates settled in for the usual middle-of-the-night alert routine. They both dozed off a few times over the next two hours. Pill awoke with a pain in the back of his neck and checked his watch. Perfect. Only nine more minutes and then time to shift to the jet. He and Oxford were at the halfway point.

The ready room hatch suddenly burst open with a loud *thwack*. Oxford bolted upright, drool flying off his chin. Scout,[16] a second-cruise RIO, entered the space with a cheerful, "Good mornin'," threw his gear on the first chair he saw, and yawned loudly.

"Damn, Scout. What's got you so cheery at this god-awful time of the morning?" asked Oxford groggily.

"Liberty call. Liberty call in about twenty-four hours, my friend."

Oxford merely sighed, as he couldn't think of Hong Kong. Not yet. The RIO had to sit strapped in a cockpit for the next two hours with no chance of flying at 0400 in the morning.

Trapper and Scout, the next alert crew, began suiting up and continued the process. Ordinarily, they would be the second-to-last alert aircrew for the day, as the regular flight schedule ordinarily commenced at 1000. But today, there was little chance of a break in the weather. The alert

---

16   Got lost while leading a group of JOs on liberty in Yokosuka, Japan.

schedule likely would continue until the ship entered Hong Kong Harbor a day or so away.

As Otter and Mustang had done exactly two hours earlier in relieving Bourbon and Austin, Pill and Oxford sleepily reviewed the logbook for Wolf 106. They finished cinching their harnesses and SV-2s and made their way topside to the jet. When the flyers stepped out of the last passageway and onto the catwalk adjacent to the flight deck, they were greeted by a veil of blackness. A ship in the middle of the ocean at night is darker than a West Virginia coal mine, especially when a thick cloud layer blocks all ambient star and moonlight. The flyers paused, allowing their eyes time to adjust to the darkness. They could barely see their hands stretched in front of their faces, protecting them from inadvertently knocking into something sharp and pointy sticking out from a parked aircraft. After a minute or two, they continued and walked to the F-14 parked on Cat 4.

Pill and Oxford stood in silence next to the jet, allowing their compadres to climb down and relinquish control. As he waited for him to drop down from the last rung of the ladder, Pill half expected Otter to turn and toss him a set of keys. Instead the pilot barely managed a "Take 'er easy," as he lazily strode toward the closest deck ladder, not even waiting for Mustang.

Pill climbed into the cockpit and adjusted the seat. The warm South China Sea air breezed past his face, as the ship was making a measly six knots. If he had been airborne for a couple of hours, Pill could have looked down and seen *Ranger* steam in a large circle. With another twenty-four to thirty-six hours before it could enter Hong Kong Harbor, the ship was going nowhere fast—well, actually, nowhere slow.

The salty air refreshed both Pill and Oxford, momentarily. For the past twenty-one hours, the flyers had been breathing recirculated air over dusty and dirty filters that had not been cleaned since the ship departed San Diego three months earlier. The last time either aviator had been topside, or outside at all, was for FOD walkdown at 0700 the previous day. Anything over a day, or more than two days without flying, and Pill, like most of the flyers onboard, felt the bulkheads closing in.

After a few minutes, the sea air was no match for the exhaustion that flooded Pill's body. The Wolfie pilot was not going to fight it. He would be asleep in less than five minutes, no matter how uncomfortable the Martin-Baker MK GRU-7(A) ejection seat felt against his back. He fastened and began tightening the parachute and harness straps.

The warm breeze and rhythmically pitching deck worked their magic. Both Pill and Oxford nodded off to sleep almost immediately. Their catnaps, however, were rudely interrupted when VA-155's AMEs began a low-power turn on an A-6 in the six-pack. As soon as the huffer fired up less than thirty yards away, the loud, high-pitched whine woke Pill like a shot of ice water across his forehead. *Great. Gonna be one of those nights.* As he reached for his skullcap and helmet to put on his head, Pill yawned loudly.

"Guess you're awake too," shouted Oxford from the rear seat.

"I am now!"

Between two low-power turns and a re-spot of Bullet 202 to the fantail, Pill barely nodded off intermittently for the next ninety minutes. His sore neck returned. The pilot checked his watch and was relieved to see 0541 illuminate. Although at that very moment the sun was likely dawning across the horizon, the thick cloud deck prevented any sunlight from penetrating. Fourteen more minutes and he and Oxford could unstrap. Add eight minutes to walk to the PR shop and shrug off his gear, two minutes to get to his stateroom, one minute to brush his teeth, and he'd be back in his rack in exactly twenty-six minutes. He stretched at the thought and felt the tightness travel down to his lower back.

"You awake?" Oxford called from behind.

"Yeah," replied Pill as he tried to shake the sleep from his tired body.

"Want to catch some breakfast?"

"Naw, I'm going straight to my rack." Pill reached for his nav bag and started organizing its contents.

Oxford turned and saw Trapper climb up from the catwalk, sauntering toward the jet. It was difficult for a naval aviator not to saunter when encumbered with thirty pounds of survival gear and a harness cinched so tight it felt as if the Incredible Hulk were pushing the pilot's shoulders through his knees.

The VF-1 aircrew had no clue, but at that precise moment, an order was about to be sent that would alter Oxford's and Pill's sleep plans for the morning. Sixteen minutes earlier, OS2 Hammer, on watch at Air Ops two decks below the flight deck, noticed a new contact pop up on his screen. The target was a fast-mover, climbing out of twenty-two hundred feet in the vicinity of Hainan Island and squawking Mode II IFF, the designator for military aircraft. It was the first such contact in over three days, as the typhoon had kept the People's Liberation Army Air Force, or PLAAF, from flying as much as it had CVW-2's planes.

Within seconds, the *USS Valley Forge* came on the net and verbally announced the contact. Simultaneously a bogey track was superimposed over OS2 Hammer's raw radar blip. The bogey track included altitude, airspeed, direction vector, and a track number, in this case, 4-Lima-2.

Chatter burst onto the previously silent audio net as additional OSs from Battle Group Echo's ships chimed in. The first bogey in days added an adrenaline rush to the watchstanders' early morning monotony. OS2 Hammer pressed a button on his console and within seconds, the Tactical Air Officer was at his side.

"Watch ya got, Hammer?"

"Just popped up, Sir. I'd bet my first beer at Joe's it's a Badger out of Youlon," answered OS2 excitedly.

"What, in this weather?" replied the lieutenant commander. "You think the PLAAF is flying in this crap?"

"I don't know, TAO. Maybe they have a break in the weather over Hainan."

"All right. I won't take that bet. Let's see what Alpha Whiskey wants to do."

The tactical operators did not have to wait long. As soon as the bogey broke ten thousand feet and continued heading east, word from "the man" unequivocally came over the net. An unmistakable authoritative voice commanded, "Launch the alert-five fighter!"

CAG stepped into combat just as the battle group admiral ordered the alert launch. Grimacing, not happy to hear that one of his birds was launching in this weather, CAG quickly walked to the status grease board to see who was flying the alert aircraft. The senior aviator's face relaxed slightly when he saw Pill, a second-cruise aviator with above-average greeny-board scores this line period, was piloting the Tomcat. CAG thought for a moment and then ordered that the E-2C launch as well. If he was going to have a fighter airborne, he might as well give the crew extended eyes and ears.

Other than rhythmically pitching in the ten-foot swells, the flight deck appeared calm. Yellow-shirts reclined and slept on the huffer next to Wolf 106. VF-1 enlisted personnel also lounged and slept on additional yellow gear near the Tomcat. Trapper and Scout were perfunctorily preflighting the jet. Oxford had unstrapped and was about to stand up and start climbing out of the jet. In the time it took to declare five short words, controlled mayhem ensued.

"Launch the Alert-Five fighter!" boomed across the 5-MC.

Like cats in a shower, the yellow-shirts and plane captain sprang into action. One minute they were sleeping—dreaming of the upcoming port call—and three seconds later they were sprinting, firing up the huffer, and prepping the Tomcat for launch. Oxford started to stand, looked at Scout, sat back down, and was about to stand again when he saw the canopy on its way down. He quickly strapped in, plugged in his helmet radio cord, and began the prestart checklist.

Pill had been caught equally off guard. All he wanted to do was get out of the jet and climb back into his rack. After four hours of alert duty through the middle of the night, the last thing he wanted to do—the absolute last thing he wanted—was to launch off the carrier in dogshit weather, fly for an hour in turbulent air, and return to land on a pitching, rolling deck in the same crappy weather.

"Shit!" Even with his helmet on and the roar of the TF-30s starting to whine, Oxford could hear Pill yelling.

"God damn it! Fuck!"

"Yep," muttered Oxford. "Should be an interesting flight."

Oxford looked down and saw Scout looking blankly up at him. Trapper stood similarly dumbfounded. When he heard the command to launch, Scout started climbing the ladder to switch with Oxford and go flying. Conversely, Trapper had hesitated long enough to give the yellow-shirt the chance to cut off any idea of an aircrew swap. It was the yellow-shirt's butt on the line if the jet did not launch within three hundred seconds of the command. He was not going to let an aircrew swap screw-up his launch. Trapper and Scout had no choice other than step away from the jet and watch the show.

At one minute, the huffer fired up, and the Tomcat's left motor began to turn. At two minutes, the left motor was running, and the generators kicked on. At three minutes, Oxford completed the alert navigation alignment and the plane captain ran Pill through the abbreviated flight control checks. At four minutes, both motors were online and the ordies pulled the pins on the Sidewinders and Sparrows. At four minutes and thirty-eight seconds, Wolf 106 hurtled down Cat 2 at one hundred forty-seven knots with Pill and Oxford simultaneously yelling, "F-U-C-K!"

Since they were EMCON, Oxford refrained from the usual check-in with departure on Button 17. Instead, they followed the vector information data-linked directly to the jet from Mother and displayed on Oxford's TID. Pill selected NAV on his MFD and was able to see steering data to the target. Without a prompt from his backseater, Pill yanked the Tomcat hard to the left, pulling five g's in a climbing turn just below the cloud layer. Ordinarily, aircraft departing the carrier pattern remained at six hundred feet altitude for five miles on the departure heading, but all bets were off for alert launches, as no other aircraft were in the pattern. The fighter needed to close on its target as quickly as possible.

Pill left the throttle in zone-five afterburner until he saw five hundred knots while passing nine thousand feet. They were still Popeye, and Pill felt the first stages of the leans. Leveling the wings and bunting the nose, the pilot slowed the rate of climb marginally. He would have enough difficulty landing in this weather and didn't want to worsen an already bad situation by having to fight vertigo this early in the flight.

"I think I have something at, ah, about two hundred ten miles," Oxford's familiar voice came across the ICS. "Looks like he's heading one-zero-zero at angels two two-point-five."

"Climbing up," replied Pill. "I can't believe they launched us in this shit." The pilot was still fired up. At least his anger and adrenaline pushed back the exhaustion—for a little while, anyway. "If this is a COMAIR, I'm gonna shit," he added.

"Naw," remarked Oxford. "I'm getting a mode-two."

"Ain't no way any PRC bomber is gonna find Mother in this goo. Why the hell did they launch us?" complained Pill.

A minute later Pill chuckled. "Did you see Trapper's face when the canopy started down? Ha! As much as I didn't want to fly, I wasn't gonna take the time to switch out. Skipper would've burned our asses if we'd busted five minutes."

"No kidding. Hey, I don't think Sunking is up here."

As if on cue, the KY-28 tone beeped, and the filtered sound of an air wing bubba came across the cryptic voice comms, "Wolf One-Zero-Six, Sunking…how copy?"

"Lima Charlie," replied Oxford.

"Your bogey is two-four-three for one-eight-five, angels two three. Buster."

Oxford stepped quickly on his left foot-pedal microphone twice. The result was two short clicks that crackled through the comm net, meaning "roger that" or "copy." Tactical military communication, or comm, was abbreviated as much as possible. The double click took approximately one second to transmit and served to eliminate redundant chatter.

Inching the throttles forward, Pill wanted to make sure he and Oxford arrived at the merge with a full complement of speed as far from Mother as possible. Oxford worked the intercept from the rear seat, while Pill placed the bogey on the Tomcat's nose.

The F-14's AWG-9 radar was the most powerful radar ever placed in a tactical fighter jet. The system was designed in the late 1960s to tackle hordes of Soviet Bear and Backfire bombers streaking across the horizon to attack the carriers. The AWG-9 was optimized for overwater operation and could track up to twenty-four targets simultaneously. The radar also supported six simultaneous AIM-54 Phoenix launches at up to six separate targets. Although impressive as a marketing ploy, in reality the weapons support system could not cool six AIM-54s simultaneously. The tremendous weight of each Phoenix ensured no more than two AIM-54s were under the belly of a Tomcat flying off the boat. On this flight Wolf 106 merely carried a 2/2/0 loadout: two Sidewinders, two Sparrows, and no Phoenix.

"Two-four-four for one-six-eight...angels two three...speed three-one-zero," chirped Sunking. Oxford thought he recognized the voice emanating from the tube of the E-2C Hawkeye, as LT John "Headache" Kennedy. Headache was one of the more likable moles in the Sunkings with an imitable call sign.

The E-2 NFOs were an entirely different breed of aviator than the rest of the air wing bubbas. Because they sat in a blackened tube with no windows watching blips move across glowing screens all day and night, at times it seemed as if they could do their job from a bunker or air traffic control tower. In reality, the NFOs performed a crucial airborne mission. Not only did the E-2 crews back up the ship in controlling the entire air wing's complement of aircraft to make sure no one flew into one another, they also ran interference from commercial aircraft, no-fly zones, and prohibited airways. During combat, the Hawkeye crews also controlled strike packages and kept a watchful eye for incoming bandits and vampires. Due to their battle space management mission, the NFOs also had top-secret clearances and worked behind "the curtain," or top secret realm with the Intel weenies. The admiral was on a first-name basis with a handful of the Sunking FOs—unilateral first-name basis, that is, with the reciprocation always being, "Aye, aye, Admiral."

Wolf 106 streaked along at four hundred forty knots while the bogey indicated three hundred ten knots. With a combined closure rate of seven hundred fifty knots groundspeed, the aircraft were covering over thirteen miles per minute. At that speed, with less than 150 nautical miles separation, the aircraft would merge in about twelve minutes, eternity for a fighter intercept.

Pill grew uncomfortable, as they were still Popeye. Oxford, his head down in the radar working the intercept, barely noticed. He switched from Doppler to pulse to see if he could break out the target. Sure enough, he thumbed the control stick and managed to paint a slight echo on the pulse display.

"Gotta be a big bomber, probably a Badger," said Oxford excitedly over the ICS. "I'm starting to paint him in pulse."

The two aircraft were now less than one hundred miles apart and closing. The RIO had not heard from Sunking in several minutes. Ordinarily, the intercept controller tracked the intercept and parroted range and pertinent data every few miles.

Both Pill's and Oxford's breathing increased, as a real-world intercept, even during peacetime, was thrilling. Pill started to see slight breaks in the clouds between large buildups.

"Wolf One-Zero-Six, be advised. Sunking's radar is tango-uniform."

"Roger," replied Oxford. "We've got it covered, two-four-five at eighty-four, angels two eight-point-five."

At fifty miles, Pill turned ten degrees to the right to obtain the desired offset to the north to maneuver behind the target's wing-line and arrive at the bogey's six o'clock position at one nautical mile at the conclusion of the intercept—optimal weapons employment range.

Suddenly, the gray abyss pealed back, revealing a spectacular blue sky. Both Oxford and Pill were momentarily blinded, as neither aviator had seen the sun in days. Both flyers squinted uncomfortably behind the clear visors attached to their helmets. The view emerging below them was quite spectacular, as Pill could see the early morning sun glittering off the surface of the South China Sea. The sun was behind them, so he did not have to fight the glare in trying to make out a speck that would eventually turn into a large piece of flying metal. With any luck, he would obtain a visual at around fifteen miles. Sure enough, he caught a quick wing or windshield flash at twenty-two miles. *Damn, I'm good!* Pill congratulated himself.

"Tally," the pilot stated excitedly.

Oxford took one last scan high and low with the radar to ensure there were no wingmen or fighter escorts.

"Roger," acknowledged Sunking. "Say type of aircraft."

"Metal," replied Oxford sarcastically. "We're at nineteen miles," he added. Sometimes, even the most seasoned E-2 NFOs got caught up in the moment and did not realize the environment their fighter brethren worked in. It was something the fighter guys never let the moles forget. Oxford would make sure to relive the "type of aircraft" query with Headache at the dirty-shirt after they recovered on deck.

At ten miles, both Pill and Oxford had their heads out of the cockpit. Pill was fixated on the growing dot in the center of his windscreen. Oxford avoided the temptation to boresight the target and instead had his head craned backward, ensuring no unobserved aircraft snuck up on the Tomcat.

Pill asked Oxford to tell them it was a Badger, as he could make out the distinctive features of the vintage 1960s-era bomber at eight miles.

"Sunking...Wolf One-Zero-Six," stated the backseater over the secure radio.

"Go ahead."

"Looks like an H-6 Badger...single."

"Weapons?" asked the AIC.

Pill stepped in. "Clean wing."

Pill increased the Tomcat's bank angle to approximately thirty degrees to maintain head-on throughout the final stages of the intercept. The idea was to remain nose-on to minimize the cross-section view the large fighter displayed in the event the target was aware of the Americans and the adversary aircrew began to visually scan for the approaching jet. Here, the bomber flew straight and level and made no movement to indicate it was aware Wolf 106 was in the neighborhood.

The Badger was a distinctive-looking bomber of Soviet design. The Chinese obtained several Tu-16s from the Soviets in the late '50s and began indigenous production in the early '60s. The wings of the Badger were mounted midway through the fuselage and swept back, tapered with blunt tips. Its two turbojet motors were mounted in wing roots extending beyond the leading and trailing edges of the wing root. The bomber's fuselage was long and slender; it bulged where the engines were mounted and tapered to the tail. The aircraft had a round, glassed-in nose and a stepped cockpit. The Badger could never be described as graceful or intimidating. In fact, it was so ugly the aircraft repelled gravity. No wonder it was named the Badger—though Warthog or Platypus would have been equally appropriate designations. Pill maneuvered the Tomcat eight-tenths of a mile in trail of the lumbering bomber.

"Don't get too close. They've got a tail gunner, you know," warned Oxford.

"Yeah, I see him," replied Pill. He thrust the throttles forward to mil, pulled the stick back, and banked to the right to join on the bomber's starboard wing.

"Easy, tiger," exclaimed a surprised Oxford, "I was getting the camera out."

"Sorry," Pill chuckled. "Next time I'll warn ya." *Yeah, right!* Some of the Tomcat pilots liked to play with their backseaters by catching them unaware and banging their heads off the canopy. So far on this cruise, Pill had nailed Oxford twice.

For the next ten minutes, Pill and Oxford moved fore and aft of the starboard side of the bomber. Oxford snapped multiple photos, including several of the copilot waving. On the previous cruise about two years earlier, Oxford had intercepted a Soviet Tu-95 Bear H out of Cam Rahn Bay, Vietnam. While escorting the bulky bomber, the aircrew seemed quite jubilant to have two Tomcats on their wing. The copilot raised a bottle of vodka and toasted the American aircrew. The bomber pilot unfolded a magazine. When they eased closer, Oxford could see it was a *Playboy* centerfold. Due to the monster propellers on the large bomber's wing, they could not get close enough to see what month. The Russians appeared almost giddy. Looking back at the intercept, the incident foreshadowed Glasnost and the breakup of the Soviet Union, which occurred less than three years later.

The PLAAF aircrew was nowhere near as relaxed, but remained professional and restrained. The bomber made several gentle turns plus-and-minus thirty degrees of their zero nine zero heading in an apparent attempt to obtain radar targeting on *Ranger*. With its antiquated surface radar system, the crew may have had an idea of the carrier's direction but could not narrow the location close enough to find the flattop or its escorts. There was substantial merchant ship traffic in and around the area where *Ranger* was currently located. The typhoon and bad weather must have been affecting the bomber's radar system. Both the Badger and Wolf 106 were nearing the frontal system Pill and Oxford had finally flown out of during the last portion of the intercept. Both aircraft began experiencing slight turbulence, as the warm air of the South China Sea began mixing with the cold front at the outer fringes of the typhoon. Pill performed a conservative barrel roll over the bomber and settled approximately a hundred yards off its port wing. The Chinese aircraft responded with yet another turn to the south; this time, however, it continued turning until it steadied up at one hundred seventy degrees. Pill took the opportunity to slide back underneath to the starboard side of the aircraft.

Ordinarily, US fighters remained between the threat aircraft and Mother. In an attempt to confuse the PLAAF crew, Pill placed 106 on the opposite side of the Badger, even though *Ranger* was east of the two aircraft by approximately 160 nm. The ploy appeared to work, as the Badger immediately turned another ten degrees to the west and steadied at one hundred eighty degrees.

For the next twenty minutes, the Badger flew north and south along the edge of the cold front. The aircrew seemed to give up searching for *Ranger* and began zigzagging southeast and southwest before turning and heading northwest. Wolf 106 was down to 8,800 pounds of fuel and needed to head back to the ship in another fifteen to twenty minutes. They checked in with Sunking and were told not to expect relief on station. In other words, another Tomcat would not launch unless the Badger changed direction and began heading for the carrier.

Oxford took an entire roll of film and relaxed. He never thought he would get bored intercepting a Chinese bomber, but he didn't have anything else to do. They had been flying form on this behemoth for over forty minutes, and he could stare at a piece of metal in the sky for only so long—even if this particular metal was flown by Communist Chinese and possessed forty-millimeter machine guns and two thousand pound air-to-surface missiles and bombs.

The Badger began descending. Pill hung on. At ninety-seven hundred feet, the bomber turned west. Pill piloted the Tomcat to the rear half of the bomber to get a better look at the tail gunner. Oxford was commenting how the empennage reminded him of an old B-17 from World War II, when he noticed flaps coming down on the large bomber's wings.

"Man, Oxford, this guy is getting slow," noted Pill. "Maybe he's trying to shake us off. I've never heard of that tactic before."

Oxford looked at the airspeed indicator and saw one hundred ninety knots.

"Doesn't he know the flying tennis court can duel with the best of them?" replied the RIO gamely.

Pill thumbed out the F-14's maneuvering flaps and continued slowing with the Badger. At one hundred forty knots, suddenly two large doors opened from the belly of the bomber.

"Oh, shit!" exclaimed Oxford, "Is he gonna drop something?" Oxford was half-expecting a bomb or missile to drop from the aircraft. But a second later, he saw four large tires and two gear struts extend from the wings of the bomber.

"Oh," replied Oxford ashamedly, "never mind."

"No shit, Sherlock! Don't worry. I won't tell the guys as soon as we hit the ready room," joked Pill.

"Seriously, what the hell is this guy doing?"

"Well, he's at twenty-six hundred feet and descending."

The exact same thought hit Oxford and Pill at precisely the same time. As if choreographed, both flyers' heads snapped away from the bomber and looked out in front of the jet. What they saw shocked the experienced aviators. Dead silence draped over the cockpit as the gravity of the situation sunk in.

"Holy shit!" Before Oxford could finish the statement, Pill already had thumbed in the flaps and pushed the throttles to mil. "What the hell is that?"

"I don't know, but I do know we're getting the fuck out of here." Pill wrapped the jet into a four-g buffeted turn and sought to egress due east, placing as much space between the Tomcat and the Badger in as little time as possible.

"Should we pop out chaff or flares?" asked Oxford excitedly.

"Nah, let's hold off. Keep your head on a swivel for any fighters."

Oxford wrapped his head around and immediately began scanning behind the Tomcat. He could see two large, parallel runways and could even make out the Badger about to touch down on the left runway. "Man, we must be on about a six-mile final. This sucks!"

"Damn, Pill, I can see combatants in a harbor next to the runway. Gotta be Jianhu frigates. What is this place?"

"I don't know. Hainan?" asked Pill.

"Naw. Hainan's huge. This is the size of Manhattan."

"Dude, how did we get out here?" asked Oxford. He was checking their six, both in the air and from the surface, confirming they were not getting shot at.

"I don't know, but let's not say anything to anyone."

"What about Sunking?" asked Pill. "How come they didn't warn us?"

"I guess their radar is still tits up."

"Oh, man," replied Pill. "You don't see any other aircraft, do you?"

"Nope."

"Don't check in with Sunking for another ten minutes or so. We can then tell 'em we're breaking off the intercept for bingo."

"Good idea."

For the next ten minutes, neither aviator said a word. They continued scanning the horizon behind them for Chinese fighters. Finally, Oxford broke the silence and checked in with Sunking. The plan seemed to be working, as there was no unusual reply from the E-2. Both Oxford and Pill could hear Sunking check in with *Ranger*, and all seemed normal.

No other American fighters were launched, as the PLAAF did not send further aircraft aloft anywhere in the vicinity of *Ranger*. Oxford and Pill were cleared for an immediate Case III straight-in recovery. The weather within a hundred fifty miles of *Ranger* remained lousy, so Pill concentrated intently for the instrument approach. The exhaustion from the all-night alert and early morning launch crept back into his body. From the rear seat, Oxford kept a vigilant backup on heading, airspeed, and altitude.

Even though he had been up all night, launched abruptly during the last four minutes of their four-hour alert, intercepted and escorted a Chinese bomber, almost buzzed a Chinese airfield, flew for over three hours in and out of turbulent clouds and had less than 2,200 pounds of fuel, Pill managed to keep himself and Oxford out of the water and onto the two-wire.

It was not until they were in CVIC debriefing the flight that their luck started to turn. The Wolfies were discussing the rendezvous with the B-6 with a lieutenant junior-grade Intel debriefer when the ship's Intelligence Officer came rushing through the door.

"You guys Wolf One-Zero-Six?" demanded the surly lieutenant commander.

"Yes, Sir," replied Oxford in his most deferential tone.

"An OS2 on the Valley Forge had you guys within five miles of Woody Airfield. Five miles!" The commander stood with his lips pursed and arms gripped ominously across his chest. The tone of his voice was unmistakably pissed. He did not have to say it, but the implied message was loud and clear: "Don't fuck this up, flyboys. If I have to draft and send out an OP-REP message, you boys will be so far up to your asses in paperwork, you'll be lucky to see the inside of a jet in this or any other lifetime." But that is not what came out. What he said was, "Now, that can't be correct, right, gentlemen?"

Oxford looked at Pill. Pill looked down. The debriefing JG looked terrified.

"Uh," stammered Oxford. "I don't think that's possible, Sir." *Think, Oxford, think. What was going on with Sunking? That's right—their radar was down, and they weren't tracking us!* "We, uh…" *Deny, deny, deny.* "The Badger did get a bit low, but, uh—"

"He lowered his gear, and that's when we had to break it off to bingo," interrupted Pill.

"That's your story?" asked the commander incredulously, as if to say, "You can't come up with something better than that?"

"I guess we could'a been near an island. There are several out there in the Paracells, but I know we're not supposed to get within twenty-five miles of any, Sir."

"So the Valley Forge's multimillion dollar SPY-ONE radar must need some calibrating. Is that what you're saying, Lieutenant?"

"Sir, um, well, we can't say for sure, Sir," stammered Pill.

The commander stood menacingly over the flyers and Intel JO seated at the small table. He hesitated and started to say something else but changed his mind; instead, he marched out of the space without uttering another word.

Oxford and Pill finished the debrief in record time. The JG sure as hell did not want to cause any more waves, so he kept his mouth shut. Oxford handed over his camera with the Badger photos to the debriefer. The aviators slipped out of CVIC before the commander returned. They headed to the ready room and debriefed the maintenance day shift, dropped off their flight gear in the PR shop, and ended up in the dirty-shirt in time for lunch. They had planned to go directly to their racks, but the shot of adrenaline in CVIC had altered their plans. The co-conspirators needed some time together to get their stories straight before talking to Bourbon, Drum, or Pole.

Two Tomcat crews in the mid-'80s underwent a comparable experience. The four junior aircrew launched off Enterprise with two AIM-54s strapped to their jets. They wanted to conduct a photo op, and while joining to get a closer shot, the two aircraft exchanged paint. Unfortunately, the left wingtip of the wing aircraft contacted the lead's weapons rail and inadvertently ejected one of the million-dollar missiles into the Pacific.

The flyers communicated over a discrete frequency and came up with a plan to explain the missing Phoenix. They adopted the Gus Grissom "it just blew" explanation. There were sporadic pulses on the caution panel, and before the pilot could turn off power to the affected missile, the rail received a spurious electrical charge, malfunctioned, and released the missile into the ocean. *Yeah, that's our story, and we're sticking to it!* It was a dubious explanation at best.

A bored mole in the back of the airborne E2-C at the time was eavesdropping on several frequencies and heard the flyers switching to the "not so" discrete frequency. Worse, this particular NFO was a disenchanted RIO wannabe who had dreamed of Tomcats his entire childhood and was beat out by three one-hundredths of a grade point in flight school. Due to quality spread, he was drafted for Hawkeyes instead of fighters. Wrong guy scanning frequencies that day.

When the Tomcat aircrews recovered onto the carrier and told their stories in CVIC, the E-2 NFO danced in with the audiotape in hand. Upon disclosing its contents, one of the RIOs ripped the tape from the mole's hand, ran topside, and threw it into the ocean. Unfortunately for the fighter jocks, the Hawkeye NFO had the foresight to make a copy in his ready room minutes prior to entering CVIC. Suffice to say, the four Tomcat flyers lost their wings and were drummed out of the navy. Pill and Oxford were anxious not to follow in their brethren's muddied footsteps.

The skipper of the Valley Forge must have been an Academy grad, as he sent a message to the battle group commander containing Wolf 106's specific lat/long posits, altitudes, airspeeds, and times down to tenths of a second. There was no denying the SPY-1 radar's computer-generated data. Oxford and Pill were in a world of hurt. The admiral had no choice. Due to the political sensitivities associated with an incursion into PRC airspace, *Ranger* was required to fire off a Navy Blue OP-REP flash message to the

Pentagon. Best case, Pill and Oxford might get new call signs out of the incident. Worst case, they could lose their wings and get a quick trip home.

The next morning, Typhoon Warren made landfall near the city of Shantou in southeastern China. The weather near *Ranger* began clearing within hours, but the remnants of Warren's low-level circulation and clouds continued tracking northwest and well inland of Hong Kong. It was surreal—after five straight days of clouds and rough seas, the water and sky melded into a majestic cobalt blue, and the sea calmed considerably. Unfortunately for Pill and Oxford, their turbulence only heightened.

As *Ranger* headed for a well-deserved liberty call in one of the premier port calls of WestPac, the VF-1 flyers were put in hack. At least they were in good company. The entire Sunking aircrew—two pilots and three NFOs—also were restricted to the ship. The admiral did not care their radar had been inoperable during the incident. The State Department had responded within twelve hours of *Ranger*'s message and requested that all involved personnel be on call to meet with the American chargé d'affaires, if required. *Ranger*'s commanding officer was not about to exacerbate an already volatile situation, so he accommodated the request. The only Hong Kong liberty Pill, Oxford, and the Sunking crew would see was through the eyes of their squadronmates.

Ranger arrived in Hong Kong Harbor at daybreak. She anchored and had liberty boats alongside by 0900. Hundreds of sailors streamed through the hangar deck and boarded the large liberty launches headed directly to Kowloon. Pill and Oxford stood the in-port SDO duties the first couple of days. On day three, they were told to muster in the formal dining room with the Sunking aircrew and ship's legal officer. A State Department rep was going to interview them.

Oxford and Pill had no idea what to expect. They were upset with the fact they were on restriction for three days and missing out on some of the best liberty of WestPac. The flyers were told to wear their SDBs, as this would be a formal meeting.

Prone to jocularity and levity, the dining room was unusually somber as the seven aviators and JAG sat quietly waiting for the government official. The officers expected an uptight, gray-haired career diplomat read them the riot act. Instead, a thirty-something-year-old man in Bermuda shorts, golf shirt, Wayfarer sunglasses, and Docksiders with no socks breezed into the room escorted by the ship's PAO officer. Pill, Oxford, Headache, and the rest of the Sunking crew didn't even have a chance to rise to attention, as they were caught off guard by the casual introduction. Within five minutes of hearing the events, the State Department representative laughed off the incident. He told them the PRC had not even mentioned the event. If the Chinese were serious, they would have heard something from one of his PRC peers, or worse, Beijing would have filed a demarche with Washington. Most likely, the local PLAAF commander was too embarrassed to report to headquarters the incursion of a US fighter into Chinese airspace.

It took another five hours before word passed down from the skipper of *Ranger*, through CAG, to the skippers of VF-1 and VAW-116, to let their people go. Pill and Oxford were free to enjoy the remaining two days in port. They made up as much time out on the town as possible, cramming one hundred twenty hours of freedom into forty-eight hours of liberty.

17

After the ship's crew spent five glorious days in Hong Kong sightseeing, shopping, and, of course, barhopping, *Ranger* steamed southwest toward the Strait of Malacca and points further west. Cruise was past the one-third point, and almost everyone on board felt comfortable in their routines—or at least as comfortable as one could get working on an aircraft carrier doing anything remotely affiliated with flight ops. The crew had just completed two successful and gratifying liberty ports and was looking forward to getting to the North Arabian Sea, or NAS, and reaching the halfway point of cruise. It was with this mind-set that the ship's crew neared the southern-most point of Vietnam close to the former US base at Cam Rahn Bay.

The ship conducted routine flight ops the third day out of Hong Kong on the way to Singapore. Spyder and Tank were scheduled for a 1200 Alert Bravo and a 1945 night AIC hop. Spyder must have been doing something right in the eyes of Bourbon because the Ops O had not put him in a late-night or early morning alert since the Philippines.

After reviewing the message traffic, Spyder was not tired and could not re-rack. Instead, he had a leisurely workout in the ship's gym at 0700, showered, and worked on several evals until it was time to suit up for the alert. He was excited to fly with his roommate. Since they were both JOs, they rarely flew together on cruise.

Spyder made his way to the ready room and watched the 1000 air-crew brief. Mop, VA-145's Intel Officer, provided the usual chatter. CVIC briefed the routine political and military situation in Vietnam and its neighboring countries. There wasn't any fallout from Pill's and Oxford's

Badger incident, and no other PRC aircraft had come out to see *Ranger*. Another ordinary day of cruise—notch 71 of 180.

As Spyder completed his second eval for a second-class petty officer in his AQ branch, the 1-MC announced loudly, "Launch the alert-five fighters now. Launch the alert-five fighters!" Spyder was not yet on alert status and had not even put on his gear, yet his heart began to pump. Aviators swung into motion around him. Bourbon and Austin, the Alert Bravo aircrew, grabbed their helmets and gear and were out the ready room door in less than ten seconds. Mauler, the SDO, dialed Air Ops. In a minute, both the XO and CO entered the ready room and immediately began harassing Mauler for information. Since Spyder and Tank were the next alert aircrew on the schedule, they quickly grabbed their gear from the PR shack and suited up, awaiting further orders.

The only information Mauler gleaned from Air Ops was that a Soviet Bear-H bomber had launched from Cam Rahn Bay, Vietnam, and was heading east. Both VF-1's and VF-2's Alert Alpha aircraft launched and were vectored to intercept the bomber. As Mauler was briefing the CO and XO, the 1-MC announced for the second time in less than ten minutes to launch the alert fighters.

"What the hell's going on, Mauler?" exclaimed the Skipper. He couldn't remember the last time four alert fighters were launched within minutes of one another.

Spyder didn't wait to hear Mauler's response, and instead, grabbed his helmet and nav bag and yanked a card-of-the-day from the SDO desk. He quickly scanned the maintenance logbook from Maintenance Control and jogged onto the deck with Tank on his heels. *Sometimes ya just gotta trust the wrench-turners.*

As Spyder and Tank popped up onto the flight deck, Wolf 102 was being placed into tension. Spyder stopped and strapped on his flight helmet while watching the Shooter punch his right arm into the air and thrust out all five fingers. Brilliant flames shot out of the tailpipes of 102's two afterburner engines. Spyder was a good fifty yards away from the Tomcat, yet the deafening noise and deep vibrations felt as if they were piercing his chest cavity directly to the center of his heart. He turned his back and searched for his alert aircraft, Wolf 107.

By the time Spyder and Tank reached 107, a yellow-shirt was next to the aircraft barking out orders. The Handler shouted for a re-spot over the radio and ordered 107 and Bullet 204 on the waist catapults. Four blue-shirts were already unfastening the chains and hooking a tractor to 107's nose gear. Spyder and Tank had to wait to perform their preflight because it was too dangerous to inspect the jet while being towed.

It took seven minutes for the flight deck personnel to re-spot 107 on Cat 3. Tank quickly slapped a VCR tape into the aircraft's recorder. Before the aircraft was fully chained down, Spyder and Tank conducted a quick walk around the jet and hopped up on the turtleback to finish their preflight. Both aircrew were amped, as neither had launched on a real-world alert or escorted a foreign aircraft. The closest either had come was five months earlier when they launched to intercept and escort a Lear Jet simulating an enemy bomber during a JTF-EX off the coast of San Diego.

Spyder quickly arranged his cockpit and climbed in. Airman Brown climbed the ladder and helped him and his RIO finish strapping in.

"Sir, do you know what's going on?" asked Brown. "Four fighters in ten minutes, that's gotta be some kind of record."

"I heard there's a Soviet Bear bomber roaming around. Not sure why they launched four fighters, though. Maybe there are more Russians out there."

"Cool. Hope you get to launch, Sir."

"Me too."

Brown climbed back down and finished prepping the aircraft for its alert status. He plugged in the huffer hose and electrical cord, which gave Spyder and Tank electrical power in the cockpit. Tank turned on the radio and switched to Strike, Button 5. A static screech filled their headsets.

"Go green," suggested Spyder on the ICS. Tank switched on the KY-58 radio, and within seconds, the screechy static turned to decipherable voices. Spyder recognized Mustang's distinctive drawl.

DAN ZIMBEROFF

"Roger, Sunking. Wolf One-Zero-Two has two bogeys three-one-zero at twelve...angels one five."

"Oh, man!" exclaimed Spyder to Tank. "They've got two out there." Spyder's adrenaline pumped, even though his aircraft sat chained onto the deck.

"Wolf One-Zero-Two, Bullet Two-Zero-One. Your bogeys are two-niner-five for fifteen, angels one seven."

"Wolf One-Zero-Two," responded Austin.

"Jesus!" shouted Tank. "It's a fucking furball out there. Those can't all be bombers."

"Think there are some fighters thrown in from Cam Rahn Bay?" asked Spyder as he grew even more excited.

"Must be."

Over the next five minutes, Spyder and Tank sat on the edge of their seat pans as they heard Mustang, Austin, and the two Bullet RIOs run intercepts on the bogeys. Spyder and Tank adjusted their cockpits awaiting imminent launch.

Slum and Mustang, with Bullet 205 on their wing, were the first fighters to go head to head with the bandits. The Wolfies met two Russian fighters at the merge.

"MiG-23s," confirmed Mustang. His voice strained as he grunted to help stave off the g-forces Slum reefed on the jet as they attempted to maneuver behind the foreign aircraft. "Wolf One-Zero-Four has...err...two armed Floggers. We're...err...engaged now."

"Roger Wolf One-Zero-Four, two MiG-23 Floggers," responded Sunking. Even the NFO in the back of the E-2C sounded keyed up.

Spyder and Tank knew they would be launched now for sure. Spyder tightened his straps and readjusted his cockpit for the third time. He and Tank completed their alert pretakeoff checklist. They sat and listened to their squadronmates mix it up with two MiGs. The aviators could hear the tension in the voices of Austin, the Bullet RIOs, and even the well-experienced Mustang. No aircraft was shooting, but they were embroiled

138

in intense maneuvering and dogfighting. From the radio calls, it sounded like the navy pilots were getting the best of the Floggers.

More time lapsed with no activity on the flight deck. "I can't believe they aren't launching us," said Tank disappointedly from the rear seat. The 5-MC blared, "Launch an alert-five fighter! Launch an alert-five fighter!"

"Finally!" shouted Spyder. But his enthusiasm was short-lived. He looked down expecting a flurry of activity from the deck personnel around his aircraft, but instead, saw everyone looking to the left of his jet. He followed their gazes and saw several blue-shirts and VF-2 personnel scurrying around Bullet 204.

"No way! They're launching Two-Zero-Four but not us?" Disappointment tugged on Spyder's words.

"Shit!" exclaimed Tank.

Spyder and Tank sat dejectedly as they watched Bullet 204 go into full burner merely eight feet away and then launch into the brilliant blue sky. They still could not believe everyone else was mixing it up with Vietnamese MiG-23s while they sat on their hands.

The sea was smooth. A bountiful sun shone down on them between puffy, scattered clouds. Soviet fighters and bombers were zorching around the sky in *Ranger*'s backyard; yet, Spyder and Tank sat in their jet chained to the rhythmically rising and dropping flight deck.

The Wolfie flyers continued to bake in the cockpit while listening to the tactical frequency as Bullet 204 entered the fray. An A-6 tanker launched to refuel Wolf 102 and Bullet 201. The yellow-shirts re-spotted another Bullet aircraft on Cat 4 next to Spyder and Tank. Just when they thought they were going to miss all of the action, they finally received the order they had been awaiting. Four minutes and forty-five seconds later, the Wolfie JOs screamed down Cat 3 in zone-five afterburner accelerating through one hundred fifty knots. After feeling the violent jerk at the end of the cat stroke signifying transition from steel to sky, Spyder remained in burner, set a steep climb attitude, and yanked the jet in a hard ninety-degree angle of bank turn to the west. He and Tank were not going to waste any more time getting to the fight.

"Radar's tits up," stated Tank matter-of-factly from the rear seat.

"No way! You can't get anything, not even pulse?" asked Spyder.

"Nothin'. I've shut it down completely twice, kicked it once, and even rubbed it gently, but got the same error message. Something must've come loose in the cat shot."

"Great!" added Spyder. His first alert launch against a gaggle of bogeys and he and Tank were lead-nosed.

"Sunking, Wolf One-Zero-Seven at angels one four. You have a vector for us?" asked Tank on secure Button 5.

"Stand by."

"Tank, keep your head out of the cockpit and check our six often. I don't want any surprises," said Spyder. "I'm keeping the master arm off for now." The Tomcat was loaded with live missiles—two Sidewinders and two Sparrows.

"Roger that. I'm already head's out."

"Wolf One-Zero-Seven, Sunking. Your bogeys are three-zero-five for sixty-eight, angels twelve-point-five. You have Wolf One-Zero-Two and Bullet Two-Zero-One in the mix. Be advised, separate gaggle two-niner-eight for eighty-one miles with Wolf One-Zero-Four and Bullets Two-Zero-Five and Two-Zero-Four."

"Roger that." Tank didn't even try to mask his excitement.

Spyder eased out of burner to save fuel and was still streaking along at four hundred eighty knots in full military power. At that speed, it would take them less than nine minutes to reach the closest furball. If they were lucky, they'd catch a wing or canopy flash at around twelve miles. He had no chance of seeing them from over fifty miles, yet Spyder still squinted through the HUD, searching for any speck of metal amid the white clouds and blue sky.

Both the tactical frequency and strike frequency filled with comms from numerous aircraft stepping over one another. Aircrew tried to adhere to strict radio discipline and not fill the frequency with superfluous chatter, but there was a lot of information to pass. Except for the major alpha strikes at Fallon, neither Spyder nor Tank had been involved in a sortie involving such a large number of fighters. This was real world with actual fighter aircraft armed with live missiles.

"Left ten o'clock, low, probably ten miles," declared Tank over the ICS.

Spyder instinctively banked the jet thirty degrees left and slightly nose low as he desperately searched the sky for the jets Tank had called out. *What? My RIO caught a tally before me!*

Spyder continued scanning the sky. "No joy. Where are they?"

"Keep it coming ten degrees left," answered Tank eagerly. "I've got two—no, three aircraft slightly nose low!"

"Got 'em!" exclaimed Spyder triumphantly.

"Bourbon, Spyder's entering the fight high from the east. Are you tail end Charlie?" asked Spyder on the front-seat radio.

"Affirm. Stay high cover. There may be more out here. Slush and I have these two Floggers cold."

"Roger."

Spyder leveled the wings and eased the throttles back a few notches. He checked the fuel gauge and saw they still had over twelve thousand pounds remaining. The Tomcat was loaded with two fuel drop tanks, which degraded its dogfighting performance but gave them much valued time on station. If required, Spyder could pickle the tanks and greatly increase the jet's aerial capability. For now, he and Tank were relegated to the bench. Bourbon directed them to remain out of the fight and continued orbiting overhead to ensure no other bogeys surprised the navy fighters dogfighting below.

"This sucks!" exclaimed Spyder. "We didn't launch and fly out here to circle overhead and watch from the cheap seats."

"No kidding," responded Tank.

As he started to bank at eighteen thousand feet about five thousand feet above the two Tomcats and two Floggers looping below, Spyder calmed. His heart rate slowed, and he felt as he did during training hops out in the Papa areas off San Diego. Unlike depictions of dogfights shown in the movies, actual ACM took place in three dimensions. Aircraft did not simply follow one another like vehicles in a car chase. As he looked below, he saw the Floggers climbing and rolling and the Tomcats alternating in and out of the chase. The aircraft looped, dove, banked, and pirouetted. At one point, the lead Flogger flew straight into the sun in an attempt to blind the pursuing Tomcats, but Bourbon offset to the south and remained above and behind the MiG.

"See anything else?" asked Spyder.

"Nope, but this is awesome. Bourbon could be gunning the brains out of those MiG bastards if he wanted."

Spyder stared down at the aircraft and saw the two MiGs extend down and westward. It looked as if they were trying to escape from the Tomcats, but Bourbon and Slush stayed on them like stink on a pig. Something caught Spyder's attention out of the corner of his left eye. He saw slight movement to his left and readjusted his gaze upward.

"Bogeys west high!" was all Spyder could muster as adrenaline shot through his body. He was surprised his mouth even worked. Slamming the Tomcat's throttles to mil, he banked the jet on its side and yanked six g's to put the bogeys on their nose. Spyder's senses calmed long enough for him to think and talk simultaneously.

He smashed the comm button on the stick, "Bourbon, two bogeys angels one eight about a mile from Wolf One-Zero-Two and Bullet. Spyder's taking 'em nose-on."

Bourbon and Slush immediately broke off their pursuit of the first two Floggers and streaked upward and to the left. If they had continued, they would have been easy targets for the advancing new MiGs. Now that Spyder had alerted them, the Tomcats had a good chance of avoiding flying in front of the second flight of Floggers.

In seconds, Spyder and Tank went right to right at a distance of less than five hundred yards with the lead MiG-23. "Merge with two Floggers!" exclaimed Spyder on the tactical frequency.

"Keep an eye on the westernmost one," Spyder instructed Tank over the ICS while he craned his head over his right shoulder keeping track of the fleeing MiG. "I'm going after dash-one." He immediately banked the Tomcat 110 degrees to the right and reefed seven g's on the jet, dropping the nose twenty degrees to keep some smack on the Tomcat. The lead MiG could not turn anywhere close to the rate of the F-14, even with its two drop-tanks. Before they had turned 180 degrees, Spyder and Tank were already inside the turning radius of the lead MiG and gaining angles each second.

"Dash-two is slightly higher...err...and to the west of lead," grunted Tank under the severe g forces. "No factor yet."

"Spyder, keep it coming," directed Bourbon on tac. "Slush and I will take dash-two and also keep an eye on the first two who bugged out west."

"Wolf One-Zero-Two flight, Sunking," interrupted one of the E-2 NFOs. "Two bogeys five west, angels ten, headed west."

Spyder was now inside thirty degrees of the Flogger's longitudinal axis and just over a mile in trail. The bogey was in prime missile range, assuming the MiG was not accelerating too quickly. The Flogger was faster than the Tomcat in a straight-out dash and could fly away from the American pilots. But the MiG pilot did something completely unexpected. He pulled hard and started climbing straight up. Spyder followed suit and moved the throttles to afterburner. The aircraft were passing sixteen thousand feet and zooming upward. He pulled seven g's initially and once again cut inside the radius of the MiG-23's loop. The Tomcat closed in on the Flogger and was now almost directly behind it. As if on cue, the MiG rolled on its belly, showing Spyder and Tank its underside, affixed with two AA-7 APEX radar missiles and two AA-2 ATOLL infrared missiles.

"This is unbelievable!" exclaimed Spyder. "Are you getting this on tape?"

"You bet! Started it as soon as we entered the fight," responded Tank triumphantly.

The Flogger continued to rise like an orca breaching out of the sea. When it reached the apex of the loop, instead of rolling back and continuing the loop, the fighter remained on its back and then pulled to wings level at twenty-one thousand four hundred feet of altitude. The green and tan camouflaged fighter was now straight and level and a sitting duck for Spyder and Tank. But Wolf 107 was screaming along in zone-five. Spyder had failed to anticipate the Flogger pilot's actions and was now overtaking the MiG at over three hundred knots. If he didn't do something quickly, they would overshoot the Flogger and then be in an extremely vulnerable position. Spyder slammed the throttles to idle, triggered the speed brakes, pulled back sharply on the stick, and shot upward to twenty-three thousand feet. He then rolled the Tomcat on its back and pulled on the stick, lowering the nose and completing the spacing maneuver. He slowly pushed the throttles back to mil as the jet reached two hundred knots.

"Dash-two is coming around right four o'clock," stated Tank.

"OK."

Spyder paused for three seconds as the Tomcat reached four hundred knots. He then banked and pulled hard to the right, dismissing the lead Flogger momentarily. The pilot let the F-14's nose drop to maintain speed and kept six g's on the jet. Within ten seconds, he had the second Flogger on his nose and continued the turn to get inside the MiG's radius. As with the first MiG, Spyder was able to cut the corner and gain substantial angles on his adversary in less than three hundred sixty degrees of turn.

"Keep it coming," stated Bourbon on strike. "Slush and I will fillet this Flogger in five more seconds."

"Spyder."

Sure enough, Spyder kept the turn on and saw the two Tomcats swoop in behind the MiG in a much better firing position. After a few seconds, Spyder discontinued his turn, leveled his wings, and accelerated through four hundred knots. He then pulled hard on the jet and streaked upward, trying to get above the fight and resume high cover.

"This is awesome," called out Tank from the backseat.

As soon as Spyder hit twenty-five thousand feet, he rolled the Tomcat on its back to look down at the aircraft below. Both Floggers bugged out to the west with Bourbon and Slush in hot pursuit. For the second time in less than five minutes, Bourbon and Slush chased off a section of MiG-23s with Spyder and Tank watching from the high perch.

"Knock it off," directed Bourbon on the front-seat radio. "Slush." The entire dogfight had lasted less than six minutes. The two Tomcats disengaged and started climbing upward toward Spyder.

"Sunking, Wolf One-Zero-Two with Bullet Two-Zero-One and Wolf One-Zero-Seven, say intentions. Wolf One-Zero-Two at fuel state five-point-six," stated Austin from Bourbon's back seat.

"Wolf flight, proceed case one recovery," directed Sunking. "Mother's at one-zero-two for ninety-three miles."

"Wolf One-Zero-Two."

Spyder joined on Slush's wing, who was flying a loose trail off Bourbon. Bourbon then directed Slush and Spyder via hand signal to switch positions, as he wanted his squadronmate as dash-two. Austin checked in with strike for the flight of three and was told to switch to Button 17. The flight was cleared to Charlie without having to Marshall overhead. The ship was waiting for them and wanted the aircraft to recover without delay.

Bourbon bustered the aircraft for the fifteen-minute transit back to Mother and entered the break at five hundred fifty knots and five hundred feet. He broke at the stern and masterfully slowed and configured the jet for landing. The department head utilized his superior flying skills to land without touching the throttles to an OK 3-wire. Not a bad day at the office for Bourbon and the other CVW-2 fighter bubbas.

After landing and securing their jet, Spyder and Tank raced to CVIC. They wanted to share their amazing afternoon of flying with the Intel debriefers and see what other hijinks their brethren had experienced. The aviators completed the debrief in under twenty minutes and almost sprinted to the ready room to share their high-energy anecdotes.

When they burst into the Wolfpack den, the aviators were greeted by a dozen peers in flight gear all talking with their hands and trying to out-shout one another. It took only a couple of minutes before Spyder and Tank realized half of the squadron had launched and mixed it up with the MiGs. Spyder and Tank dove right into the gaggle and began telling their tale along with Bourbon and Austin. The ready room atmosphere mimicked the locker room of a Super Bowl championship team. The aviators were all speaking over each other in an effort to retell their encounters dogfighting the MiGs.

After dinner, all of the VF-1 officers assembled in the ready room to formally debrief the afternoon's intercepts. They discovered a total of eight VF-1 and seven VF-2 fighters had launched and intercepted twelve MiG-23 Floggers and two Bear-H bombers out of Cam Rahn Bay, Vietnam. The flyers were told by CVIC debriefers that the pilots and aircraft were not Vietnamese, but Soviet. The Russians had a Flogger det at Cam Rahn Bay and for some unknown reason had decided to come out and play with *Ranger*'s air wing. The large-scale impromptu intercepts were unprecedented. Never before had a carrier air wing intercepted more than four Soviet fighters during a single mission. The *Ranger* flyers speculated that the Flogger squadron CO must have been retiring and wanted one final fling before riding off into the sunset. Whatever the reason, the afternoon was a career highlight for several of the aviators who retired or left the navy prior to the Gulf War and 9/11.

Mauler was in a sour mood the entire afternoon and evening, as he was one of the few VF-1 flyers who did not participate in the fun. Not only did he not get into the air and mix it up with the Soviets, but he also had been virtually chained to the SDO desk putting out myriad fires. He'd battled all day with the Maintenance Master Chief, Strike Ops, and Handler in getting enough VF-1 jets re-spotted and into the air.

After musing about the intercepts for hours in the ready room, the Wolfies realized all had flown well against the MiGs except for a single VF-1 pilot. The JOs kidded that at that precise moment, the Soviets were probably back at the Cam Rahn Bay Officers' Club sipping their version of Thermonuclear Specials and reliving the day's events from the Soviet perspective.

"Comrade Leninski," kidded Slum in a mock Russian accent to the group. "Those American pilots are very, very good aces. Yes, they all got behind us and flew our tails off except for that single F-14 with the bright red Wolf on its tail. Yes, comrade, he must have been the junior-most pilot of the squadron—ah, how you say it...F-N-G?"

"Little did they know," shouted out Austin, "that was our skipper!"

The ready room broke out in laughter, as Pole was the lone American pilot who had allowed a Flogger to get behind him.

"Now, Slum," responded Pole seriously. "Hell if I let him get behind my three-nine line. At worst we were neutral."

"I'm not sure, Skipper," interjected Drum. "I coulda sworn I saw the MiG on your tail."

"No, XO, that must have been Bullet Two-Ten. He was having trouble."

"Whatever you say, Skipper," replied the XO dutifully.

For the remainder of cruise, VF-1's commanding officer had to downplay the fact he was the only CVW-2 pilot who had allowed a Cam Rahn Bay Flogger to maneuver aft of an F-14's wingline. The fact Pole was a former F-4 Phantom pilot may have had something to do with it, as the venerable F-4, like the MiG-23, was far from a turning machine. In any event, it provided plenty of ammo and laughs for VF-1 during Foc'sle Follies at the midpoint of cruise.

✳ ✳ ✳

The aviators of Carrier Air Wing TWO found themselves in dire circumstances less than two weeks later. *Ranger* had transited the Strait of Malacca after a port call in Singapore and was on its final leg to the NAS and Gonzo Station. The closest land was the Maldive Islands off the southern tip of India, over a thousand miles to the southeast. The navy called this "blue water ops"—flight operations when the carrier was outside of divert airfield range, meaning if an aircrew experienced an inflight emergency, they would have to try to recover on the ship or eject next to it.

The flying was routine, almost boring, as there was no land and few merchant ships to overfly. Like Bill Murray's character in *Groundhog Day,* some of the crew began to feel as though the same day kept repeating itself over and over.

Spyder was scheduled with Tank again as a spare for a 1945 night AIC hop. As they sat through the 1745 brief, the 1800 cycle launched precisely on schedule. Spyder always found it difficult to concentrate on the CVIC brief when sixty-thousand-pound jets catapulted off the deck merely feet above his head. The junior Intel officer provided a succinct brief, as there was not much information to pass while *Ranger* steamed westward in the middle of the expansive ocean. No foreign combatants were within five hundred miles. About the only data of any interest was a tropical depression off the western coast of India building sea states in *Ranger*'s path. By morning, the ship would be in moderately heavy seas. Presently, the boat was pitching in mild six- to eight-foot swells. Once again, the highlight of the brief was the BOTD—in this case Penthouse Pet of the Month for June. Spyder's mind wandered to the bikinis on the beach back home in San Diego.

After the brief and review of the maintenance book, Spyder followed Tank up the ladder well to the catwalk near the stern of the ship. They stepped up onto the flight deck and searched for their jet. After several minutes of shining their lights on other Tomcats, they found and preflighted Wolf 106, the spare aircraft spotted aft of the island and six-pack. Spyder finished his walk-around preflight and hopped up on the turtleback of the mighty Tomcat. As he looked at the expansive wings, fuselage, and stabilators, he was not surprised the F-14 was also affectionately known as the "flying tennis court." The pilot took a few minutes to look out at the pitch-black sea. After so many days and nights cruising through the Philippines, Hong Kong Harbor, and the Strait of Malacca, he was not used to seeing the void of darkness that enveloped the ship. *Yeah, I'm definitely OK staying as a spare and not launching tonight.*

Even though the Tomcat was not parked over water, Spyder kept to his usual routine and let Tank preflight the top of the jet. He climbed into the cockpit and prepared for engine start. Since he and Tank were the mission spare, they were the last to receive power and start from the yellow- and blue-shirts. Spyder took his time setting up the cockpit before finally clicking the parachute fasteners. He enjoyed the respite from his usual harried engine starts and pre-flight checks.

✳ ✳ ✳

At the same time Spyder and Tank were setting up their cockpits, Pole and Austin were entering the Marshall stack at seven thousand feet from the preceding launch. Slum and Scout were assigned the next higher altitude block, or eight thousand feet. The section of fighters had finished a routine AIC flight with two Bullet aircraft. It was the point of cruise, transiting between major landmasses, where the flying was mundane and far from thrilling.

"Skipper, we've got seven-point-one of gas. I calculate max trap with our two-and-two loadout at four-point-two," stated Austin over the ICS.

"That's what I got. Since we're blue water ops, I won't dump until after we've pushed."

"Roger that. Say, you wanna bet on a push time?" Austin looked at his watch and saw it was 1935.

"Sure," responded VF-1's commanding officer. "The usual soda?"

"You're on."

✳ ✳ ✳

The Bullet section checked in with Approach on Button 17 and was assigned nine thousand feet and ten thousand feet, respectively. Scooter and Soup were in Bullet 205, with VF-2's skipper and a JO pilot in Bullet 204. Scooter and Soup played a similar game to Pole and Austin. Scooter bet his department head RIO a Diet Coke their push time would be 1950. Soup took the bet, as he calculated in his head a 1956 push time. Readjusting his cockpit lighting, the pilot began reviewing the final landing procedures. He imagined the final ten seconds of landing, including finessing the throttles, anticipating the burble over the deck and making a final subtle lineup correction, repeating this process in his mind several more times while waiting for Approach to announce the push times.

✳ ✳ ✳

"Dude, who were you writing a letter to earlier?" Tank asked over the ICS. The two flyers were finished with the engine start and system checks and were waiting to see if either Pole's or Joker's planes broke.

"Uh, no one in particular," Spyder replied.

"Dude, really?"

"No one. Just a friend from college." Spyder tried unsuccessfully to avoid Tank's inquisition.

"Does she have a name?"

Spyder capitulated. "Laura."

"Ha, I knew it. Have any photos?"

"No, dammit!"

By now, Spyder had heard and felt the first aircraft launch off the bow cat. He and Tank had a front row seat for the launch about to commence at the waist cats. A half dozen aircraft sat parked on the stern awaiting their turn to launch. Both Wolf 112, Pill's jet, and Wolf 107, Bourbon's bird, were behind the Intruders and likely would be the fourth and fifth jets to launch. As Spyder looked over 112 and 107 to see if he could see any problem with the fighters, he heard and felt the roar of Jackal 502 go to mil power on Cat 4. Spyder looked forward in time to see the Shooter pump his fist in the air and then bend down and touch the deck. A second later, the mighty Intruder shot forward with a loud *whoosh* and was off into the night sky. Immediately a yellow-shirt began taxiing the third Intruder onto Cat 4. The jet's outline faded in and out of the steam rushing down the deck from the first launch. The Intruder on Cat 3 then went into tension with another loud roar. Spyder and Tank's Tomcat shook slightly from the vibration and kinetic energy flowing through the flight deck. The troubleshooters looked over the jet one last time and gave their thumbs-up. The Shooter repeated his launch sequence. As the Shooter's hand touched the deck, the catapult petty officer pushed the button and released the catapult's piston along with seventy-two thousand pounds of foot-torque power. The jet jerked forward, rushed down the track and launched into the night sky to join his squadronmate in lumbering flight.

✳ ✳ ✳

"Ninety-nine aircraft, Approach, stand by for push times," stated the controller on Button 17. In response, Austin and each of the other eleven sets of aircrew in the Marshall stack grabbed their pens and prepared to write down their push times. The controller identified each jet in roll-call fashion with associated push times in one-minute intervals. Each aircraft acknowledged their time and established orbits to hit the initial approach point, or IAP, on speed, on altitude, and on time. The aircrew had a strict plus or minus ten-second window from which they had to commence their approach or suffer the wrath of Approach Control and ridicule from air wing aviators listening on the common frequency.

✳ ✳ ✳

"Man, I pooched that one!" exclaimed Scooter to his RIO. "What, now I owe you three Diet Cokes, right?"

"Yeah. And it's only gonna go higher," replied Soup teasingly. He glanced at the fuel ladder notations on his kneeboard card and jotted down some fuel calculations. "We're about twenty-two hundred pounds heavy. We'll want to start dumping as soon as we commence."

"OK, will do," responded Scooter. He was still going over the landing procedures in his mind, trying not to psyche himself out. The first butterflies began to dance in his stomach.

✳ ✳ ✳

Spyder and Tank were enjoying the light show as the first two Wolfies launched in full afterburner from Cats 3 and 4. Ordinarily he would have shielded his eyes to avoid searing his night vision, but since it looked like he wasn't going flying, Spyder stared at the fire-belching TF-30 motors in their full brilliance. Raw fuel-engulfed flames shot out at least ten feet behind each motor in a pyrotechnician's dream display of intense red, orange, and yellow bursts reflecting off each piece of metal and Plexiglas in sight, adding to the radiance of the show. It was a highly impressive performance, reminding him of a July 4th fireworks demonstration; however, this one was merely twenty yards away and included heart-pounding vibration with full-on surround sound.

✳ ✳ ✳

Austin checked his watch for the third time in ten seconds and saw he and Skipper had fifteen seconds left before their push time and they were at three hundred thirty knots with three miles to go.

"Looks like we're gonna be about ten seconds late," stated Austin over the ICS.

"I'm tapping burner now," responded the skipper. "We'll be a bit fast, but right on time."

Exactly fifteen seconds later, Pole and Austin were the first aircraft to commence the Case III recovery. "Wolf One-Zero-One commencing at four-nine, six-point-three," stated Austin succinctly on Button 17.

"Roger Wolf One-Zero-One," replied Approach.

"I'm holding off dumping for a few more miles," said Pole over the ICS.

"Roger that."

✳ ✳ ✳

Though both Wolfpack jets had launched minutes earlier, the deck personnel had not yet shut down Spyder's and Tank's jet. The Tomcat's engines continued to turn while the flyers sat strapped in their harnesses watching continuation of the 1945 launch. Spyder saw the two Bullet aircraft taxi into position. Bullet 209 taxied onto Cat 3 while Bullet 203 was being taxied by the yellow-shirt behind Bullet 209 on its way to Cat 4. Spyder and Tank were looking straight at the scene as it unfolded before them. The next sequence happened so quickly neither officer had time to react.

Because it was an older Forrestal-class carrier, *Ranger* did not use jet blast deflectors, or JBDs, for its waist cats. This meant aircraft had to remain at least fifty feet behind a standard launch and a hundred feet behind an afterburner launch. As Spyder and Tank gazed forward, they saw the Shooter place Bullet 209 in tension before 203 was out of the way. As soon as 209's pilot pushed the throttles to military, the exhaust of the twin TF-30 motors flowed back onto the rear stabilators of the sister jet crossing behind the launching aircraft. In the blink of an eye, Bullet 203 spun two hundred seventy degrees and faced backward toward the stern. Worse, the momentum from taxiing to Cat 4 and being spun by 209's exhaust careened the jet onto the catwalk and almost directly over the side of the ship.

Bullet 203's right mainmount thrust partially through the port catwalk, and the jet hung precariously on its starboard drop tank. The jet was listing at about a twenty-degree angle toward the ocean sixty feet below. With each roll of the ship, the aircraft rocked back and forth, perilously close to teetering into the sea.

"Shit!" exclaimed Spyder over the ICS. "They're about to go over the side!"

Both he and Tank sat helplessly, as they were still strapped to a turning jet thirty yards from the stricken Tomcat. At any instant, Spyder expected to see the canopy blow and two bright flashes from Bullet 203's ejection seats.

The VF-2 flyers, Pie and T-Bone, looked down at the dark water rushing sixty feet below. They knew if they punched out, there was a high probability due to the angle the cockpit leaning toward the ocean, that they would be ejected onto the surface of the ocean. Breaking a neck or drowning in a half-deployed parachute were not especially appealing alternatives. They decided to stay with the jet—at least for the moment.

✳ ✳ ✳

"Ninety-nine aircraft, ninety-nine aircraft, max conserve. Stand by for further instructions," Approach announced over Button 17 and Button 6 simultaneously.

"What the hell?" exclaimed Austin over the ICS to his skipper.

"Ya know, I had a feeling. I was about to start dumping fuel, but something told me not to."

"This has never happened to me before, Skipper. Do we continue the approach or return to Marshall?"

"I bet back to Marshall. Why don't you wait a few seconds, and if Mother doesn't direct us, give Approach a holler."

No sooner had Pole finished his sentence than Approach directed all of the recovery aircraft to return to their previously assigned altitude blocks in the Marshall stack. The controller also queried each aircraft's fuel state. A Rustler, Jackal, and Bullet aircraft had started dumping and were the low fuel state aircraft. Approach redirected the three jets to the bottom of the stack and rerouted the other aircraft to higher altitude blocks.

✳ ✳ ✳

"Shit!" exclaimed Soup. "Stop dumping."

"Securing the switch," responded Scooter. "We're at thirty-four hundred pounds. What's our max trap?"

Soup was ahead of his pilot and had the number written down. "Twenty-four hundred. We should be OK, as long as Approach doesn't fuck around with us anymore."

Neither aviator was overly concerned, although it was never comfortable being jerked around at night that close to landing.

"What's going on?" asked Scooter. "What should we do?"

"I'll ask Approach. In the meantime, level off, and keep your eyes out of the cockpit. Do you see Wolf One-Eleven?"

Scooter scanned the night sky and could see the distinctive red blinking lights about three miles ahead and slightly lower than the Bullet aircraft. "Yeah, I have a tally."

"OK. Make sure you don't lose him. I'm turning the radar back on."

✳ ✳ ✳

Pie and T-Bone were long past shitting bricks. Both flyers' nervous systems were now in sheer survival mode. Their senses peaked as they communicated over the ICS and talked with the Air Boss. The Boss assured them flight deck personnel were scrambling to tie down the jet with every available tie-down chain. The crew had already shut down both motors.

"Lightning Eleven, bring it in close port side," the Boss ordering the HS-14 helicopter plane guard to fly close abeam the port side of the ship, just in case.

At least half of the flight deck personnel who were working the launch near the waist cats swung into action and were fighting to keep the Tomcat with its two-man crew from slipping into the sea. Flight directors quickly shut down the three remaining aircraft that had been waiting to launch. With the launch suspended and sailors running across the deck, there was a high risk of FODing an engine or injuring a sailor.

✳ ✳ ✳

"I can't believe how fast Two-Zero-Three spun around. Did you see it?" asked Spyder over the ICS.

"No, I missed it. I was kind of daydreaming, and the next thing I knew, it was going over the side. What happened?"

"I think they were taxiing him behind the other Bullet aircraft and must have placed his wingman in tension before he was clear."

"Wow, thank God. It looks like they're gonna tie her down before she goes over."

A yellow-shirt finally got around to Spyder's and Tank's jet and shut them down. No one seemed to know what to do with the remaining aircraft scheduled to launch, as the deck personnel were still scrambling to save Bullet 203.

Spyder saw a member of the crash and salvage crew jump onto Tilly and scramble up to her driver's compartment. Tilly was a large, heavy-lift flight deck crane that usually sat abandoned aft and port of the island. Spyder and Tank were parked two aircraft away from the bright-yellow, gangly looking apparatus. The heavy machine jerked from its parking space and lurched toward Bullet 203.

Spyder noticed a large amount of fuel spilling onto the flight deck from one of 203's punctured external fuel tanks. The crash crew, fully outfitted in silver hooded asbestos protective gear and complete breathing apparatuses, started a flow of AFFF from their crash truck onto the flight deck. After what seemed like eternity, the Tomcat's canopy finally raised, and the Bullet aircrew slowly and methodically unstrapped, safed their ejection seats, and with the assistance of two yellow-shirts, gingerly climbed down from the cockpit. The entire time the jet rocked and rolled in cadence with the ship.

As both Pie and T-Bone hit the flight deck, Spyder could see a sense of relief sweep over their bodies. It looked as if both aviators were about to kneel down and kiss the deck. Instead, they were rushed from the landing area down to the Bullet ready room for a detailed debrief. Though Pie and T-Bone were safe, twelve aircraft low on fuel were airborne and could not land as long as Bullet 203 was lying crippled half in the landing area and half on the catwalk, dangerously overhanging the black ocean.

✳ ✳ ✳

The Air Boss conferred with the Handler to determine what to do with 203. Approach redirected all airborne aircraft to marshall on the 085 radial, with the jets with the least fuel in the bottom of the stack. Bullet 205, with Scooter and Soup, had the third lowest amount of gas and was placed at nine thousand feet. Two Intruders had less fuel and were placed at seven thousand and eight thousand feet, respectively. Austin and the skipper were up at fourteen thousand feet, as they had a comfortable reserve of gas. The airborne aircraft were not given revised push times, as the flight deck personnel were still battling to remove 203 from the landing area and Approach did not have an exact recovery time from which to gauge new push times.

Anxiety increased in the bridge, Pri-Fly, Approach and throughout each ready room. With a dozen aircraft from the earlier cycle still airborne burning hundreds of pounds of fuel each minute, and with the ship in blue water ops, few options remained. If the deck personnel could not move 203 in time, they would have to push her over the side to clear the landing area for the recovering jets. Other than a punctured drop tank and a scratched mainmount, 203 was a perfectly good sixty million dollar jet. The captain hoped he would not have to make that decision. The senior chief in Approach Control advised the captain they had about nine minutes left before they had to start the recovery; otherwise, several aircraft would be desperately low on fuel. There was only one tanker airborne, Rustler 403, and he only had enough fuel onboard to gas two, maybe three jets. CAG was in Approach Control and checked the status board. He was agitated to see there was no KA-6D on alert. He immediately called down to VA-155 and ordered an A-6E with a D-704 pod fueled and an aircrew to man the jet in the event another tanker was needed. With the uncertainty surrounding the status of Bullet 203, neither the captain nor CAG wanted to launch another aircraft into the night sky—not even a tanker—unless absolutely necessary.

✳ ✳ ✳

"Uh, Soup, I'm not feeling real comfortable here. We're at twenty-eight hundred pounds sitting at nine thousand feet, number three in the stack.

How 'bout finding out where the recovery tanker is," suggested Scooter. Perspiration started to bead on his forehead. He turned up the cockpit a/c a few notches.

"Yeah, I was hoping Approach would start us down by now. You heard what I did on the front seat radio. Sounds like Pie and T-Bone had quite a ride. I bet they'll have to change their flight suits when they get back to the ready room."

"Yeah, no shit. I can't—"

Scooter was interrupted by the Bullet skipper on the front seat radio, "Scooter, say state?" The young pilot had been alternating the front seat radio between Tower and Bullet discrete.

"We're at two-point-eight, Skipper. Soup's about to holler for Texaco."

"All right," replied the Bullet CO in a terse tone. He was preoccupied listening to the events transpiring on the deck. He also felt concerned by Bullet 205's rapidly diminishing fuel state. The skipper had confidence in Scooter, but his junior officer was still a first-tour nugget.

Soup queried Approach on the status of Texaco and was told to stand by.

"Great," exclaimed Soup over the ICS. "We'll sit here for another ten minutes and run out of gas while you work the problem!" Scooter dabbed at the sweat now pooling on his face.

✳ ✳ ✳

"Get Two-Zero-Three hooked up to Tilly now!" shouted the Air Boss over the 5-MC. "I don't give a damn if the drop tank is secured. Move the damn jet this instant!" The Boss was hearing it from both CAG and the captain of the ship and needed Bullet 203 cleared in the next six minutes. The crash crew had not yet secured the fuel leak from the Tomcat's port drop tank, and JP-5 continued to flow onto the flight deck. Time was running out. Flight deck personnel rushed to tie the straps and chains onto Tilly's lanky arm before word came to abandon rescue efforts and push the jet into the water.

"Boss?" asked the Mini-Boss seated next to the Air Boss up in Pri-Fly, "What about the missiles?"

The Air Boss stopped, slammed down the two headsets he had in both hands, sat back, closed his eyes, and came unglued. "Shit!" he shouted to no one in particular but loud enough to rattle the space. Several petty officers cowered and took a step away from the corner of Pri-Fly, where the Air Boss and Mini Boss were seated. If they could have, the enlisted personnel would have melted into a dark recess. The Boss was rapidly running out of ideas and time. He took a deep, audible breath and opened his eyes. "Mini, get CAG Ordnance on the line now!"

Bullet 203 had two live, state-of-the-art AIM-9M and two AIM-7F air-to-air missiles under each wing. If the jet were pushed overboard, there would be a risk the Soviets or Chinese could recover the jet and missiles and exploit the technology from these weapons. After an AIM-54A was lost overboard in the Atlantic back in the early '80s, the navy spent more than twenty million dollars searching and recovering the single missile with a mini-sub to protect the weapon from falling into the Soviets' hands. *Ranger*'s officers sure as hell didn't want to repeat the exercise if the captain ordered the jet over the side.

The Air Boss looked at his watch and saw they had less than four minutes remaining. "We're fucked!"

✳ ✳ ✳

"Jackal Five Hundred, push at time zero-eight. Rustler Four-Zero-Seven, push time zero-niner. Bullet Two-Zero-Five, proceed immediately overhead Mother and join on Rustler Five-Zero-One at angels two-point-five and take two-point-oh. Rustler Four-Ten, push time one-zero. Wolf One-Eleven—"

"Great! I'm heading down now to beat the Jackal commencing his approach," stated Scooter decidedly over the ICS to his RIO.

"I'm scanning the radar and will lock up Texaco as soon as I've got him," replied Soup. Both aviators' nerves eased slightly now that they had been assigned a refueling tanker.

＊＊＊

"Skipper, we're pushing at time one-five. Adding six hundred pounds for the approach, I've got us over the deck with four thousand pounds, just under max trap. We're looking good, Skipper," stated Austin confidently to his CO.

"Piece of cake. Hope they clear Two-Zero-Three in time."

Pole readjusted his cockpit lighting rheostats and twisted his head back and forth in an effort to clear his mind. He had over thirty-five hundred Tomcat hours and eight hundred carrier landings, yet the pilot still needed to focus and prepare for each and every recovery. He mused this likely would be his last cruise in the cockpit and wanted to make sure he did not screw the pooch. Two weeks before, while piloting an F-14, CAG had landed eight feet right. The Tomcat's starboard wingtip sheared right through an Intruder's nose cone. Even with hundreds of traps in his logbook, Pole made sure he was on the top of his game.

＊＊＊

Spyder and Tank could leave 106 and return to their ready room at any time following shutdown, but neither aviator wanted to miss the show. They were far enough away from 203 so as not to get in the way. They both felt as if by simply observing the activity first-hand, they were in some psychic way providing assistance.

"Hey, Spyder, look to your left. I think I can see Jackal Five Zero Zero at about eight miles," said Tank on the ICS. Though their engines were shut down, Spyder had made sure the plane captain left the electrical power on the jet so the aircrew could speak to one another over the ICS and monitor the radios. Tank and Spyder had both Approach and Tower frequencies dialed in.

"Yep, I'd say they have less than three minutes to raise and tow Two-Zero-Three out of the way or she's going over the side."

In addition to the crash and salvage crew, at least a dozen other flight deck personnel worked under, around, and on top of Bullet 203. For the first five minutes, they tried desperately to fasten the jet to the flight deck in an effort to stop her from sliding into the sea. Now they were attaching large straps and chains from the jet to Tilly and unhooking the original chains that fastened the jet to the deck. Several chiefs shouted orders over one another to the crews. The Air Boss added his terse orders by way of the 5-MC. Tilly shifted from side to side and spewed large diesel plumes. More yellow-shirts, blue-shirts, and plane captains scrambled to re-spot aircraft that had not launched and now fouled the landing area. Before any of the airborne jets could land, these aircraft needed to be towed around 203 and Tilly to the bow. Presently the landing area looked more like a NASCAR pit row than aircraft carrier runway.

✳ ✳ ✳

"Scooter, I've got Texaco locked at six miles, angels two-point-five," remarked Soup to his pilot.

"Got him. Good job! Looks like he's headed at us. This might just work out. I'm gonna take a slight offset to the north and if we're lucky, we can join without any major hiyakas."

✳ ✳ ✳

Spyder looked back to his left and could identify the port and starboard lights from the approaching Intruder. He guessed the aircraft was at five miles, or about two minutes from landing. Looking forward, he saw Tilly clearing the landing area with the stricken Tomcat in its clutches. FOD walkdown commenced immediately from the stern and made its way rapidly up the landing area. Spyder and Tank jumped down from their jet and joined the group. The fifty or so sailors and officers hoped to catch any fragments of 203 or any other metal object that might foul the landing area.

"FOD walkdown participants, you've got thirty seconds to finish!" bellowed the Air Boss on the 5-MC. "Jackal Five Zero Zero is at two miles. Hurry it along and then secure immediately to the bow. Now move it!"

Under the number-four wire, Spyder picked up what looked like half of a chain link. *This would have torn the shit out of a motor. Hope the other half isn't around here.* He and the rest of his shipmates quickened their pace and got to the end of the landing area as the Jackal BN called the ball. The sailors and officers sprinted out of the landing area. The Boss signaled a green deck to the LSOs precisely five seconds before the lead LSO was going to have to pickle the recovery and send the Intruder back around the landing pattern. The flight deck personnel had performed astonishingly well in saving Bullet 203 with mere seconds to spare.

Spyder and Tank entered the starboard catwalk just as Rustler 500 snagged the three-wire and pulled it noisily along the flight deck. The Wolfies quickly made their way back to VF-1's ready room to find out who had been in 203.

* * *

Scooter and Soup ran the intercept perfectly, with Texaco turning wings level from his orbiting turn as Scooter joined. The BN immediately began circling with his red-lensed flashlight, indicating he was extending the refueling basket from the drogue. Thirty seconds later the BN gave the OK signal, and Scooter dropped back to begin the mechanical mating ritual. He extended the Tomcat's probe and set up approximately ten feet behind the steel basket. The A-6 began a gentle left turn to remain orbiting above the ship. Scooter matched his rate of turn and barely touched the throttles forward. After stabilizing about three feet from the basket, Scooter inched the throttles forward and made a play with his rudders for the basket. During this evolution, Soup was essentially useless. Ordinarily, the RIO's main job during tanking was to keep his head on a swivel to ensure no other aircraft ran into them, as the pilot was fixated on the probe and basket trying to merge the two.

"Gotcha!" exclaimed Scooter. He performed flawlessly on the first attempt and pushed the probe three feet forward past the detent. He remained in position and waited for the brightened yellow light on the drogue to shift to green, showing positive fuel transfer. He waited several agonizing seconds. The light did not change.

"Shit! We're not getting any gas."

"Rustler Five-Zero-Nine, we're still showing yellow," stated Soup disappointedly on Approach frequency.

"Yeah, that's what we're showing here too. Why don't you back out and we'll recycle and then try it again. It worked fine earlier tonight."

"Roger," replied Soup.

"Ever feel like it's not your day?" asked Scooter to his RIO. He backed out of the basket and offset to the left, making sure he wasn't directly behind the drop tank and drogue when the basket recycled. After the Jackal BN cycled the basket and gave the OK, Scooter rejoined and attempted to plug the basket. Soup didn't think it was a good time to advise his pilot, but they were down to seventeen hundred pounds of fuel, or about twenty-five minutes of flying time.

On his first attempt to replug the basket, the probe rimmed the basket and flung it into the side of the jet with a loud *thump*. Both Scooter and Soup held their breath as Scooter throttled back and danced away from the basket. Fortunately, the basket remained attached to the hose. A pilot's biggest worry during inflight refueling was to hamfist it and accidentally tear the basket from the hose and suck it into an engine, thus FODing the motor and causing catastrophic problems, including possible engine fire and subsequent ejection.

"No problem. I'll get it this time," assured Scooter more to himself than his RIO. Sweat was now nearly flowing into his eyes. He blinked hard and glanced at the fuel gauge and saw it drop below fifteen hundred pounds. He performed a Hail Mary blessing discretely so Soup would not see him in the front-seat mirrors. The pilot subconsciously bit his lip as he guided the probe directly into the center of the basket. He pushed the throttles and moved the basket forward. The light remained yellow. Scooter's heart began racing.

"Uh, Houston, we've got a problem here," remarked Soup on Approach frequency.

"Unknown aircraft, say again," replied the controller.

"Approach, Bullet Two-Zero-Five. We've got a sour tanker and we're at one-point-four."

"Bullet Two-Zero-Five, repeat fuel state."

"One-point-four."

The radio went silent. Both Scooter and Soup could imagine the GQ bells going off in Approach Control as they took in the seriousness of the situation. After five seconds of deafening silence, a more senior Approach controller spoke.

"Bullet Two-Zero-Five, cleared heading zero-seven-five degrees down to angels one-point-two for short final and immediate recovery. You'll be vectored between an S-3 on short final and an E-2 at eight miles."

"Roger. Two-Zero-Five is down to one-point-two heading zero-seven-five," replied Soup. He tightened his seat pan straps, lowered his sleeves, and put on his oxygen mask. "Piece of cake, right, Scooter? A walk in the park."

"Yeah, right." Scooter realized the enormity of the task ahead. Depending upon how far Approach extended their downwind, he and Soup would have one, possibly two looks at the deck before flaming out. He had no alternative but to trap on the first attempt.

"Bullet Two-Zero-Five, I'll be turning you final in about twenty seconds. You have an E-2 Hawkeye at eleven o'clock at six miles," directed Approach.

"Roger that," responded Soup. They were at twelve hundred feet altitude two miles from the boat. Soup could see scattered lights from the ship at his left eight o'clock position. He could not make out the outline of the boat in the darkness. There was little ambient light as it was a quarter moon with a ten-thousand-foot scattered layer. *Ranger's* flight deck was pitching six to eight feet.

"Bullet Two-Zero-Five, turn left to final heading two-five-five, cleared bull's-eye approach, contact paddles button six."

"Two-zero-five."

"Gear and hook coming now," stated Scooter over ICS. He had refrained from lowering the landing gear until the last possible moment to reduce drag and save as much fuel as possible.

"Roger that," replied his RIO.

Soup felt the gear lock into place as Scooter leveled the jet on a heading of two hundred fifty degrees. He leaned to the left and looked over Scooter's left shoulder to see the hook and gear indicators in their down positions. Glancing at his TID, the RIO saw the bulls-eye needles were centered. At least they were starting the approach on glide slope and glide path, even if it was merely four miles behind the boat instead of the usual twelve miles for a Case III recovery.

"Confirm final airspeed at one thirty-six," asked Scooter.

"I got one thirty-seven," replied Soup.

"Roger that."

"Bullet Two-Zero-Five, this is paddles. Heads up. We're gonna target you for the two wire." Scooter recognized the voice of "Bug" Roach, CAG paddles and one of the most experienced LSOs in the navy. The pilot's anxiety meter ratcheted down one notch—now only at nine on a ten-point scale. Scooter and Soup were on hot mic, and Soup could hear his pilot breathing heavily.

"Just like every other landing thus far on cruise, fly the ball to touchdown," comforted Soup over the ICS.

Soup checked the bull's-eye needles and saw they were dead-on slope at just under two miles, but the glide path needle was moving rapidly to the left.

"What the fuck!" exclaimed Scooter. Before Soup could respond, paddles came over the radio.

"Scooter, the ship's in a turn fishing for some wind. Keep it coming left. I'm trying to have the captain steady up."

"You gotta be shittin' me," added Scooter dejectedly over the ICS.

"Do the best you can flying the needles. Don't look outside yet," said Soup.

The RIO checked his nav readout and saw they were at three-quarters of a mile. "Two-oh-five, Tomcat ball, one-point-two."

"Roger ball Tomcat. Keep it coming left. You're on speed," responded Bug.

The ship was still in a turn. Right after the S-3 recovered, a seven-knot breeze from the west completely died out. The OOD was grasping for five knots of natural wind, as the ship increased its internal speed in a race to achieve the minimum twenty-four knots across the deck for Bullet 205 to recover at its current fuel load and weight. If *Ranger* did not obtain that wind-over-deck airspeed and the Tomcat recovered, it could pull the arresting gear out of the stanchions. Or if the jet boltered, it might not have enough landing area to make it back into the air.

"Ship's steady," exclaimed Bug. "Keep coming left, and add a bit of power." But it was too late. Scooter had been trying to catch up with the ship's turn from the outset. When *Ranger* suddenly stopped turning, he already had a big play to the left and overshot the final heading. Even Bug missed it.

"Right for lineup!" shouted Bug over the whine of the Tomcat's engines, now less than three hundred yards from the stern of the ship. As soon as the words left the LSO's mouth, he knew Scooter could never catch the significant right-to-left drift. "Wave it off! Wave off!" Bug pickled the bright red wave-off lights.

Both Scooter's and Soup's hearts missed a beat. The thundering Tomcat, with gear and flaps down, lumbered fifteen feet over the fantail and LSO platform in mil power as Scooter fought to climb. The roar and vibration of the motors pierced the hearing protection worn by every sailor on the flight deck.

Soup didn't waste a second. "Bullet Two-Zero-Five's on a wave-off." Not waiting for Approach to respond, Scooter immediately began a gradual left turn downwind.

✳ ✳ ✳

The ship's captain rang the Air Boss and asked him how long it would take his people to rig the barricade. "Five, six minutes," responded the Boss over the intercom. "Get it done in four!" demanded the CO. The boss instantly yelled into the 5-MC, "Rig the barricade! I say now, rig the barricade. This is not a drill. You have four minutes to rig the barricade!"

Flight deck personnel sprinted into action. If they had moved quickly thirty minutes earlier in securing Bullet 203, they now moved twice as fast to take out the stanchions, cables, and nets and place them across the landing area. Unlike the mad dash to save 203, for this evolution each person had a job and knew exactly where to go and what to do. They knew they had a jet and aircrew in trouble and had to break their best record by at least two minutes. Current *Ranger* flight deck personnel had never rigged the barricade in less than five minutes. But the lives of shipmates were never on the line during this cruise before, either.

The E-2, with an ample reserve of fuel, was directed to orbit overhead at three thousand feet.

CAG chimed in from his chair in Flight Ops. "Scooter, this is CAG. We're gonna hook you in on final at two miles. We're rigging the barricade now. It's your and Soup's choice. You can either fly by the port side of the ship and eject alongside, or try to bring it aboard in the barricade," announced Air Wing TWO's most senior aviator on Tower frequency.

Scooter didn't hesitate or confer with his RIO. "We'll bring her aboard, CAG."

"Roger that. Air Boss promises me the barricade will be ready for you. I'm handing you back to paddles. Good luck, son."

"Thanks, CAG."

In their combined flying experience—over twenty-nine hundred hours and one hundred ninety traps—neither Soup nor Scooter had been in a situation even remotely this hazardous. They were minutes—possibly seconds—from flaming out. Soup looked down and saw the fuel indicator passing nine hundred pounds total on its way down. He knew the gauge was only accurate to plus-or-minus five hundred pounds per side, meaning they should flame out at any moment.

"Scooter, if we lose an engine, remember to set ten degrees attitude, maximum of fourteen degrees angle of attack. Step on the good tapes, go to mil on the good engine, and—" Soup was interrupted by Bug back on the Tower frequency.

"Scooter, we don't have time for the full barricade brief. Approach has you at two miles. Begin your turn now. Remain at six hundred feet. We've got the lens set for a steeper glide slope. Fly the ball no matter what. Do not go high. As soon as you make the deck, I'll call 'cut,' and I want you to cut power. Got it?"

"Yes," replied Scooter. At this point, he was too busy wrestling rattle-snakes in the cockpit to be scared. Basically, he was flying a day pattern at night—flying manually only six hundred feet above the water in a turn, dirty, scanning from the boat to his HUD to the engine instruments. One or both motors would be flaming out at any moment. And there was that barricade thing hanging out there too.

"Final heading is now two-four-zero," stated Bug.

"Good job in the turn," coaxed Soup over the ICS. "You've got twenty degrees to go before final bearing." Soup only heard Scooter's heavy breathing in response.

✳ ✳ ✳

"Two-Zero-Five's at a mile, Boss," stated the Mini to the Air Boss. The Boss had been riding the flight deck personnel hard over the past three minutes. The barricade was laid out over the landing area but was not yet raised.

"Get it raised now!" he shouted over the 5-MC. "Tomcat on a mile final!"

If the barricade wasn't raised and secured in the next sixty seconds, Bullet 205 would have to overfly the landing area and Scooter and Soup would have no choice other than to eject into the blackness alongside the ship.

✳ ✳ ✳

"Scooter, you're a tad high," stated Bug over Button 6. Scooter pulled a handful of power for a couple of seconds and then eased it back slowly. Soup called the ball at three-quarters of a mile with six hundred pounds of fuel. By all indications, at least one motor should have flamed out.

"Right for lineup." Scooter was flying anything but a textbook approach. Fortunately, the ship was steady this time around. Scanning from the ball to the landing area, the pilot saw the barricade for the first time, shooting a ping of fear through his body. He had never thought much about taking a barricade, and now he was seconds away from crashing into the steel and nylon net at over one hundred fifty miles per hour.

When both Spyder and Scooter were in flight school, an A-3 Skyraider off the *USS Nimitz* had attempted a barricade landing while in the Mediterranean. It began as an ordinary recovery during an ordinary night during an ordinary Med cruise. But as often happens with carrier operations, in an instant the ordinary turned deadly. The junior pilot was having difficulty and had boltered five consecutive times. Rather than divert the electronic spy plane to shore, the ship's captain and CAG ordered a barricade landing. At the stern, the pilot got spooked and added instead of cut power. The large, twin-engine aircraft climbed just enough for its landing gear to snag the top of the barricade. The steel cables severed the landing gear and slowed the jet below flying speed. The aircraft bounced once on the flight deck and careened sideways into the sea. All eight crewmembers perished. Scooter wanted to make sure he did not similarly screw the pooch. He would follow Bug's guidance all the way through touchdown and into the barricade. *Piece of cake, Scooter. Just listen to Bug.*

"Barricade's clear. You've got a green deck!" exclaimed the Air Boss to Paddles over the Tower frequency. Scooter swore he could see sailors sprinting out of the landing area as he dipped his right wing and made a final play for the deck.

"Easy, easy," coaxed Bug. The Tomcat was flying a steeper approach than usual and looked as if it was going to strike the fantail. At the last moment, the stern of the ship dropped in a wave trough and the jet's landing gear cleared the ramp by eight feet.

"Cut! Cut! Cut!" yelled Bug.

Scooter did as ordered and threw the throttles backward, the exact opposite of what he had been trained to do his entire flying career. He maintained attitude on the jet and did not want to lower the nose and risk a hook skip. The flyer felt the Tomcat crash onto *Ranger's* flight deck and simultaneously saw the barricade rush blurrily toward the windscreen. His initial reaction was to go to military power, like every single previous carrier landing he had flown. But he remembered Bug's directions and remained at idle. The pilot braced for impact into the barricade. In an instant both Scooter and Soup were slammed forward into their restraining straps. Scooter unconsciously shut his eyes and did not see the barricade swallow the jet. Within a second, he and Soup were thrown backward into their ejection seats. He shut down both motors as he heard Bug instruct over the Tower frequency to turn off his engines.

For the second time that evening, *Ranger's* crash and salvage team rushed to a Bullet aircraft to help evacuate its aircrew. Scooter and Soup were fine, but they needed help extricating the Tomcat's canopy from the top cable of the barricade. VF-2 and flight deck personnel assisted the crew in securing the aircraft. Ten minutes later Scooter and Soup were in the Bullet's ready room receiving high-fives and kudos from their skipper, CAG, and each officer in their squadron. Even the ship's captain stopped by to congratulate them on a job well done. Each of the air wing's aircraft was safely on deck.

It was not until an hour later when Scooter was alone in his stateroom that his legs began to shake uncontrollably. He sat aimlessly watching a PBA bowling tournament on the ship's television station while he waited for his legs to calm. It took almost two hours, but they finally did around 0100, when his roommates returned from working out.

The next morning Scooter thanked his RIO for his high level of professionalism and assistance. He also sought out Bug and thanked him, as well.

"Just another day on WestPac, huh?" they all joked.

"Yeah," replied Bug, slapping Scooter on the back. "Now about that overshooting start on the first pass."

18

Spyder stood up and excused himself to make another head call. Rolls joined him, as the junior officer also needed to give back some of the beer he had consumed. As he entered the head and stood in front of a urinal, Spyder tried to remember how he felt when he was Rolls' age.

"Rolls, you are enjoying the hell out of the navy and your life right now, right?"

"Sir?" asked Rolls from three urinals away.

"You know this is the time for you to max your fun meter, right?"

"Oh, I realize that, Commander." Both officers stared straight ahead at the blank tiles in front of them.

"Sure, you'll get older, start a family, have new challenges and opportunities. You may or may not leave the navy. Whatever you do, you'll never have as much fun as you will during the next few years flying off boats and raising hell in foreign ports with your squadronmates." Spyder zipped up his trousers and stepped to the sink to wash his hands.

"Yeah, I know," responded the junior officer. "In ten years when I'm flying the Kennedy-to-LAX route for United, it won't be the same as it is in my squadron flying Growlers off the *Stennis*."

Continuing to wash his hands, Spyder looked at his own reflection in the mirror. His hair had receded an inch or two and was starting to turn gray around the edges. He worked out regularly, but he had recently started feeling the aches of middle age. He glanced over at Rolls' reflection and saw a walking military recruitment poster. Spyder looked back down and rinsed his hands a second time. *Did I ever look like that? Did I ever feel on top of the world back then, or was I too busy living it to stop and look around?* The images of being back in the cockpit flooded his mind. He thought back to Pam, and several women from the Miramar O'Club whose names he'd long since forgotten. Other than the recent divorce, Spyder's life was going along swimmingly. He looked back to his days flying in the navy with a combination of remorse and joy, longing, yet fulfillment. When he left the active duty navy, he closed a chapter of his life never to be repeated. His time as a naval aviator would be remembered as one reads a book, almost as if it had happened to someone else. Retelling the stories to Rolls and Drone rekindled feelings and emotions Spyder had not felt in several years. The senior reserve officer splashed cold water on his face.

As Rolls grabbed the door to leave the bathroom, Spyder stopped him. "Rolls, you know most grown men would give their left nut to do what you do? And gobs of women would sleep with you if given half a chance."

Rolls looked back at Spyder and wondered where had that comment come from.

"Don't you forget it, Lieutenant. Savor every moment," Spyder added. Rolls nodded and headed out into the passageway stumbling for something to say.

Neither officer said another word on their short walk back to the table. Rolls was the first to break the silence. "Hey, Commander, I saw the patch on your flight suit. How was Top Gun?"

Broken out of his reflective mood by Rolls' question, Spyder responded immediately. "Yeah, Flash and I got to go after our first cruise in VF-1. It was a terrific experience and some of the best flying I did in my entire career—comparable to combat over in the desert. We worked our butts off. We studied and flew from sunup to sundown and briefed and debriefed three or four hours for each flight hour, or so it seemed. The instructors worked their asses off too. But I'll tell you what. There are no more professional officers in the navy and marine corps than Navy Fighter Weapons School instructors. I felt really privileged to have the opportunity to train with them."

But rather than talk more about Top Gun, Spyder wanted to continue talking about his time in VF-1, almost as if he was reliving that chapter, after all.

19

When Spyder made his first WestPac cruise, the Middle East was relatively peaceful—assuming the words "peace" and "Middle East" can ever be used in the same sentence. The Iran-Iraq war had been over for several years, Indian-Pakistani tensions were at a low level, and even Israel was getting along with its neighbors, temporarily. Numerous carriers spent their three-month line period in the NAS, with nothing to do but steam in watery circles.

It was always hot—-Africa hot—-and extremely humid. A constant inversion layer hung from three thousand feet to the surface that rivaled the Los Angeles smog basin. The mixture of sand and dust often necessitated Case II recoveries, even in the middle of the day. Flying below five thousand feet was unbearably hot, monotonous, and boring. Flights were restricted to international airspace, at least twelve miles off the coast of any country, and more often a minimum of twenty miles. These restrictions translated into many mind-numbing SSC and high-altitude AIC missions.

Spyder recalled one particularly nasty 1300 launch when the environmental control system of his Tomcat failed. The flight director taxied the Tomcat near the fantail so the AMEs could troubleshoot the system. The canopy was raised to allow the second-class petty officer to work from the inside, while another troubleshooter worked on an exterior panel. For forty-five minutes, Spyder and his RIO breathed hot jet exhaust from eighteen jets turning during taxi and launch. The air stung his eyes and burned his throat as if he were a firefighter battling a blaze without an oxygen mask. He sucked on O_2 for a while but did not want to use up much of the air since they were scheduled for a double cycle. Plus the oxygen did nothing for his burning eyes.

Spyder and his RIO missed their hop and had to continue turning while watching all eighteen aircraft catapult off the ship. After another fifteen minutes of troubleshooting without a fix, Spyder finally was allowed to shut down and climb out of the jet. He was greeted by blasting heat radiating off the steel deck. When he walked, his feet squished from the perspiration pooled in the bottom of his boots. He shook a couple of droplets of perspiration off his nose and looked at the dozens of enlisted personnel working on the flight deck day in and day out, twelve to eighteen hours per day. He reminded himself how dedicated they were and how lucky he was to have gone to college and taken the officer route. Back in the PR shack, Spyder quickly stripped off his flight gear, checked in with the SDO, and headed for the showers.

The air conditioning on *Ranger* was overworked and barely eked out perceptibly cooled air. And the showers—when there was enough water to shower—worked at three, four, or five levels. The mist from the showerhead felt as though it escaped from the ship's showerheads at 3,000 psi and 1,000 degrees. On a good day, the showers on the O-3 level only took off three layers of skin, on a bad day, five layers. Today, after baking in the Tomcat for over an hour and pouring himself out of his flight suit, Spyder was rewarded with a level-five shower.

✳ ✳ ✳

Occasionally while on WestPac, a host country invited the navy to engage in a major air exercise. Thailand was a regular player, as was Oman. Countries such as South Korea, Pakistan, and Australia also provided opportunities for limited engagements, including 2v2s or 4v4s. On his first cruise, Spyder was fortunate to participate in a comprehensive, large-scale Alpha Strike that included virtually the entire air wing attacking Thumrayt Airfield in Oman.

Prior to the strike, several air wing aviators flew off the ship to spend a night on the beach to liaison with their Omani Air Force counterparts. VF-1 sent Tank, who came back to the ship with a particularly noteworthy bilateral exchange experience. After an intensive morning meeting going over ingress altitude deconfliction, frequencies, tanking orbits, and surface-to-missile engagement zones, Tank looked forward to a lunch break. He finished feasting on some local lamb cuisine at the mess hall and was strolling through the aviators' club with another JO when an older gentleman wearing a full tribal robe entered the room. The flyers didn't think much of the man, other than realizing he was not a pilot and likely not military.

As Tank meandered around the room perusing photos of various Omani Air Force operations throughout the years, he noticed the gentleman suddenly quite close to him. Tank was not concerned because the man was his grandfather's age, even if he had no clue regarding Western culture's idea of personal space. It only took a matter of seconds before Tank was introduced to Oman's sense of personal space. While Tank read about a 1974 air strike against insurgents across the border in Yemen, the stranger conducted his own strike. Now a foot to Tank's side, the man casually reached his hand out from his robe and began massaging Tank's derriere. Jumping two feet to his left, the navy officer cocked his fist ready to strike. The man got the message, his innocent smile replaced with a frown, as he exited the room in a huff. Tank wasted no time returning to the afternoon planning session.

No further bilateral relations occurred during the remainder of the strike coordination—at least nothing admitted by any of the other air wing aviators. Carrier Air Wing TWO was ready to launch the Alpha Strike. The basic rules stated *Ranger* was given a target, Thumrayt Airfield, and a window of opportunity, 0730 to 0900, to strike.

The Omani pilots were actually British citizens, a practice stemming back several decades. The British had great influence on the military development of Oman. Sultans used British military expertise and manpower to secure their rule. The Sultanate of Muscat and Oman Air Force was established in 1959 with British aid. The Brits remained in the country after training a skeleton group of Omani pilots. England also supplied

Oman with all of the desert country's aircraft. In the early '60s, the Omani government began hiring mercenary pilots from Great Britain.

The mercs were paid well in British pounds and Scotch—some of the former and more of the latter. They flew often and low, and occasionally engaged in cross-border combat missions. What more could a young British fighter pilot full of spit and vinegar desire? None of the former mercs were allowed back into the Royal Air Force, as they were tagged too high of a flight risk. Imagine that—too insane to fly Harrier jump-jets off British aircraft carriers.

The mercs were crazy in the minds of the Carrier Air Wing TWO pilots. Not "loco" crazy, but "strap on a rocket, light your hair on fire" crazy. The Brits flew far lower than the American flyers dared. In fact, the mercs flew entire missions without climbing above two hundred feet, something unimaginable in the US military's fixed-wing community. The mercs did this for the most basic reason: survival. They flew outdated aircraft designed in the '50s without sophisticated weapons or defensive countermeasures systems. The pilots flew across ground as flat as a dish plate. Even an antiquated radar early warning system could pick out an airplane flying at medium altitude a hundred miles away, which gave anti-aircraft gunners and SAM batteries ample warning. Thus, the Brits adopted tactics—including flying camel-hump low—that kept them alive.

The mercs took off in ground effect, raised their gear, climbed twenty feet to overfly the perimeter fence, and then tried to maintain that altitude for the remainder of the flight until it was time to land. As the American pilots thought the Brits were insane for flying the way they did, the mercs thought the Americans were crazy for flying off a pitching, moving carrier deck. There was enough shared respect between the Brits and Americans to fill pitchers of beer and tumblers of Scotch during the prestrike planning socials at the Thumrayt pilots' bar.

Over 98 percent of the air wing flyers had never flown in combat, so simulated strikes such as the Thumrayt Airfield strike, along with missions flown against the EW ranges in CONUS, were the closest the attack guys came to feeling the adrenaline and exhilaration of war. The fighter guys had gotten their rocks off a month earlier with the Cam Rahn Bay ACM det. But they too were looking forward to mixing it up with the OAF's Jaguars and Hawker Hunters. The entire ship was abuzz with excitement in anticipation of the Omani strike.

Spyder and Mauler clambered up to the flight deck in darkness, as sunrise wasn't for another two hours. Even at 0420 in the morning, the ambient heat of the NAS began to permeate their flight suits. The Wolfies' Tomcat was on the bow, so they entered the flight deck from the forward-most hatch and catwalk. Spyder blinked on his flashlight and aimed it on the fuselage fin, hoping to spot 110. A sailor in flight deck gear recognized Spyder and walked over to him.

"Hey, Sir! Beautiful mornin', eh?" the figure stated joyfully—too joyfully for that point of cruise. The crew had not seen port for over a month and was still at least thirty days away from the rumored Australian port call.

Spyder flashed his light on the brown-shirt's vest. "Oh, hey, Smitty. What are you so cheery about this morning?"

"Well, Sir, 'cause of the strike we cut out a whole bunch of mainte-nance and re-spots this evening. As soon as the launch is over, I get to hit the rack."

"Good on ya. Enjoy the break," said Spyder. He knew the enlisted personnel deserved any break they could get. Spyder never forgot how much the eighteen- and nineteen-year-old kids enjoyed the excitement of naval aviation. It was these fresh-faced young adults just out of high school who comprised the true backbone of the navy. Sailors worked eight to sixteen hours per day under some of the most extreme conditions imagin-able for pay considered laughable by mainstream America. Furthermore, they didn't have the opportunity to personally share in the product of their work. At least a kid in Arkansas who worked day and night on his '69 Ford Mustang could jump behind the wheel and light the tires on fire when fin-ished with his motor overhaul. But a third-class petty officer aviation me-chanic who spent two days on a dual engine change-out didn't get to hop in the jet and take it for a check ride. Surprisingly, this lack of reciprocal gratification rarely impacted their dedication or performance. Spyder often found himself in awe of the "can do" and resourceful attitude these young men exhibited day in and day out, both at sea and ashore.

The comprehensively detailed and well-choreographed ballet known as US Navy aircraft carrier operations proceeded exceptionally well in launching the Thumrayt strike. The F-14 Tomcat's start, control checks, and taxi from the bow to forward of the island were uneventful—if uneventful could be used to describe any facet of carrier ops. The flyers, squadron personnel, flight deck crews, and yellow-shirts were hitting on all cylinders four months into cruise.

Spyder and Mauler half taxied and half slid behind JBD number two on the starboard side of the bow catapult. Several aircraft had already launched into the pitch-black sky, as the sun was not scheduled to rise for another fifty-two minutes. *Ranger's* flight deck pitched rhythmically in the six-foot swells. The Tomcats from the bow were in the last group of aircraft launched. A handful of Intruders launched from the waist and port bow cats. Bullet 203 sat poised in tension in afterburner and was about to spring forward. *KAAWOOSH!* In mere seconds, the Tomcat faded into the abyss, except for the glow of its twin TF-30 afterburner motors, which remained lit until the aircraft was safely airborne and climbing. As the JBD lowered, a burst of steam passed over and around Spyder's and Mauler's cockpit.

Spyder focused intently on the yellow-shirt who directed him to taxi forward quickly. The pilot simultaneously scanned his engine instruments, viewed his wingtips in his peripheral vision, and made sure to keep the yellow-shirt in focus. Apparently, Spyder was not paying close enough attention, as the flight director stuck his right flashlight wand into his left hand and then jerked it upward into the air, signaling the Tomcat pilot to "pull his head out of his ass." *Wow. Good morning to you too, Ted.*

In the backseat, Mauler saw a deck hand run to the side of the jet and point a box lit with the number 660 toward the backseater. The RIO circled twice with his flashlight, confirming the Tomcat was sixty-six thousand pounds gross weight for launch. Although the weight of each jet was passed to the Catapult Department prior to each launch, inevitably about a quarter of the time the weight was incorrect when the individual aircraft taxied to the catapult. Sometimes the aircraft's weight changed due to added ordnance, other times for equipment modification, and sometimes someone within the deck department was exhausted and simply screwed up.

As wind-over-deck requirements differed for each type of navy jet, catapult personnel had to adjust the amount of acceleration and end speed the system needed to hurl a jet down the two-hundred-ten-foot track with enough smack to launch the aircraft into the sky. A lot had to go right to launch a jet successfully from an aircraft carrier—only one link in the long chain needed to break to put a crew in the water.

When Wolf 110 taxied to the cat and the crew performed their final checks, Spyder focused intently upon the yellow shirt. The director slowed his hand movements, and Spyder reacted to the subtle movements as if he were a pianist studying a concert conductor. Mauler looked to the side and confirmed over the ICS when he observed the wings moving forward. Spyder acknowledged and asked his RIO if he was ready to go.

"Rock and roll," answered Mauler excitedly. "Let's blow this popsicle stand."

The director placed his wands together a final time, and Spyder and Mauler felt the jet's nosewheel lock into place. The director motioned for Spyder to lower the F-14, and Spyder did so. The Tomcat's nosewheel strut compressed, and the jet's nose lowered. With flashlight wand in hand, the Shooter thrust his arm upward into the air animatedly five times. The VF-1 pilot responded by methodically moving the throttles past the mil detent into the five stages of afterburner. The Tomcat shook with tens of thousands of foot-pounds of kinetic energy as raw fuel shot into the tailpipes of the Tomcat. Both pilots avoided looking at their mirrors as the bright glow from the twin afterburner motors reflected and lit the area around the rumbling jet like a bonfire. Spyder glanced one more time at his engine instruments, saw each gauge in the correct location, and flicked on 110's exterior lights, demonstrating he and Mauler were ready to launch. No matter how many times he had been through the drill, Spyder's heart raced, and he could feel the hairs rise all over his body in the moments preceding a carrier launch. *Come on, baby. You wanna go flyin' this morning.* The Shooter kneeled down and touched the deck with his wand. A second later, Spyder and Mauler were kicked in the ass by ninety thousand pounds of torque. In 2.2 seconds, Wolf 110 was hurtling down the bow of *Ranger* at over one hundred seventy miles per hour.

"Yeehaw!" yelled Mauler from the rear seat.

Spyder merely grunted as he tried to retain focus on the engine instruments; his eyeballs pushed back into the recesses of his skull. At the end of the cat stroke, the flyers felt a sharp jolt as the jet leapt off the deck. Once his eyes reset and vision cleared, Spyder scanned the flight instruments in the black void outside the cockpit to confirm the Tomcat was indeed flying away from the water. He saw good tapes on the motors and a slight positive climb rate. *Yeah, we're flying.* He kept the jet in afterburner until passing two hundred feet, just to be sure.

The fully laden Tomcat climbed in the hot, humid air and Spyder flew the Case III departure to Texaco, orbiting overhead Mother at eight thousand feet.

* * *

Following the mission, by the time Spyder and Mauler landed, taxied to the bow, parked, and shut down, both flyers were beyond mere exhaustion. The adrenaline from the strike and carrier landing wore off quickly. Following their fifteen-minute debrief with CVIC, the flyers had to endure another hour-long gaggle air wing debrief.

"Think CAG'll miss us if we head straight to our racks?" Spyder asked Mauler as they dragged themselves tiredly toward CVIC.

He wanted to agree with his junior pilot, but Mauler knew better. "CAG might not, but Bourbon and XO would have our asses."

"Yeah, you're right. Oh well. It was worth a try," yawned Spyder. Sleep had to wait another two hours.

20

On day 138 of cruise, *Ranger* was relieved on station in the Gulf of Aden by *USS Midway*. Battle Group Echo left the Gulf and headed southeast to destination unknown—at least unknown to the crew. As much as the ship's crew longed for Perth, no news had leaked from the bridge about the rumored Australia port call.

After close to a week of transiting the Indian Ocean, *Ranger* ventured into the sacred realm of King Neptune, ruler of the underwater world. The excitement of Wog Day was exacerbated by the fear of the unknown. Energy aboard ship was conspicuous and manifested itself through spontaneous yelps and shouts throughout the evening prior to the celebrated event. The official Wog Day initiation began when Davy Jones was sighted—the day before the ship actually crossed the equator.

On behalf of King Neptune, Davy outlined special watches and dress codes for both shellbacks and pollywogs. The watches were absurd creations such as Coriolis Swirl Watch, Bow Watch, or Chief of the Smoke Watch, "to make sure the ship does not make smoke in excessive quantities, which might offend King Neptune." Special lookout watches were designated for the "Line." The men on duty for these watches were required to wear bizarre outfits and were equipped with silly instruments, such as binoculars made of two rolls of toilet paper, and had to follow strict rules of conduct, including shouting ridiculous warnings every fifteen minutes at the top of their lungs.

Later that night a wog talent show was held in Hangar Bay 1. The Wog Queen Pageant, ordained by Davy Jones, crowned the best-looking pollywog Wog Queen, who could then sit on King Neptune's court. A group consisting of a pollywog from each ship's department and aviation squadron was selected to participate in a fashion and talent show for the shellbacks. The pollywogs were dressed as women and performed seductive or comical dances, songs, and acts. The wog who was crowned queen was the one who most convincingly portrayed a woman.

Spyder and a good number of Wolfies made their way to the hangar bay for the show. The flyers could not believe their eyes. Spyder realized he had been captive at sea with over five thousand men for way too long when he saw what was displayed that evening. The contestants had shaved all their body hair, including legs, arms, and underarms and wore everything from see-through lingerie with long blond wigs and spiked heels, to classic 1940s-era dresses to short skirts and absurdly massive plastic breasts. The sailors gyrated, pranced, and sang with conviction. At the conclusion of the competition, a diminutive, effeminate YN3 from the ship's Admin Department was crowned Wog Queen. By the end of the show, Spyder could only shake his head and mumble to himself. Flash and the rest of the Wolfpack aviators who witnessed the event were similarly astounded. "Must be a blackshoe thing," added Tank.

The following morning at 0338, *Ranger* officially crossed "the Line" and entered the domain of King Neptunus Rex. The official events were not sanctioned to begin until 0700 reveille, but many of the enlisted shellbacks did not get the word and began hazing the two thousand-plus *Ranger* pollywogs at 0339.

At 0401, shouts and yells of "Slimy wogs!" and cracks of Shillelaghs awakened Spyder and his two roommates. The JO pollywogs stared at the top of their racks for the next two and a half hours listening to the enlisted shellbacks "walking" their wogs with dog collars and leashes down the passageways on hands and knees—fearful that at any moment their shellback VF-1 squadronmates would bang on the stateroom hatch to summons them.

At 0650 the Wolfies' time had come. The piercing sound of a metal trashcan bouncing down their passageway announced the welcoming party. Immediately, shouts of "Get up, slimy pollywogs!" and "Wake up! It's your special day," rang through the spaces. Spyder's stateroom door flung open, and Mauler and Killer entered loudly. They both wore headbands and had on t-shirts with skulls and crossbones colored on them. "Get up, slimy pollywogs!" repeated Mauler. "Pollywog Tank, you are mine. Put on this leash!" Mauler threw a dog collar and leash to Tank.

Spyder jumped down from his rack and assembled with Flash and Tank. All three officers had prepared before going to sleep the night before and stuffed the backsides of old trousers with paper towel padding. They wore long-sleeved t-shirts and affixed makeshift kneepads out of foam and strips of duct tape to ease the pain from having to crawl on their hands and knees for hours upon hours throughout the day. The roommates were shuffled into the passageway on all fours with the rest of their pollywog compadres. The entire group of sixteen officers shuffled down to the ready room. During the transit, they were constantly crawling under, around, and over other pollywogs "owned" by scores of shellbacks. Cracks of Shillelaghs, shouts, laughter, and pandemonium filled the passageways.

When they finally arrived in the ready room, the pollywogs saw that the chairs had been piled to one side and there was a large open area in the center of the room. Spyder saw his Skipper, XO, and most of the Department Heads watching from the back bulkhead as Mauler, Killer, Pee Wee, Scout, and Banger—all second cruise aviators and shellbacks, ran the pollywogs through their paces. For the next two hours, Spyder and his wog brethren were subjected to shenanigans of the crudest detail. Raw eggs were shoved down their pants and then hit with Shillelaghs, allowing the raw goo to slide everywhere—repeat—everywhere. Shaving cream, silly string, and cheap women's perfume were poured on their heads and every bare spot of skin. Cooking oil was placed on the deck, and the group was forced to split into teams to try to play knee football and create human pyramids on the slippery surface. Slum nearly broke his arm when he fell off the pyramid onto his elbow. Mauler wrapped it with a gauze bandage and ordered him back into the revelry.

The worst part of the ready room was the "truth serum," consisting of the most foul and disgusting liquid imaginable. Each squadron and department on the ship had its own recipe. VF-1's formula consisted of sour milk, rancid orange juice, rotten eggs, Tabasco sauce, sugar, coffee grounds, and only God and King Neptune knew what else. Each pollywog was required to drink a full glass of the ghastly mixture. Suffice to say, fourteen of the sixteen Wolfies threw up after attempting to down the first few gulps. The two who didn't, Austin and Tank, should have regurgitated, as their faces remained a pale shade of green for the next hour.

The antics in the ready room were far and away the easiest part of the Line ceremony for the VF-1 wogs. While in the ready room, the Wolfies were under the domain and control of squadronmate shellbacks. At 0845, when they were directed out of VF-1's space, Spyder and his peers were subjected to the wrath and hostility of an entire ship full of shellbacks. The officer pollywogs were special targets for many enlisted shellbacks who used Wog Day to try to level the playing field or avenge a perceived past wrong. Shouts of "officer wog" constantly rang out through the passageways, eliciting heightened yelps of joy and hardened Shillelagh whips from the enlisted shellbacks.

The VF-1 pollywogs were "walked" on their hands and knees the entire length of the O-3 level and returned to the fantail. Shuffling down to Hangar Bay 2, the aviators were grouped with hundreds of pollywogs from all over the ship. The group remained on their hands and knees on the hard anti-skid surface. Spyder felt the skin being pulled from his fingers each time he inched forward. He had long since discarded the padding on his posterior, as it was discovered 8.2 seconds after he had left the safe confines of the VF-1 ready room. Shouts of "padded wog" had preceded him, allowing additional ass whoopin' for it.

While herded like cattle on all fours in the hangar bay waiting their turn on the flight deck, Spyder witnessed and endured a variety of abuse. All of the wogs underwent racial profiling—hell, every kind of profiling, for that matter. The Mexican sailors had bottles of hot sauce and jalapeños poured down the backs of their trousers into their underwear. A sailor from Maine who was next to Spyder had rotten lobster from last month's surf and turf night stuck in his clothes. Eggs that had been stored in Hangar Bay 1 since the Philippines were cracked open and dropped on and around Spyder. The smell was so revolting that he and several sailors around him lost it and began puking on themselves. The vomit hung from bodies and lay throughout the hangar bay deck. The sounds of shellbacks yelling, singing, and snapping Shillelaghs filled the air.

A sailor wearing pink bunny ears in front of Spyder heaved while crawling through the rotten eggs and puke. Spyder tried to crawl around the horrid mess, but there was no place to go. He suddenly felt something hard and slimy fall onto the back of his neck. He was almost afraid to discover what it was but reached back with his hand and pulled something thin and gooey from his skin. It took him several seconds before he recognized the form as a rotten slice of ham filled with mold spores and maggots crawling in and out of the meat that had been thrown from some shellback. It probably reeked, but his olfactory glands remained overwhelmed by the rotten eggs and vomit. He flung the ham slice, feeling half sorry for the pitiful wog upon whom it landed. Something was now crawling down Spyder's back, and he ripped off his shirt to get at it. He swiped at his back and whatever it was, likely a maggot from the ham slice, was thrust away.

Spyder and the other Wolfie wogs were stuck on the hangar bay for seemingly eternity. They finally made their way onto the aircraft elevator, along with about a hundred fellow wogs. A warning siren blared, and the elevator rose slowly to the flight deck. The instant the elevator stopped, the wogs were immediately greeted by a new group of shellbacks emboldened by the elevator full of virgin wogs. The real fun was about to begin.

For the next two hours, Spyder was subjected to outrageous obstacles and behavior. The experience only worsened the further along he went. The first challenge was a hundred-yard tube that created a maze along the flight deck. Dark and restricted, the flyer couldn't see five feet in front of him. He was pushed into the tube with the ten thousandth Shillelagh crack across his backside and immediately was overcome by a wretched, slaughterhouse-like odor. When he finally emerged from the other side ten minutes later, Spyder had encountered two severed pig heads, animal intestines, and a host of rotten, decayed, and moldy food. He'd climbed through enough puke in the tube to impress a roller-coaster attendant.

At the exit, Spyder was greeted by two large shellbacks who directed him to a trough filled with some form of liquid. At first, Spyder thought it was water to wash off the putrid mess all over his hair, clothes, and body. But as soon as he was allowed to stand, he saw the trough was filled with more than simply water. Brownish bubbles filled the surface. Spyder's nostrils were introduced to yet another fetid stench that emanated from the trough. "This one is real simple, wog," declared a shellback. "All you need to do is jump in and completely dunk yourself, including your head."

Spyder didn't hesitate and jumped right in. Frigid and salty water covered his body. His feet immediately sunk into some type of slimy, soft, noodle-like consistency. He was not sure if it was squid, animal intestines, or what, and he sure as hell was not going to open his eyes or feel around to identify it. After quickly dunking his head, the flyer jumped right out of the trough. As he pushed with his legs, his feet slipped on the bottom, and he almost dunked himself a second time. Several shellbacks roared with laughter.

"Like the shit so much ya wanna stay in, huh?" asked the second shellback. *You mean "shit" figuratively, right?* Spyder grimaced, gripped the edge of the trough and pulled himself out onto the deck. He was dripping in cold, slimy liquid. The breeze on the flight deck further chilled his skin. Spyder wondered if his sense of smell would ever return following the day's events.

"Now back on your knees, and crawl over to the dreaded Davy Jones's lockers!" ordered the first shellback.

Spyder did as he was told and crawled twenty yards to the next group of shellbacks. A dozen pollywogs awaited him in front of four pine coffins. Spyder could see two wogs to a coffin covered with rotting food and vomit from the hundreds of sailors who preceded them. *How can anyone have anything left in their stomach to puke?* Two large shellbacks stuffed a plywood lid on each of the coffins, and a group of other shellbacks started banging on the sides with Shillelaghs and mallets. After a minute or so, the coffin lids were removed, and the sailors spilled out of the boxes, full of rotten food and puke. The sailors were then ordered to mimic a sixty-nine position in front of the cheering shellbacks. Spyder barely endured the coffin. He refused to sixty-nine with another sailor and went straight to the next obstacle amidst cries of "pussy wog" and cracks of Shillelaghs across his backside.

The Wolfie had to wait in a long line on his hands and knees for close to a half-hour, as there was a logjam of pollywogs in front of him. When he finally made it to the front of the line, he saw a row of twenty or so men seated in chairs. He recognized the first group as finalists from the previous evening's Wog Queen contest. The pollywogs were forced to kiss the hand of these "queens," who wore dresses, makeup, and wigs. The next group was a series of overweight chief petty officers who sat bare-chested on chairs in a row adjacent to the ship's superstructure. Rotten food, shaving cream, and truth serum was smeared on their extended bellies. The pollywogs were directed to "kiss" each chief's belly. As a wog rose off the flight deck and placed his head near a swollen gut, a chief would grab the wog by the back of his head and smear it in the slime of his belly. The scene was repeated with the last two individuals seated at the end of the line, Davy Jones and King Neptune.

Spyder got through this "reception line" as fast as he could. As soon as he finished, he was dismissed by King Neptune and welcomed to the privileged world of the shellbacks. He and the other pollywogs around him sprinted to the fantail, stripped naked, and threw their clothes into the sea. Spyder then walked naked down to his stateroom, grabbed a towel, shampoo, and soap, and waited in line for a shower. He took a ten-minute level-three shower, the longest shipboard shower of his life, washing his hair three times. When finished, he swore he could still smell the stench of puke and rotten food.

Later that evening, Spyder and the remainder of the VF-1 newly ordained shellbacks gathered in the ready room and retold their Wog Day stories. Mauler, Banger and the other veteran shellbacks sat back and laughed heartily. Killer showed a video taken earlier in the day. The back of Spyder's throat continued to burn from the truth serum he had drunk hours earlier. He and the other former pollywogs didn't have much of an appetite and barely touched their dinners. Almost everyone was in their racks by 2100, with the absolute craziest days of their military careers finally behind them.

21

"Wow!" exclaimed Rolls. "Your experience with Wog Day is tough to comprehend in today's navy. From what I've heard and read in the *Navy Times*, they sure have toned it down. Nowadays they run DC Olympics, perform a PT obstacle course, and have to wash airplanes and such. I don't think any of the hazing is allowed anymore. I doubt anyone would be allowed to hit one another with Shillelaghs."

"It's not like anyone was 'hit' with Shillelaghs," responded Spyder defensively. "I mean, sure, on the backside. But it's not like it left more than a slight bruise or welt. I think—"

"Commander, do you honestly believe in today's navy a sailor could whack a shipmate to a degree where a bruise or welt was left and the CO wouldn't be relieved?" interrupted Rolls. "I mean, come on, Sir. You read the paper."

"I can't explain it. It was all good-natured fun and—"

"OK, counselor," interrupted the junior pilot, "I'll let you make that argument in front of the CNO and court of public opinion."

Spyder smiled and sighed. "You're right. I can't connect my active duty experience with today's sailors. Talk about a generation gap." Spyder looked around the emptying club and searched for something else to do. He spotted a pool table in an adjoining room. "What do you say we play a game of pool?"

"Sure."

Spyder and Rolls got up from their table and walked to the pool table. No one had played all night. While Spyder pulled a stick from the wall, Rolls racked the balls.

"I don't suppose you ever played crud, eh, Rolls?" asked Spyder, already knowing the JO's answer.

"Uh, no."

"Nine ball?"

"Umm."

"Never mind. Let's stick with eight-ball."

Rolls finished racking and let Spyder break. The commander struck the cue ball smartly and pocketed two striped balls. As Spyder continued to shoot, Rolls asked him about his favorite port call.

"Ooh." Spyder paused from shooting and smiled widely. "Not even a close call."

22

Four days after Wog Day, Spyder was awakened in his rack by a loud rattling noise and shaking throughout the stateroom. In his sleepy haze, he thought the ship was headed back to the Gulf of Aden for combat or some other contingency ops. He hopped out of bed and turned on the television to the ship's data channel. He quickly saw that *Ranger* was headed 170 degrees at 22 knots. The carrier was headed somewhere—rapidly—but it wasn't anywhere toward Iran or the Middle East.

Tank peeked his head out from behind the curtain of his rack. "What's up, Spyder?"

"I dunno, but we're headed south."

"Do you think?" asked Flash excitedly from his rack.

"Oh, man!" exclaimed Tank. He jumped out of the mid-level rack. Flash quickly followed from the lower rack.

The three aviators threw on their flight suits and boots and headed toward the ready room.

Virtually the entire *Ranger*town crew had looked forward to a rumored port call to Australia even before the ship had left San Diego to begin WestPac. As soon as the lines were cast and the tugboats pulled alongside in North Island, the crew's collective thoughts and hopes had shifted thirteen thousand miles westward to Perth. Four months and ten thousand miles later, Spyder and his squadronmates found themselves agonizingly close to realizing their dream port call.

As soon as the three squadronmates burst into the ready room, they were welcomed with a shout from Otter, the SDO, "We're going to Australia!"

Flash broke out into a jig and sang out repeatedly, "We're going to Australia...we're going to Australia!"

Crewmembers walked and jogged down the ship's passageways banging on hatches and bulkheads spreading the word. Within minutes, the Wolfpack ready room was filled with joyous officers high-fiving one another.

Later that day, the crew was informed they would be the second US Navy aircraft carrier to visit Australia that year, as the *Constellation* had beat them by two and a half months. Every *Ranger* sailor was too pumped to care. "That's all right," Spyder overheard a senior chief boatswain mate on the mess deck announce. "Now the Aussie women will be all warmed up!"

Five days later and three days sailing from Perth, in a formal ready room ceremony officiated by the CO, Drum was anointed party scout for Perth and given a budget of $10,000 from the VF-1 officers' mess to arrange a bodacious squadron party and admin for six days and nights.

In a brilliant display of foresight, the officers of VF-1 had ordered extra squadron merchandise to sell on cruise to fund their in-port admins. Squadron t-shirts, golf shirts, ball caps, and coolie-cups were especially popular. But the hottest item, hands down, were the Wolfpack panties, complete with the squadron's mascot wolf head emblazoned on the center of the crotch. What better gift for that wife or girlfriend who was sleeping alone ten thousand miles away? The sailors ecstatically received the panties back from their wives or girlfriends after they had been worn, passing these gems around to their buddies for a sniff test. Though they probably could have doubled their profits, the Wolfpack officers refrained from reselling this "slightly used" merchandise. The VF-1 officers' mess netted over $12,500 the first four months of cruise selling items almost exclusively to the three thousand enlisted personnel of the ship's company and one thousand enlisted airdales.

At 0500 the next morning, the XO boarded the COD with a cashier's check in his pocket and the trust of thirty-two VF-1 officers to do them right.

Three days later, the air wing flew a series of low-level hops over the western Australian outback to maintain pilot currency prior to the week-long liberty. Before planning these missions, CAG had a personal meeting with each of the air wing skippers. He informed them of a major *faux pas* from the *Connie*'s air wing. Apparently VF-154's skipper had what he thought was a flash of brilliance. In order to better advertise his squadron's party, the CO had the squadron's Admin Department make up a thousand flyers rigged to deploy from the Tomcat's speed brake. The CO arranged with his CAG to overfly Perth at the end of a low-level mission. Everything worked according to plan—well, almost.

The paper invitations were completed and bound to the inside of the speed brakes. The low-level portion of the flight was flown to perfection, and the section of Tomcats was cleared by Perth ATC to overfly the city at an altitude of five thousand feet. The skipper descended to one thousand feet and flew directly over several office towers. The CO deployed the speed brakes directly overhead, causing the flyers to rain over the bustling city. The two Tomcats were barely out of earshot from the ground when the Australian controllers' phone lines lit up with calls from surprised civilians. Back onboard *Connie*, the skipper claimed he misunderstood the controller's accent and was certain he had been cleared down to a thousand feet—plausible deniability, yah right!

✳ ✳ ✳

The evening before *Ranger* pulled into port, flight ops were scheduled to cease just past midnight. Spyder completed his hop at 2145 and stayed up to watch the double feature roll'em. Watching the movie beat lying in his rack staring up at the darkened ceiling, too excited to sleep. The night before liberty call, the twenty- and thirty-year-old sailors felt the same anticipation, excitement, and wonder as children did on Christmas Eve. But instead of awakening to a room full of presents, the men of *Rangertown* awoke to a city full of beer, women, and six days of unadulterated freedom.

Mustang, as VF-1's senior watch officer, had worked the watch bill earlier in the cruise to ensure none of the single officers had to stand a watch while in Perth. Spyder, Flash, Tank, Trapper, Austin, Otter, and the other single officers had done double duty in Hawaii, Hong Kong, and Singapore, hoping for reciprocation in Australia. Their gamble paid off, so Spyder and his roommates packed their bags for a week away from Mother.

Since the port in Perth was not equipped to handle a super carrier, *Ranger* anchored approximately a half mile offshore and relied upon liberty boats to shuttle sailors and equipment back and forth. This same system was utilized in a large number of foreign WestPac ports, including Thailand, Diego Garcia, and Hong Kong. Each country had its own indigenous armada of liberty boats. In Thailand, it was speedboats straight out of James Bond's *Dr. No*. Diego Garcia used World War II-era landing craft. Perth, like Hong Kong, utilized private bay cruise boats.

By the time Spyder, Flash, and Tank ate breakfast and changed into their SDBs, the liberty-call line already snaked its way past Hangar Bay 2 into the adjoining Hangar Bay 1. Fortunately for the VF-1 aviators, Drum had more than taken care of his officers' mess. He notified the SDO and word was quickly passed to all Wolfpack officers to assemble immediately at the fantail. The squadron members circumvented the three- to four-hour liberty line and walked directly to a private liberty launch rented by Drum. As soon as the group of officers boarded, they were greeted by a bevy of women, cases of chilled beer, and a live band playing rock 'n' roll from the forward deck.

As the VF-1 liberty launch pulled away from *Ranger*, some of the officers were already arm in arm with a few gals and waved good-bye to their shipmates in the standard liberty line on the carrier. The sailors longingly watched the fighter pilots sail toward shore amidst the sound of live music and scent of perfume wafting across the water and into the hangar bay. Several of the sailors in line provided the international gesture of goodwill and diplomacy to the Wolfpack aviators.

"Look! They're flipping us off," exclaimed Pill to no one in particular. "Shoulda gone to college!" he yelled toward the ship.

"Nice," remarked Flash. "Quite classy."

"What do I care? I'll be shit-faced in ten minutes."

"You're shitty now," added Spyder.

Before the liberty launch was even clear of the carrier, the Wolfies popped open beers and began socializing with the dozen women onboard. As the boat made its way to Fremantle and up the Swan River toward Perth, it instantly transitioned into a true booze cruise. It didn't take long for the officers to begin getting lit, as they had not consumed much alcohol over the past few months. The women drank their fair share of Scotch and acted as tour guides as the boat passed local landmarks and points of interest. After two hours, the launch slowed near a dock at the outskirts of downtown Perth. As the boat was tied to the dock, a red double-decker bus pulled alongside. The booze cruise seamlessly shifted into a pub crawl, where the Wolfies and their female escorts visited four of Perth's finest watering holes.

At 1800, the double-decker bus arrived at the entrance of the Perth Parmelia Hilton Hotel. Nearly all of the VF-1 officers had their own hotel rooms. The hardest part of sleeping in a hotel after months aboard *Ranger* was adjusting to the calm, serene quiet. Since everyone's brain was acclimated to suppressing the noise of thirty-ton aircraft slamming onto the deck eight feet above their racks, the squeal of the arresting gear, the constant clanking of chains sliding across the steel deck, and the pounding of wrenches and hammers throughout the ship, it took a few days before the officers slept uninterrupted in the four-star hotel—for the limited time they actually spent sleeping.

Spyder had just enough time to throw his bag on the bed, shower, wipe a beer stain off his left pant leg, and slip back into his SDBs. He called Flash and Tank and made sure his two squadronmates had not fallen asleep. The air wing party was in a ballroom at the hotel, so at least they did not have to travel anywhere. All three aviators still had a buzz on as they entered the ballroom at 1855. Unlike civilian social events, an officer who cared even slightly about his career would not be "fashionably late," especially when the admiral was attending.

Spyder, Flash, and Tank went straight to the bar and ordered a round of XXXX Gold, the locals' beer of choice. A steady stream of navy officers and Australian military and civilians entered the ballroom. Spyder quickly scanned the room and saw many attractive women. Though extremely friendly and cordial, none of the dozen or so women from the booze cruise had interested the young flyer. He was in the ballroom for less than five minutes when a handful of women captured his and his squadronmates' attention.

"I'm going on a MiG Sweep," Spyder said to both Tank and Flash. He left his buddies to cruise alone looking for a woman to talk to in the growing crowd. Instead, Spyder ran into three Bullet flyers and stopped to say hello. As he did, two female Aussies walked by and both smiled at Spyder. He quickly excused himself from the Bullets and walked directly up to the women.

"Good evening," he said confidently. "Are you ladies enjoying yourselves?"

"We just arrived, but it looks to have some potential," replied the strawberry blonde in a thick Australian accent.

Spyder was a sucker for both Aussie and British accents. "I've only been in your country for ten hours, and I'm already ready to move." He smiled at the blonde. Both women laughed politely.

"That's what all the American sailors say after months at sea," remarked the brunette.

"Is that so? You've met some of my shipmates, have you?"

"A few months back, I believe," replied the brunette teasingly. "*USS Constellation*, correct?" she added.

"Very good," Spyder remarked sincerely. "A decent ship manned by adequate sailors and capable officers, but nothing compared to *Ranger*. In fact, I—"

"Hey, Spyder, who are your friends?" interrupted Flash, appearing out of nowhere.

"Umm," stammered Spyder.

The strawberry blonde extended her hand to Flash. "My name is Wendy Roberts. Nice to meet you."

"Bill Akins," said Flash as he shook Wendy's hand.

Spyder reached out to shake the brunette's hand and introduced himself. The brunette, Jules Whittier, reciprocated with a friendly smile.

The two officers and late-twenty-something Aussies talked for the next fifteen minutes. Spyder and Wendy gravitated to each other, as did Flash and Jules. A mutual attraction permeated the air, or so the flyers thought. The pairs walked through the buffet line and then sat down at an empty table to eat and chat. The women handled their liquor well, as neither showed any impairment after several Glenlivet Scotches.

After dinner, the couples began dancing to a Beatles' medley. After several songs, they took a break. When they got to the table, Wendy turned to Spyder and thanked him for the dances and conversation. Jules had similar comments for Flash. The two women pecked the respective officers on their cheeks and disappeared into the large and now lively crowd. The Wolfie flyers turned and stared blankly at one another. *Not again!* Images of Tomcat ball flooded Spyder's mind.

After a few awkward seconds, Flash finally spoke. "What happened? I thought we were doing well. Did you fart? I thought I smelled something."

"No! Must've been your dorky dancing, dude."

"Yeah, real funny," replied Flash disappointedly.

The now dejected aviators started walking through the throng of bodies looking for a squadronmate or two to commiserate with. But everywhere they turned, the aviators saw Wolfies hooked up in pairs or groups of women. Flash elbowed Spyder, "Look. Even Pea's hooked up," gesturing to the dance floor. Pea, a VF-1 RIO, was far from the most attractive officer in the navy. If he were a woman, people would have said he fell out of the ugly tree and hit each branch on the way down. But now he was having the last laugh, slow dancing with an attractive brunette.

In a matter of minutes, Spyder and Flash went from having fun and believing they were scoring with a couple of hot Aussies to feeling like outcasts among their peers. The flyers walked around the ballroom one last time. They spied Pole and Drum dancing with two forty-something-year-old women. Slum, Mustang, and Scout were with two Bullets and a group of women.

Flash decided to change venues and head to the admin to see if his chances were any better up there. "I can't believe our first night in Australia is going like this," he said. "Everyone but us is going to get lucky. I still have nightmares about Tomcat Ball. Hell, even Pea's gonna get laid."

"Doubtful. Don't give up yet. It's only eleven o'clock. Besides, we can always hit the bars if it doesn't improve."

"All right. Catch up with me in the admin," replied Flash.

Spyder felt self-conscious being alone that late in the evening, so he left the hotel to grab some fresh air. The young officer walked several blocks and happily took in the fact that he finally was back on land. Suddenly nausea set in, as the twelve-pack of beer and multiple cocktails from the party, booze cruise, and pub crawl caught up with him. He staggered back to the Hilton, making it to his room just as he got sick. After brushing his teeth and tearing off his uniform, the pilot was fast asleep two minutes after his head hit the pillow.

∗ ∗ ∗

Spyder spent the next two days with his squadronmates walking around Perth and Freemantle by day and attending squadron parties and checking out the local bar scene at night. At the Wolfpack party two evenings later, several hundred guests packed the small ballroom. At the peak of the evening, there was barely enough room to walk through the crowd. It felt like being back at the Miramar O'Club on a Wednesday night. Spyder finished dancing with an Aussie he had met minutes before and made his way through the crowd to the bar to get a drink. When the pilot stepped in line, he felt a tap on the shoulder and turned.

"Still enjoying our country?" asked a woman with a very friendly smile.

"Oh, hey, yeah, you bet." It took a moment for Spyder to recognize Wendy from the air wing party the first night of liberty. "How about you? Did you have a good time the other night?" The Aussie looked stunning in a tight, black cocktail dress that showed off her long, trim legs. The dark dress contrasted well with her strawberry blonde shoulder-length hair.

"Yes, both Jules and I had fun. There were a lot of people to meet."

Spyder decided to act coy. He imagined Wendy probably expected him to buy her a drink, but he did not offer. He was about to excuse himself to get his beer and return to the other Aussie woman, when Wendy unexpectedly offered to get him a drink. *In that case…*

Spyder and Wendy spent the rest of the evening talking, dancing, and drinking. Jules was there as well and spent her time talking to various aviators. Spyder pegged her as the type who craved attention and wanted to flirt with as many guys as possible. Flash spoke with her for a few minutes but decided she was up to her usual game and politely excused himself to return to another local he had been scoping out.

When hotel security finally shut down the party at midnight, over a hundred people remained. The party spilled out onto Mill Street, as many groups and pairs walked toward a line of bars down the road from the hotel. Spyder took Wendy to a balcony overlooking the Swan River. The flyer doubted their chemistry. He was extremely attracted to her, but wasn't sure how she felt about him.

As they stood together admiring the view, Spyder noticed goose bumps on Wendy's arms. He placed his arm around her and glanced down and kissed her. He felt her body tense for a moment, and then relax. They kissed a couple more times. Wendy was the first to speak. "I'm sorry. It's just that, well, I ended a three-year relationship some time ago and haven't even wanted to think of men. Umm, I am really attracted to you, and, well…"

Spyder took her in his arms again and kissed her passionately. She responded by wrapping her arms around his neck and pressing herself against him. After kissing for several minutes, Wendy stepped back and asked Spyder if he wanted to go back to her house. He didn't need to be asked twice.

Wendy and Spyder spent the next four nights and three days side by side. She showed him all of the popular tourist sites around Perth and drove him to the edge of the western outback for a picnic lunch. They spent one day driving along a coastline that reminded the California native of Big Sur. Spyder petted koala bears in the wild, gagged trying to eat a vegemite sandwich, walked along the Sunset Coast, hiked through the Perth Hills, and met several of Wendy's friends. He fixed a plumbing leak in her bathroom, and she reciprocated with a homemade candlelit dinner. Wendy was far from the ice princess who had blown him off the first night he met her.

The couple spent their last day together lounging in bed in the morning and then aimlessly walking in the city and strolling through the Perth Zoo. They went back to Wendy's house for a final dinner and lay on the floor next to a fire. For the first time in his short navy career, Spyder did not want to go back aboard ship. Sure, most liberty ports ended prematurely as far as he was concerned, but it was not too difficult to give up the alcohol binge and return to flying. This time Spyder felt as if he were really going to miss Wendy. He wanted to stay in Perth with this woman and continue their intimacy. But both Wendy and Spyder knew he really didn't have a choice. He reluctantly gathered his jacket and a few items he had bought earlier in the day and drove to the pier. They stayed in the car until the very last moment. Wendy tearfully said good-bye and gave him one last passionate kiss and hug. He turned, waved good-bye, and boarded the last liberty launch back to *Ranger*.

The ship was moored a half-mile from shore, and liberty expired at 2300 in the evening, yet there still were hundreds of people, mostly women, lining the pier waving to the American sailors. Almost as many women stood on the pier waving good-bye in Perth that July evening as had been back in February when the ship departed San Diego.

23

"Sounds like it's really true what they say about Australia," remarked Rolls. "We're supposed to go there when we leave for WestPac in June. I sure hope we make it."

"You and six thousand of your shipmates," responded Spyder.

He and Rolls finished their game of pool. The two officers walked back to their table and sat down to finish out the evening.

"Commander, you were around during Tailhook, right? I mean you—"

"Ohh," interrupted the former aviator. "You don't really want to get me started on that, do you? I was beginning to wind down."

"Well, if you really don't want to, that's fine. I thought it was around the time you've been talking about."

"OK, OK. But let's get a couple of fresh beers first." Spyder walked over to the bar and bought two more Coors Lights. The bartender struck up a short conversation, and Spyder found out her brother was a navy pilot stationed in Florida. He paid for the beers and walked back to join Rolls.

After sitting back down, Spyder took a swig from his beer bottle and began the infamous tale of Tailhook.

24

Tailhook. Mention of the name would forever rankle naval aviators who were on active duty in 1991, the year the annual fun-in-the-sun frolic in Vegas ran head on into a confluence of events that brought national news and disgrace to the navy. Prior to the ignominious events of the '91 convention, "Hook" was promoted among the fraternity of navy and marine corps carrier aviators as the annual pilgrimage to the desert to renew bonds, rekindle friendships, and gain insight into developmental weapons systems. In reality, the primary motivation for most of the two thousand-odd Tailhookers who attended the yearly convention was the four consecutive days of booze, sun, gambling, and lighting one's hair on fire in Sin City.

* * *

"We understand you were at Tailhook last year," stated the Naval Investigative Service agent dressed in starched white shirt and JC Penney's dark suit.

"Yes?" responded Spyder curiously. He was in the process of checking into his new assignment in the Pentagon after thirty days of leave and was surprised the NIS had tracked him down in the labyrinth of the world's largest office building before the pilot could even find his own office. Tailhook was starting to make the back pages of a few newspapers and had not yet blown up to the major conflagration it did later that year.

"Mind if I ask you some standard questions?" inquired the agent in official government-speak. Must be hard to sound normal while carrying a badge and Glock 22.

"Sure."

The agent escorted Spyder to a vacant office, opened his briefcase, and took out a short stack of papers. He sat down behind a small desk and had Spyder sit in a chair across from him. The office featured typical austere government minimalism: metal desk, two metal chairs, empty bookcase, and requisite photo of President George Bush, Sr.

For the next twenty minutes, Spyder was subjected to a series of inane questions about the gauntlet and various unnamed and unidentified officers. Spyder's favorite questions surrounded a composite sketch of a short-haired Caucasian male in his mid- to late twenties.

"Do you recognize this man?" asked the agent.

"Sure," replied Spyder.

The agent straightened up and became visibly excited. "You do? Was he part of the gauntlet that night?"

"Yep, he and about two thousand other guys," added Spyder sarcastically. "You do realize that you just showed me a rough sketch of a nondescript young white guy with short hair. That covers about eighty percent of naval aviators. You're gonna have to do a lot better than that."

The agent slouched back in his chair. "Yeah, I know. I gotta do this, ya know?" pleaded the investigator.

All in all, Spyder was impressed that the NIS had even found him, considering he had moved across country and was checking into an entirely new command. The line of questioning, however, seemed ridiculous.

"Do you know Cowboy? Was he there?"

"Sure, about four of them, but I didn't see any of them during the night in question."

"No, Sir, I did not see anyone pinch, fondle or assault any women."

"No, I did not observe any criminal behavior."

"No, I did not see any senior officers attempt to stop the drinking."

"For God's sake, it was Tailhook!"

"Yes, I would agree to take a polygraph."

After ten more minutes of going through the motions, both the agent and Spyder had had enough.

"Thank you, Lieutenant. I'll type up my notes and send them off to headquarters."

"OK."

"Thanks again for your time. I don't think you'll hear any more from us."

The NIS agent could not have been more wrong. Over the next six months, Spyder had to endure three additional longwinded, exhaustive interviews that resembled interrogations. And he hadn't even been in the hotel during the night in question.

✳ ✳ ✳

Tailhook's roots dated back to Rosarito Beach, Baja, Mexico, in 1956 when a small group of San Diego-based naval aviators hit the beaches of Baja for well-deserved R&R. The pilots wanted to reestablish friendships with peers they had trained and schooled with but had not seen for months or years due to the military's method of reassigning personnel across the globe every three years. The first meeting had fewer than forty participants. Two years later the group incorporated in the State of California as a nonprofit organization with the official purpose of fostering, developing, and studying carrier aviation. The real reason was to drink beer, party, and tell "There I was…thought I was gonna die" sea stories. The annual convention shifted to Las Vegas in 1963.

Membership was open to anyone who had made an arrested carrier landing. Ninety-nine percent of the activities for the organization involved the annual convention. Undoubtedly, there was some charter or legal document filed with the State of California probably stating the mission of the not-for-profit organization was to foster and promote the interests of navy carrier aviation, but mention "Tailhook" or "Hook" to any naval aviator, and images of Vegas, booze, gambling, and partying surely flooded the mind.

Tailhook was set up similar to other civilian conventions. There were official symposiums, lectures, and an entire exhibition hall filled with defense contractor products and paraphernalia. The "Hookers" spent hours browsing the booths speaking with the product reps, and examining the new products, such as helmet-mounted gunsights, flight simulators, and state-of-the-art cockpit ergonomic developments. The defense contractors were no dummies, as they brought along as many young, attractive spokesgals as the Big Three displayed at the Detroit Auto Show. These beauties passed out free t-shirts, ball caps, beer cozies, and other convention stuff. By the end of the day, attendees could accumulate up to two large bags stuffed full of swag.

During the weekend, several professional development symposiums were offered, allowing interactions with senior navy officers and an admirals' panel featuring the Undersecretary for Air Warfare and several deputies and aviation admirals scattered throughout the fleet. The Chief of Naval Operations, the navy's most senior officer, was in attendance, though not a member of that particular admirals' panel. The Secretary of the Navy also shared in some of the festivities during the conference. The expo included a Saturday evening banquet and several breakfast and luncheon events.

The Tailhook Association reserved a block of twenty-two "hospitality" suites on the third floor of the hotel adjacent to the pool patio deck. The rooms were located on a mezzanine level, with decks spilling out onto a larger patio that eventually led to the main hotel pool. During the day, the scene resembled a concrete-beach pool party. During the evening the rooms and hallway were packed with revelers. Each suite was rented by an individual squadron that brought their own geedunk, including squadron drinking banner, zappers, t-shirts, mugs, and other fraternity-type merchandise. Most of the squadrons maintained a theme or sponsored an event for the duration of the convention. At a bare minimum, a squadron brought a large-screen television and played cruise or det videos edited to rock 'n' roll music. Some of the larger squadrons had more elaborate setups.

Marine RF-4 squadron VMFP-3, the Rhinos, offered a particularly memorable drinking dispenser. Several years prior to 1991, the squadron had concocted a drink dispenser where a large gray dildo drooped from a four-foot plastic rhino. In order to tap the keg, one pulled the penis and watched rum punch flow from the phallic apparatus into a cup.

Other squadrons had similar, but not as raunchy, drinking devices. Most of the squadrons sponsored a different drink. Attendees could start at one end of the hallway and make their way from room to room, grabbing a free cocktail at each one. Frozen margaritas, daiquiris, Mai Tais, beer, White Russians, Cubi Point Specials, and numerous other drinks filled the suites and hallway floors. Squadrons tried to outdo one another with entertainment in the rooms, including strippers, dancers, and even prostitutes performing lurid sex acts on each other and select audience members.

Additional extracurricular activities were plentiful—an adult Disneyland cornucopia. One of the most popular was leg shaving, with an emphasis on bikini cuts. VF-33 opened their bathroom to any young lady who desired such personalized salon treatment. Women stripped to their thongs or panties and were shaved by a throng of aviators vying to satisfy. Lines of women formed for this crowd pleaser, with men spilling into the hall cheering on the amateur cosmetologists.

VAW-110, the E2-C Hawkeye RAG, proved tough competition to VF-33. The Hawkeye drivers and NFOs even went so far as to advertise unabashedly with a large banner that read "Free Leg Shaves!" posted on the sliding glass doors of their suite in plain sight of large portions of the pool patio. The Firebird flyers assembled their "booth" adjacent to the sliding glass doors so it was clearly visible from the patio. The "booth" consisted of a chair for the woman being shaved, an equipment table, and stools for the two male naval officers who performed the act. The elaborate ritual included the use of hot towels and baby oil, as well as massaging of the woman's legs and feet. Aviators lined up to lick the women's legs to ensure the highest "quality control."

By 2200 on both Friday and Saturday nights, the rooms, suites, and hallways were absolutely jam-packed. The area was as crowded, hot, sweaty, and charged as a stadium mosh pit. By midnight, the carpeting throughout the floor was soaked in slopped beer and alcohol. Hundreds of people spilled out onto the patios, cheering and talking loudly. Thumping music blared from boom boxes, stereos, and televisions. Though frenetic and highly charged, Hook '91 was no different than previous years.

By Saturday night Spyder, Tank, Scooter, and Flash needed a well-deserved break from the excesses of the event. Between the four JOs, they had experienced eleven previous conventions. After two straight nights and days of partying and drinking, their bodies and livers demanded a respite. It hadn't been that long ago the four had been partying to excess in the Philippines and Hawaii on the way home from the Gulf War. Rather than subject themselves to yet another night and early morning in the Hilton, the flyers decided to grab a sushi dinner across town.

After dinner, the squadronmates took a taxi back to the Riviera, where they gambled until well past midnight. They then hit the rack without ever stepping foot in the Hilton on the fateful Saturday night. It was a capricious, yet fortuitous, decision that quite possibly saved the four Wolfies' military careers.

* * *

While the VF-1 aviators gambled and slept at the Riviera Hotel, their aviator peers made history, or more appropriately, infamy. The acts should not have been a surprise to the navy brass. It was well known throughout the naval aviation community that the annual Tailhook convention included excessive drinking, general rowdiness, and wild parties. The Navy Inspector General had filed written reports from previous years, which included detailed descriptions of debauchery, explicit sex acts, and wanton property damage.

In the weeks and months that followed Hook '91, national headlines included the Clarence Thomas-Anita Hill sexual discrimination scandal and the William Kennedy Smith-Patricia Bowman rape trial. American women were taking on the "old boys" network like never before. The time was ripe for challenging male-dominated institutions. After the testimony of Anita Hill at the Clarence Thomas confirmation hearings, sexual harassment became, almost overnight, the quintessential women's issue of the early '90s. On that fateful Saturday night, amidst claims by several female attendees, including an admiral's aide, of groping and sexual assault, the Tailhook gauntlet thrust the navy into this national debate and helped keep the torch of political discourse and *Washington Post* headlines brightly lit for many scintillating months.

Congress held up each navy officer's promotion for close to a year while NIS and DoD's Inspector General completed their comprehensive investigations and submitted their reports on the Hill. Dozens of officers who were not even at Tailhook were subsumed into the political witch-hunt. Multiple senior officers' careers were destroyed merely because they attended Tailhook '91. The majority of these men had absolutely no involvement whatsoever with the infamous gauntlet. Curiously, the CNO and Secretary of the Navy survived the storm and continued serving out their respective tours, even though they were at the Hilton that Saturday evening and had ample information from previous conventions on what regularly transpired.

25

"So did you know any of the guys who got busted at Hook?" inquired Rolls.

"A few, including a former skipper," Spyder replied.

"What happened?"

One of my former skippers was the CO of the F-14 RAG at Miramar during Tomcat Follies when several students forgot to take down a prop used for one of the Friday evening skits at the club. The next morning, a group of retirees sat enjoying their Saturday morning eggs Benedict and mimosas when the staff opened the drapes and revealed a view of the club's courtyard where the follies had taken place the night before. Not surprisingly, several wives were aghast when they saw a large sheet of plywood painted with a vulgar poem that expressed the sentiment of the military officers during that time period. The poem went, "Hickory dickory dock...Pat Schroeder can suck my cock!'"

"Who's that?" asked Rolls.

"She was a congresswoman from Colorado who was pressing the women-in-the-military agenda—a real wave maker," said Spyder emphatically.

As the words left his mouth, he caught a glimpse of a young woman entering the club. When the figure was ten feet away, Spyder recognized Drone. She had changed out of her flight suit into denim jeans and a turtleneck sweater that simultaneously showed off and hid her figure.

"Hey, Drone. Whatcha doing back here?" asked Rolls. He was almost as surprised as Spyder at seeing his squadronmate suddenly reappear.

Drone ignored Rolls and went straight after Spyder. "You really don't get it, do ya, Sir? It's not the same male-bonding, testosterone-driven navy anymore!"

"Oh boy," replied Spyder sarcastically. "I thought you had to get up early in the morning."

"Suffice to say I couldn't sleep."

Spyder sighed heavily. "You know, Drone, we were about to get out of here and head back to the Q for a pizza. You're more than welcome to head back with us." Spyder hoped Drone would decline his invitation.

"Sure, Commander. I have no problem joining you as long as Rolls is there with us. Can't imagine anyone thinking anything inappropriate would occur," she added in a voice thick with sarcasm.

"Very well. Let's do it." Spyder ignored the insouciance from the junior officer.

Spyder walked over to the bar and handed the bartender his debit card. She smiled provocatively at him and made sure to touch his hand while handing him the receipt. He smiled awkwardly at her as he stuffed the receipt into his back pocket.

The three officers then left the club and headed across the street to Spyder's room. The suite contained a small lounge area with kitchenette. Spyder reached into the fridge and grabbed three beers. He twisted off the tops and handed the first to Drone.

"Sorry, Lieutenant. No wine coolers."

Drone smiled mockingly. "What, no glass?" she fired back. Spyder couldn't tell if she was joking. He gave up trying to figure her out and simply pointed to a clean glass on the counter. Drone declined.

"So you picked a great time to rejoin the party," replied Spyder. "Rolls and I just finished talking about Tailhook."

Drone sat upright, obviously warring with herself again. She bit her lower lip and looked as if she was about to jump out of her seat. Instead, she took in a deep breath. "I don't believe ya. How do ya know the exact buttons ta push?"

"A talent my ex-wife swore I acquired over the years. Maybe one of the reasons we're no longer married." He smiled. "Well, that and four WestPac deployments."

"Ah, of course! Divorced. What a surprise," Drone remarked with seething sarcasm.

Spyder merely raised an eyebrow and smirked. Drone glared back silently but with an expression that shouted, "Men!"

Spyder refused to comment, so Drone continued.

"I spent an entire semester studyin' the social context that led up to Tailhook and the subsequent fallout on the navy," she stated. "It was—"

"Don't tell me," interrupted Spyder. "Women's studies class?"

"Yeah, and...?"

"And, I don't know. Maybe it's just a bunch of femists with an agenda and an axe to grind conjuring up a political firestorm."

"It's feminists, not femists," growled Drone. If she had regained her composure a few seconds ago, her temper had returned and was now in the danger zone.

"You men can have your ol' boys' networks for generations and generations," she said, her voice rising. "Yet whenever a woman desires to level the playin' field, she's labeled a feminist bitch." Drone pursed her lips.

"Are you done?" he asked calmly. The senior aviator did not give her a chance to respond. "All I was saying is that not every man is sexist and not every naval aviator is a pig."

Spyder sat back and grabbed his beer, waiting for Drone to reply. He sneaked a glance at Rolls. Spyder caught Rolls' eyes and ascertained immediately the JO wanted no part of this clash.

Rolls' opinions and political views lay somewhere halfway on the spectrum between Spyder's and Drone's. Rolls' generation was some years away from Spyder's, but he thought that some of the senior officer's points remained valid. Besides, he had no interest being out front flying the women-in-the-military banner, so he sat on the periphery and watched the fireworks while casually sipping his beer.

"Is that so?" asked Drone, trying to ignore the fact that her squadronmate wasn't stepping up in her defense. She was well practiced in this debate. "Then why are there so few female TACAIR pilots and only a handful of women submariners?"

"Lieutenant, it's hard enough putting women on small boys. You know how much the navy is spending retrofitting subs to accommodate women? Ever been on an LA-class nuke? There are a total of three heads for the hundred forty crewmen. The total living area is the size of a three-bedroom house. You can't sneeze without spittin' on eight sailors."

"I know, I know," interrupted Drone. She had heard it all before. "And you can't integrate the races in the navy, and you can't have women serve in combat," she added.

Spyder looked at Rolls. "Jump in here any time."

"No way, Sir. You've got the lead."

"Suit yourself," he remarked. *Wuss!*

Spyder turned back at Drone. "Do you know how long it took to fully racially integrate the navy? How many race riots there were during the transition? Admiral Zumwalt stayed the course over a nearly mutinous navy for years. Years! As for women in combat, clearly females are as competent to fly airplanes and drive ships as males. In fact—"

"Wow, how mature of you to concede that point," Drone interrupted.

Spyder again ignored her commentary and continued to press his point to this young, fiery female officer. "The issue has never been whether women have the physical ability or stamina. It's the cultural impact on the forces. I'm not blaming women because it's probably more to do with the male ego. But how do you think your presence has affected the ready room of your squadron?"

"Positive, of course," responded Drone vigorously. "I'd like to think that I have different perspectives and life experiences that are assets. And most importantly, I'm a darn good ECMO."

"I'm sure you are," said Spyder sincerely. "But how do you think your addition to the wardroom has been for the wives of the married officers? Do you think any of the single officers would like to date you? How about the enlisted, especially the eighteen- and nineteen-year-old testosterone-laden airmen straight out of high school or Kansas farms? Think they might have some frisky thoughts on day one hundred one of cruise while in the middle of the Indian Ocean without a port call in site?"

"That's not my problem. Y'all know about the navy's rules on fraternization. They have to keep their peckers in their pants."

Rolls about spit out the gulp of beer he was drinking. He had not heard any word close to an expletive, other than "ay-yarse" come out of Drone's mouth in the year he had known her. Spyder remained unfazed.

"I don't give a darn what they think, as long as they don't act," added Drone.

"But that's not the point," replied Spyder. He had been down this path before, too. "Do you think it will affect their work? Will Third Class Petty Officer Schmukatelli spend more time fixing or prepping your aircraft than Rolls' here because you're an attractive woman and he's an ugly mutt?" Spyder winked at Rolls.

"That wouldn't be right," pleaded Drone.

"Who cares what's right?" Spyder shot back. "An eighteen-year-old's libido is a heck of a lot stronger than his intellectual discipline."

Spyder continued, not pausing to allow Drone to respond. "And what about Rolls here? What if he or one of the other male JOs in your squadron wanted to date you? Think that might affect the way they treat you as compared to the other JOs? Think it might affect the overall integrity and good discipline of the unit? This isn't Ford making F-150s here. We are the US Navy. Our mission is to break things and kill people."

Now that the clash had transformed into an intellectual debate, Drone was more at ease. Nothing Spyder argued surprised her. She chose her words carefully.

"Commander, why should I have to care about Rolls' libido or any other male in the squadron? Women work shoulder to shoulder with their male counterparts in offices and businesses in every city in the country. Been working out pretty well for the past fifty years, right?"

"But they don't work ten thousand miles from home isolated on a seven hundred-foot ship or a thousand-foot carrier working twelve- to eighteen-hour days performing highly stressful jobs, possibly fighting a war, with ninety percent of the crew under the age of twenty-five."

Drone thought about that comment for a few seconds. "Yeah, what about cops? Male cops have female partners in every PD force in the nation. There's plenty of stress, and they get shot at too."

"Excellent point, Lieutenant. Let's talk a minute about police officers. Do you know law enforcement has the highest infidelity and divorce rate of any job there is? And Officer Jones gets to go home to the missus every night."

Rolls chuckled. Drone turned and glared at him. He avoided her stare by looking down.

"Let me cut to the chase," stated Spyder matter-of-factly. "Rolls, ever fart loudly when a woman was present?"

"No," answered the young flyer uncomfortably.

"Ever yell 'Zit!' when a squadronmate walked into the ready room in the morning with a prominent pimple on his face and women were around?"

"No."

"Ever go barhopping in Pattaya or Hong Kong on liberty and end up at a tug 'n' scrub massage with your female squadronmates?"

"Uh, what's a tug and scrub?" asked the neophyte aviator.

"Seriously?" Spyder shook his head disappointedly. "OK, how about a legitimate massage parlor?"

"Nope."

"Ever sit around the Q while on det drinking beer and playing cards while badmouthing women with your female squadronmates? Or how about barhopping, trying to pick up chicks? Do that with your female squadronmates?"

"Well, actually, yeah, kind of. We'll all go out to the bar, and sometimes the gals help us decide who to try to pick up," remarked Rolls.

"See?" interjected Drone. "Sometimes we help 'em out. And let me ask Rolls a couple of questions while we're at it." She turned to her peer. "Ever talk to one of your female squadronmates about girlfriend problems in order to get advice from another woman?"

"Sure. I even asked you about Catherine a couple weeks ago." Rolls started enjoying being part of the debate.

"Ever have a female squadronmate act as a designated driver for a bunch of guys too drunk to drive home on a Friday or Saturday night?"

"Yes."

Drone turned back to Spyder. "So what's your point, Commander? Because the guys have to act somewhat civilized because there are female officers around is a bad thing? Women in the military have helped raise the conduct of the forces and left the Neanderthals behind." Drone crossed her arms in front of her.

The senior officer responded strongly. "You don't get it, Lieutenant. There's a reason we're called the 'armed forces' and not the 'benevolent forces.' Our military is designed to forcefully defend our country and project power, not to be designated drivers or fraternity and sorority pin pals.

"And yes, naval aviators are sometimes Neanderthals, tough on each other. It's part of the life, like drinking coffee to stay awake on oh-two hundred alerts or getting drunk on liberty. It helps cut the tension and release some of the pressure. So does coarse humor at the most inappropriate times—juvenile behavior to offset the immense responsibility we have dropping bombs, launching missiles, and killing people. So the navy ready room has transitioned from a locker room to the Oprah Winfrey show. Great! I cannot see how suppressing natural male tendencies and testosterone serves us."

Drone and Spyder continued to stare at one another.

Spyder continued, "Getting back to the bigger question. How about on cruise? You know, six to eight months away from home. Boredom and routine for weeks on end, stressful combat. People act differently, especially young, active, single sailors amped on hormones.

"Three years ago I was assigned to the *USS Shiloh* for two-week reserve duty. *Shiloh* was the first Aegis-class cruiser to be integrated. I had dinner with the XO and Chaplain. Turns out within the first six months, they had to reassign three female enlisted and one female officer out of a total of fifteen enlisted and seven officers due to inappropriate conduct and two pregnancies—two pregnancies on a combatant warship in the first six months! And yes, Drone, they also reassigned several male enlisted as well," said Spyder to appease the junior officer.

"For the nightly movie, two of the female officers showed up in flannel pajamas and bunny slippers. Bunny slippers! It's a goddamn warship! Officers are supposed to lead by example. You tell me what kind of message that sends to the other officers and enlisted on that ship?"

Spyder's use of expletives set Drone back. For the first time all evening, she failed to come up with a retort.

"Are you serious, or are you making that up?" asked Rolls.

"I'm dead serious," replied Spyder. He turned back to Drone. She didn't know what to say as her eyebrows furled and she chewed on her lower lip.

"And let's not beat around the bush. This isn't Starbucks. The US Navy is a killing machine. Our mission is to put bombs and missiles on target, on time."

Spyder paused to read Drone's face. "See?" He pointed at her. "I can see you don't like my choice of words."

"No. No, I don't. It's not all we do. Combat constitutes, what, a fraction of our time? What about humanitarian missions, power projection, keeping sea lanes open, and such?"

"Good academic answer," replied Spyder. He refused to relinquish the soapbox. "But when we are asked to fire missiles or drop bombs, we don't hesitate because we're a military organization through and through. We are trained for every combat contingency. And I will tell you the broad inclusion of women into the warfighting communities has softened our stance and made us less lethal."

"Huh?" Drone shook her head. She instantly turned flushed-on-the-neck mad. "Are ya sayin' because women are part of the organization the navy has become weaker? You have to be kidding."

"No, I'm not. I've seen it with my own eyes—lived it. The navy is becoming less tolerant of warriors and killers and more accommodating of managers and bureaucrats. We're rapidly becoming IBM. You've heard the latest navy mantra. The buzzwords include 'best business practices,' 'managerial transformation,' and 'integrated efficiency.' This business— this corporate BS—has replaced time-proven concepts such as 'lethality,' 'shock and awe,' and 'blitzkrieg.'"

"Commander, don't ya think you're exaggerating a bit?" asked Rolls.

"No, I don't." Spyder insisted.

Drone jumped back into the debate. "It's been fifteen years since the navy placed women in tactical jets. We've been deploying on ships and in ready rooms for well over a decade. I'd say it's been worked out by now. I think your concerns are no longer valid. And like I said before, the navy's a whole lot better because of us."

"Maybe, maybe not; time will tell. But let's wait for the next social cataclysm. Let's see how this openly gay serving thing works out."

"Oh, geez," groaned Drone. "Don't tell me you're homophobic and sexist." She cocked her head and raised her eyebrows.

"Don't go there, Lieutenant," shot back Spyder. "I'm merely saying maybe there are limits to the full integration of elite combat units. You've read the news and seen the reports. What about the record number of rapes and blatant harassment currently happening within all of the military branches these days?"

"You're proving my point for me," responded Drone triumphantly. "There are still a whole lot of men that still don't get it. Treating women like objects or inferior subordinates."

"Well, that I can agree with you," replied Spyder. I certainly agree that there is no place in the navy—or society—for harassment or abuse."

Having debating hotly for the past ten minutes, both Drone and Spyder paused and breathed deeply. Rolls took the opportunity to interject. "You know, I don't think either of you is going to change the other's mind, even if we stay here all night."

"Agreed," both Drone and Spyder stated at the same time. They both chuckled, having agreed on something for the first time all evening.

"Okay," said Spyder. "Since neither of us is going to win this debate, let's call it a night." He reached for his beer. But before taking a gulp, he remembered something. "You know, I've been telling you both too many stories of my flying days over the past several hours, but I never got back to telling you about Otter and Austin. Let me finish the evening with their story."

26

VF-1 returned from the Gulf War in June 1991, well after the ceasefire and long past America's victory parades. The squadron was able to participate in a highly impressive twenty-nine-plane low-altitude fly-over of downtown San Diego commemorating the triumphant return to Miramar. Over three hundred family members, friends, and west coast aviators assembled on the tarmac in front of Base Ops to greet the war heroes following their landing.

It was Spyder's second cruise, so he was senior enough to make the fly-off and enjoy the postlanding party. Once the SoCal June gloom burned off, the typical, sensationally sunny summer day emerged. When they finally landed as dash-3 of the fourth division of Tomcats, Spyder and Flash jumped out of their jet and were immediately handed a twenty-four-ounce "oil can" Foster's Lager from Otter. The junior officer had left the boat in Hawaii and flown to Miramar on a commercial flight in order to coordinate the squadron's homecoming. He also offered each aviator a red rose to give to a spouse or family member.

Spyder saw his mother came running from the crowd to greet him. She had an Uncle Sam red-white-and-blue hat and waved an American flag enthusiastically. He greeted her warmly, and they hugged for close to a minute. His mother seemed to pinch him, almost as if verifying it wasn't a dream. Six months of the most anxious fears imaginable by a parent were finally released. She wept with joy and relief upon seeing her only son safely home from war. Spyder's father and sister caught up a minute later and joined in the homecoming celebration.

After partying to live music and copious amounts of alcohol and food under a temporary tent assembled on the tarmac, Spyder hugged Flash,

Tank, and a few other squadronmates good-bye and went with his parents back to his house. He found his Vette waiting for him in the garage, completely washed and waxed. Spyder's parents and sister stayed for another day and helped Spyder start the decompression and acclimation period of adjusting from frenzied ship-borne to calm shore-based life.

The entire squadron enjoyed thirty days of leave. A skeleton crew remained in the hangar, though there was no flying. The squadron's jets were scavenged for essential electronic warfare systems, and several of the newer jets were transferred to squadrons due to deploy within the next few months. Within three weeks of returning to Miramar, VF-1 was down to seven jets, compared to the eleven aircraft it possessed on cruise.

While on cruise, Spyder and his squadronmates had spent their spare time discussing what they would do upon their return. As an unattached bachelor, Spyder decided to live large and had pre-purchased a Harley Davidson Fat Boy while in the Philippines. He was scheduled to pick up his baby in Las Vegas the second week of his leave period. Nothing sounded better that hitting the road alone. After being in such close quarters for so long, Spyder was looking forward to wide-open roads and spaces. Southwest Airlines got him to Vegas, where he promptly stepped off the airplane and took a cab straight to the Harley dealer.

The plan was perfectly simple. From the dealership, he began riding east. Over the next twelve days, he rode through Colorado, up into Montana, back south through Colorado, to Utah, then west into Arizona and through California to San Diego. He camped, hiked, and put over four thousand miles on the Hog experiencing some of the most picturesque roads in the Land of the Free. Although he kept mostly to himself, Spyder met people, made friends, and became reacquainted with the country he missed so much while on deployment and fighting in the war.

Upon return from a truly memorable trip and month-long leave period, Spyder was willing and able to return to the squadron. He was re-energized and ready to climb back into the cockpit. Tragically, it wasn't long before bad things started to happen. Two months after coming home from cruise, "Stinky," a VA-155 pilot stationed at Whidbey Island, was on the flight schedule for a routine low-level day hop with a brand-new bombardier/navigator. It was the BN's first flight in VA-155. Stinky, a war hero who had distinguished himself through meritorious flying during the Gulf War, was one of the top sticks in VA-155. More importantly, he was well liked by everyone in the air wing and had a Gap-ad family with a gorgeous wife and three beautiful kids under the age of five.

Stinky was the lead of a two-plane Intruder section flying VR 1350, a scenic low-level through the Cascade Mountains in Washington State. At a turn-point over Keechelus Lake, one of the Three Sisters lakes near Cle Elum, Stinky took full advantage to do some flat-hatting. He performed a tuck-under turn. Tragically, he miscalculated the maneuver. A fisherman on the lake reported seeing the Intruder flip on its back while its nose dropped down directly toward the water. The jet's left wing-tip caught the surface, and the 25-ton flying machine cart wheeled into the water. The plane vanished below the surface in seconds. Two days later navy divers found Stinky's body still strapped in the cockpit. It took four more days before the nugget BN's body was discovered submerged nearly a mile from the crash site.

Flying navy jets was dangerous enough when everything worked correctly and people followed the rules. The margin between life and death, especially around the boat, was often razor thin. When good people did foolish things, it only seemed to cheapen life. Maybe it was simply a defense mechanism, but military pilots often criticized colleagues who died in aircraft due to "pilot error." It made it easier for an aviator to climb back into the cockpit the next day after a deadly mishap snuffed out a good friend if the pilot thought he was invincible and would never be so careless. After hearing the news about Stinky, Spyder didn't feel that way. He was simply sickened to lose a highly respected and esteemed shipmate.

Three months after VA-155's mishap, CDR John "Bug" Roach, CVW-2's former CAG LSO and a living legend among naval aviators, was flying a routine training mission off the California coast. A true icon who waved jets from the LSO platform on the flight deck in snakeskin cowboy boots, Bug was a commander with an eccentric handlebar mustache. His

'72 Hog chopper with suicide chrome handlebars matched his personality and his facial hair. On a sunny October day in 1991, Bug was flying an A-4F for VF-126 in an ordinary 2v2 ACM mission against two Tomcats. Following the ACM engagements, and while returning to Miramar from the Warning Area, Bug's motor suddenly shut down. He was at altitude and had plenty of time to run through the NATOPS EPs and attempt to restart the engine several times. When it became apparent that he was not going to get the single-engine aircraft's motor back, he slowed the jet, leveled the wings, and prepared to eject. His last words reportedly were, "What a lousy day! Well, I gotta get out of here. I'll see you guys."

At five thousand feet while straight and level at a hundred sixty knots, he pulled the handle. His wingman was less than a quarter mile away and saw the canopy separate, the ejection seat fire, and Bug ride the rails to a safe distance from the gliding aircraft. Terribly, after seat separation, Bug's parachute tangled, and he failed to get a good chute. He tumbled downward sickeningly and hit the water at close to one hundred miles per hour, with the impact breaking his back. A navy forensic pathologist surmised the pilot survived the ejection but died soon after hitting the ocean. Bug had lived through three separate Vietnam combat tours off three separate carriers, survived combat missions and another tour off the *USS Ranger* in the Gulf War, and amassed over five thousand flight hours and a thousand carrier landings. And although he died doing what he was born to do, it was difficult to accept that the living legend was killed flying a routine training mission over Southern California due to a mechanical malfunction.

* * *

Post-war tragedy continued to be a part of Spyder's world when only a month after Bug's death, another disastrous incident occurred. CVW-2 was back in Nevada for its predeployment Fallon det. It was during the second week that a junior VF-2 aircrew mismanaged their fuel and flamed out less than 20 nm from the airfield. Although the aircrew ejected safely, a perfectly good jet was sacrificed to the Nevada desert. Less than six months after CVW-2 had returned home from the Gulf War, the air wing had lost three jets with three fatalities, leaving the remainder of the officers and enlisted reeling from the tragic crashes. It was not supposed to happen that way, with several aviators surviving a combat deployment only to die in peacetime at home. It was in this context that Otter and Austin manned up for a routine 2v2 night AIC mission over the Dixie Valley in Fallon. They were dash-2 on Trapper's and Oxford's wing.

"Otter" was a prince of a guy who was well liked by everyone, squadronmates as well as air wing bubbas. He was about as moderate as they come—controlled and balanced, confident but not egotistical. His squadronmates described him as "a solid stick, but not a water-walker." Handsome and athletic, he exhibited a dry sense of humor that revealed itself at the most surprising times. It was difficult to find anything wrong with the Indiana-raised pilot who maintained his Midwestern values down to the core.

On the other hand, "Austin" was outrageous. He loved drinking, WWF wrestling, and everything about living in San Diego. Though raised in Michigan, the RIO embraced San Diego with open arms. If there was a party, Austin knew about it and often was the first to arrive and last to leave. He balanced a carefree wild side with street and book smarts. Austin was gregarious and was often the center of attention at the bar or squadron party.

Otter and Austin were quite a team. Otter's quiet self-assuredness was offset by Austin's brash behavior. The two aviators were always bickering in a good-natured, sibling sort of way that was a constant source of entertainment to squadronmates. They were both second-cruise lieutenants who had been paired together for the Fallon det, and were highly proficient, well-qualified aviators and Gulf War combat veterans.

The mission began uneventfully with the brief, man-up, preflight, and takeoff all proceeding on schedule. The moonless night offered up a scattered layer of clouds at twenty-five thousand feet. The desert looked black as charcoal.

The two Wolfpack Tomcats took off eight minutes prior to the Bullet section and were to orbit near the EW range and await contact by the E-2C controller. At altitude, the lights of Fallon sparkled in the distance like fireflies. The Wolfies were headed northeast at seventeen thousand five hundred feet over the Clan Alpine Mountains when Oxford, the RIO in the lead aircraft, checked in with the airborne controller. A Hawkeye NFO reported the Bullet flight was "wheels in the well" and climbing.

Oxford was ready for a routine training flight. He and Trapper had come off two days of intense strike planning and a trip to Reno the night before that left them both with minimal sleep. Oxford, like every other pilot, was used to working on little sleep, and the pure oxygen refreshed his lungs and cleared his brain.

The Wolfie section continued northeast and was now ten miles from Chicago, code word for the orbit point. The Bullet flight checked in with Sunking and Trapper was about to kiss off Otter and Austin so they could take a tactical position when Otter came up on the front seat radio.

"Trapper, Otter. I've got a problem. We're, uh…stand by." Otter's voice held its usual professional tone. Both Oxford and Trapper instinctively looked to the right and saw Wolf 112 begin descending and falling off to the starboard side of their aircraft. The Tomcat's anticollision lights were operating, but it was too dark to see anything else. Trapper waited another couple of seconds before calling.

"Otter, Trapper. Say again."

Silence.

Trapper started a gentle right turn. "Otter, I'm coming right at twenty-two thousand feet."

As both Trapper and Oxford searched the sky below, they suddenly saw a tremendous explosion that filled the night sky from below.

"No, no, no!" groaned Oxford over the ICS.

"Holy shit!" exclaimed Trapper.

As if to reassure himself what he had just witnessed was not real, Trapper broadcast several more times on the front seat radio for Otter.

Silence.

Finally, Oxford came up on the intercept frequency.

"Sunking, Wolf One-Zero-Seven. We're declaring an emergency and requesting you initiate a SAR." Both Oxford and Trapper were praying their squadronmates and good friends had ejected and were at that very moment floating down in the cool night air onto a mountaintop or ridge.

"Say again?" replied the AIC controller. Since the two fighters were flying a tactical formation, only the lead aircraft had its transponder on, which meant the E-2C was only tracking Wolf 107. If the Hawkeye NFO's crew had changed radar modes and concentrated their scan pattern, it might have been possible for them to break out the second aircraft, but they had no reason to do so for this mission. Oxford's call caught the Hawkeye crew completely off guard. They scrambled into action. As the AIC controller in the rear communicated with Oxford, the right-seat co-pilot was on the radio with Fallon tower requesting they launch the alert SAR helo.

Trapper jumped onto the intercept frequency with Sunking. "We think our wingman went down. He reported a problem over the radio and then we saw a large fireball below us. We're orbiting that location now. Request you mark our position and initiate a SAR now!"

"Roger, Wolf One-Zero-Seven. We're in contact with Fallon tower and Salt Lake Center. Can you see any chutes?"

"Negative. It's too dark."

"Roger that. Stand by for further instructions."

Oxford and Trapper craned their necks and squinted, desperately trying to see any sign of a parachute. But all they could see was a black void, with a light orange and yellow glow from the Tomcat's remnants burning on the ground. From twenty thousand feet the smoldering area on the ground was merely the size of a silver dollar. But even the small flicker created a glimmer in an otherwise pitch-black night. The two flyers kept scanning the area around the fire, hoping and praying for any sign of their squadronmates.

In addition to communicating with Fallon tower and Salt Lake Center for the SAR effort, Sunking tuned 243.0, the universal emergency guard frequency, into one of their many radios in hopes of hearing Otter or Austin come up on their PRC-90 survival radios.

Silence.

Thrasher 40, the SH-3 alert helo, came up on frequency and checked in with Sunking. The helicopter pilots utilized night-vision goggles to navigate the hazardous terrain and avoid towers and other obstacles on the ground.

"Wolf One-Zero-Seven, Bullet Two-Zero-Four. Anything we can do? We're at angels one five, fifteen miles west your posit."

"Uh, I don't think so," replied Oxford. "We've got thirteen-two of gas, so we can hang around for quite some time."

"Roger that. We'll depart to the west and stay clear."

"Bullet Two-Zero-Four, Sunking. Fly heading two-niner-zero. Once overhead Los Angeles, clear to run AIC as long as you stay well clear of Wolf One-Zero-Seven's posit."

"Roger, King. But I think we'll RTB as soon as we've burned some gas." The Bullet aircrew did not feel like flying, knowing their sister squadron had lost a jet and possibly an aircrew.

"Trapper, think they made it out?" Oxford asked over the ICS.

"God, I hope so." Trapper descended down to fifteen thousand feet to see if they could get a better look at the crash site. He dared not go any lower, as they were flying near the Clan Alpine Mountains and Stillwater Range with mountain peaks upward of thirteen thousand feet.

"Wolf One-Zero-Seven, Sunking. We have taken SAR command. We're overhead angels two four. We've got the SAR helo inbound with an ETA of twenty-five minutes. Both Fallon and Reno hospitals have been notified and are standing by. Fallon Base Ops is looking for your CO and Safety Officer. State your fuel state and intentions."

"Oxford, let's stay out here as long as we can. I don't feel like leaving Otter and Austin out here alone."

"Damn straight."

The flyers were arcing around the sky at seventeen thousand feet and two hundred thirty knots in a fighter plane, unable to do a damn thing to help determine the status of their squadronmates, yet neither Trapper nor Oxford was going to leave their wingmen.

"King, Wolf One-Zero-Seven. We're gonna continue orbiting till the SAR is complete or we hit bingo fuel. State is twelve-point-five."

"Roger that."

Oxford and Trapper didn't say much to one another as they continued to fly circles over the location where Wolf 112 went down. The fire died out, leaving the area shrouded in blackness. The flyers looked down into the void, hoping, wishing, and praying Otter and Austin would come up on guard at any moment. Maybe the Wolfie crew lost their radios in the ejection. Every few minutes Sunking made a call in the blind on 243.0 querying Otter, Austin, and Wolf 112.

Silence.

"Trapper, this is the skipper on tac. How you and Oxford doing?" The CO had arrived at Base Ops and was now radioing Wolf 107 on the Wolfpack tactical frequency.

"Hey, Skipper. We're fine, but we haven't heard anything from either Otter or Austin. It doesn't look good," responded Trapper in a solemn tone.

"Did you see any chutes?"

"No, but it was really dark."

"What's your fuel state?"

"We're at eleven-point-five, Skipper."

"OK. I want you to stay out there until you hear something or reach two-point-five. Then RTB. I understand the SAR helo with a medical officer is about fifteen minutes out. And Trapper, what happened? Did Otter or Austin say anything?"

"They were having a problem, and then we saw them in a descending turn. A few seconds later we saw a huge fireball."

"Jesus." Pop paused. "OK. I'm monitoring this frequency and guard. Let me know when you hear something."

"Roger that, Skipper."

"Trapper, why don't you and Oxford say a prayer while you're out there."

"Yes, Sir," interjected Oxford. "Already did."

The SAR helo reached the crash site but was unable to land due to the steep terrain. The crew hovered all around the site and flashed its light beam over the area. There was no sign of Otter or Austin.

After fifteen more minutes of searching without results, Trapper and Oxford returned to Fallon, upset they had no idea why their wingman had crashed. They felt helpless to assist in the SAR effort.

At daybreak, two HH-60 Seahawk helicopters from Strike Rescue squadron HCS-5 flew to a rocky ledge fifteen hundred feet below the crash site. The helos were able to offload eight personnel, including the base Operations Officer, Safety Officer, VF-1 CO, and crash and salvage experts. After dropping off the SAR personnel, the helicopters scoured the mountainside and proximity for hours, searching from low altitude in the event Otter or Austin had ejected at a high altitude and had been blown from the crash site.

Snow covered the January mountainside. The SAR group took its time and was extremely cautious hiking up the side of the mountain. Sadly, there wasn't much to see, and there was absolutely no sign of life. Nothing on or in the ground resembled an aircraft. A large, black pit, approximately fifty feet in diameter and four or five feet deep, stood out from the snow pack. The area looked as if a small meteorite had crashed and scorched the earth. Since the site was above the tree line, no trees or brush were present. The largest identifiable piece of Wolf 112 was a six-inch tube of steel, apparently part of the nosewheel strut. It took some digging and about three hours, but the SAR group was able to identify parts of two ejection seats. Apparently, neither Otter nor Austin had attempted to eject—either that or the ejection process failed.

Complete JAG and mishap investigations were initiated concurrently. Exhaustive recovery efforts complicated by the snow and mountainside were completed, and, surprisingly, a sizeable amount of the aircraft was brought back to a hangar at Fallon and painstakingly examined by forensic engineers and safety investigators.

After many weeks of meticulous research and study, the Mishap Investigation Review Board determined the cause of the crash. Even though the largest piece of the aircraft recovered was the size of a hammer, the investigators concluded that there had been an electrical short in a wire bundle near the combined side hydraulic pump. The bundle chafed, and a wire fused itself to the pump, arcing electricity and super-heating the hydraulic fluid to over a thousand degrees. The entire hydraulic system suffered catastrophic failure, leaving Austin and Otter without any flight controls. Unlike Willy's and Bucket's mishap in the RAG, Wolf 112 underwent an immediate loss of all hydraulic pressure. The MIR board was unable to theorize why neither pilot ejected. From what the investigators had been able to recover from the jet, the ejection systems appeared to have been assembled and maintained properly. The answer was a mystery that Otter and Austin took to their graves.

27

"So they never found out why Otter and Austin failed to eject?" asked Rolls.

"Nope. I have my own theory," replied Spyder. "Remember the VF-2 jet I told you about, the one that flamed out twenty miles from the airfield?"

"Yeah."

"Well, I think both Otter and Austin had that mishap in the back of their minds. It's night, pitch dark, and without warning, they suffer a catastrophic hydraulic failure, but they don't know that. They see a bunch of cockpit lights, and they start working the emergency. Austin breaks out his EPs from his leg zippered pocket, and Otter looks down at the annunciator panel. Otter thinks he's still controlling the jet, but it doesn't have any hydraulics, so it starts flying where it wants to go—down.

"They don't realize what's happening because there's no horizon. There's just enough 'g' on the jet to make them think they're flying level. And there might be some vertigo induced by Austin reaching down and pulling out his EPs and Otter trying to reset and read annunciator lights down on his right side. By the time Austin breaks out the pocket checklist and finds the right page and Otter confirms and resets the lights, it's all over, and they hit the mountain."

"Whoa, it could've happened that quick," said Rolls morosely as Drone sat by quietly, listening.

Spyder continued in a mellow tone, "What I think is they were too focused on saving the jet instead of saving themselves. Their first reaction was to work the emergency and solve the problem instead of flying the airplane and getting out if they didn't have time. It was a damn shame to lose two great warriors—two great friends."

Spyder's eyes watered. He brushed them with the back of his hand and then quickly reached for his beer. Rolls grabbed his as well.

"Seems like you knew quite a few naval aviators who died, Spyder," Drone said sympathetically.

"Yeah, guess I did. I knew Otter and Austin the best because I cruised with them and lived with them for close to two years. Thank God neither was married or had kids."

"How 'bout during the war? Did you lose anyone in the Gulf War?" asked Rolls. "You didn't tell us any sea stories about your time in the Gulf."

Spyder took a moment before answering Rolls' question. He looked intently at both junior officers and then spoke solemnly. "You've both heard all about it before from instructors in the RAG and at Fallon and from probably a few senior squadronmates of yours. Hell, today you've got a whole new generation of flyers who flew over Iraq and Afghanistan, though there wasn't much air defense in either of those campaigns."

Spyder paused before continuing. For the first time all evening, he struggled to articulate his thoughts.

"War isn't something you start talking about over a few beers in an officers' club bar. God willing you'll never have to experience sustained combat. But if you do, you'll realize that you can never accurately explain the feelings that course through your veins every hour of every one of those days. The profound anxiety, excitement, boredom, and raw emotion—being pulled in ten different sensational directions at once—are difficult to convey to anyone who hasn't been there. There's the juxtaposition of feeling invincible and elated after a successful strike against a target heavily defended by a sky full of SAMs and AAA, and then landing back onboard the ship less than an hour later and feeling distraught finding out an A-6 whose pilot and BN lived two hatches down from your stateroom never made it back. After the war, the crew's remains were shipped home in a shoe-box sized canister. No, it's not something you talk about over a few beers."

The lines on Spyder's face slowly diminished. He swallowed hard, pushing down the twinge that arose from his gut when talking about Austin and Otter and the brief insight into the Gulf War. He stood up and lifted his beer bottle once again. "Here's to all of the naval aviators who made the ultimate sacrifice so the rest of us can continue living free."

Rolls lifted his bottle and toasted with Spyder and Drone.

"You know," Spyder went on, "it's not going to be too much longer before we won't have to toast fallen aviators. Sure, there'll always be pilots, but much of our combat missions are being transferred to UAVs. Just look how many air force and naval aviation squadrons and platforms have been slashed in the past couple of decades."

"It's not that bad, Sir," remarked Drone.

"Really? Do you know that two years ago, for the first time in its history, the air force purchased more unmanned aircraft than manned? Today, the navy has operational pilotless helicopters based out of Coronado and is completing testing of the X-47B UAV bomber."

"I didn't," responded Drone. "But I think we'll have to discuss that another time. I'm tired and really am getting up early in the morning. I'm glad I came back to try to straighten y'all out, but I really have to go now." Drone stood up.

Rolls looked at his watch and stood up too. "Yeah, I'm going to turn in, too."

Spyder rose from the couch. "OK. It has been a long night. It's also been a pleasure to meet you both. But before you go, please give me the honor of making one final toast."

"Sure," responded Rolls. The three officers met in the center of the room and raised their beers.

"Here's to the navy in the twenty-first century. Two hundred and thirty-four years of tradition unimpeded by progress! It's your navy now—good luck and god speed," he added, toasting the next generation of naval aviators.

"Thank you, Spyder. And good luck to you too," said Rolls. The officers *clanked* their bottles together.

"Likewise," added Drone. And for the first time all evening, Spyder noticed Drone smiling.

The two junior officers shook Spyder's hand and left the suite. Spyder closed the door behind them, walked into the bedroom, and started to undress. He pulled out his wallet from his pants pocket, and the o'club receipt fell to the floor. While picking it up, the former fighter pilot noticed handwriting on the back. He looked closer and saw that the bartender had written down her name and telephone number. *Ha!* he thought while grinning widely. *I'll be damned!*

THE END

AUTHOR'S NOTE

Spyder is a fictitious person, an amalgamation of numerous naval aviators of his time. The cockpit scenes, although based on factual events, are similarly fictitious, as I was not in each aircraft described in this story. Names of actual officers in VF-1 and other squadrons have been altered to protect the confidences and privacies of these individuals. The only aviator whose name was not altered was CDR John "Bug" Roach, a true icon and larger-than-life legend of naval aviation taken from us prematurely.

Today, women in the US military serve in virtually every combat role, including in fighter and bomber aircraft, submarines, and infantry units. It's only a matter of time before women will be serving shoulder to shoulder with their male counterparts in SEAL and other Spec-Ops units. But integration of women into the formerly male-only units did not occur without trials and tribulations. Assimilation of women, and now openly gay and lesbian personnel, into an effective fighting force reflecting not only our society as a whole but the "best of the best" of our elite combat units takes time.

Just as there is much more to a pilot than hand-eye coordination and Hollywood-style bravado in multimillion-dollar F-14 Tomcat fighter jets, there is much more to the story of naval aviation than mere cockpit exploits. The true story transcends thirty thousand feet. Sending a man, and now woman, ten thousand miles from friends, family, and home for six to nine months at a time to fight a war or simply enforce the peace—a pilot who lives on a daily basis within inches or seconds of a horrific, fiery death in a uniquely compressed, harsh environment—leads to extraordinary experiences. It is not that naval aviators are made differently—just that their combined experiences produce a story of devotion, commitment, and passion, of both *esprit de corps* and human spirit.

With much humility, I have tried in these pages to capture the story of naval aviation as it existed during the last generation of male-only airborne warriors at the end of the twentieth century.

GLOSSARY

- **AAA:** or "Triple-A," anti-aircraft artillery.
- **AIC:** Air Intercept & Control. Flight missions to identify and track unknown and hostile aircraft.
- **AOM:** All Officers' Meeting.
- **AOR:** Area of Responsibility.
- **ARTCC:** Air Route Traffic Control Center. FAA's official designation for controllers who control instrument-filled aircraft flying between airports.
- **ASF:** Advanced Strike Fighter. The proposed next generation joint fighter/attack aircraft platform.
- **Bandit:** Confirmed enemy aircraft. See also *bogey*.
- **Basket leave:** Term describing the process of submitting a leave chit to one's command that would not be processed unless the individual was injured on leave. If the leave was uneventful, then the leave chit would be torn up.
- **BCD:** Birth Control Devices. Colloquial term for the military-issue large, black-framed eyeglasses.
- **BDA:** Bomb Damage Assessment. Former term to describe postattack analysis of a target to determine extent of damage inflicted by weapons on target—much better to analyze than body counts.
- **BN:** Bombadier/Navigator; NFO crewmember in an A-6 Intruder.
- **Boat:** The navy's slang term for an aircraft carrier. Destroyers, frigates, etc. are known as ships or "small boys," while the flattops are colloquially called "boats."
- **Bogey:** Unidentified aircraft, possible bandit.
- **Boola-Boola:** Term for a direct hit of a target involving a missile exercise. See also *splash*.
- **Blackshoe:** A Surface Warfare (SWO) or submarine officer ("Bubblehead").

- Bolter: Verb used to describe when an aircraft attempts to land but misses the cable and climbs back into the patter.
- Brownshoe: A naval aviator. Aviation officers are authorized to wear brown shoes with their khaki uniforms, whereas Surface Warfare and Submarine officers wear black shoes.
- Bulkhead: Wall.
- Buster: Expedite or fly as fast as possible.
- CACO: Casualty Assistance Calls Officer. Officer charged with personally informing next of kin of a fallen service member's death; provides continued support to the grieving family and funeral assistance.
- Case I, II or III recovery: Classification of carrier approach: Case I is visual overhead; Case II is a modification between Case I and III where aircraft begins in marshal stack and instrument approach until under the cloud ceiling, where pilot proceeds with Case I visual recovery; Case III is an instrument approach all the way to calling the ball at three-quarter of a mile behind the ship (always used at night).
- CAVU: Clear And Visibility Unlimited. Shortened term to describe idyllic flying weather.
- COD: Carrier Onboard Delivery. Twin-engine, turbo-prop carrier aircraft used to deliver parts and passengers.
- COMFITWINGPAC: Commander Fighter Wing Pacific, the commander of all fighter aircraft in the Pacific theater for admin control of air assets ashore.
- CONUS: Continental, or contiguous, United States.
- CQ: Carrier Qualifications. The required number of carrier landings to certify a pilot or keep him current to land on an aircraft carrier.
- CVW-2: Carrier Air Wing TWO.
- Diode: An electronic device that restricts current flow chiefly to one direction. Also used colloquially as a derogatory term to describe a military officer who puts his career and self-interests ahead of his peers and squadronmates.
- Dirty-shirt: One of the officer cafeterias onboard ship used for less formal dining.
- ECMO: Electronic Counter-Measures Officer; NFO crewman in an EA-6B Prowler.

- EP: Emergency Procedures.
- Fitrep: Fitness Report. Written annual report of an officer's performance.
- Fleet: Navy active-duty forces, including the ships, submarines, and aircraft squadrons that comprise the sea service's forces.
- FNG: Fucked-Up New Guy. Slang term to describe a brand-new member of a squadron, applicable to both enlisted personnel and officers. See also *nugget*.
- FOD: Foreign Object Damage. Generalized term to describe ingestion of any foreign object into a jet engine, thus resulting in damage or destruction of the engine.
- FOD Walkdown: Line of personnel who walk along flight deck or airfield tarmac searching for and removing FOD items.
- Geedunk: Candy or paraphernalia.
- HUD: Heads Up Display. Digital instrumentation electronically superimposed on a portion of the windscreen so the pilot can view target and flight information without having to look inside the cockpit.
- Huffer: GTC-85. Ground equipment utilizing a small turbine that forces air into a jet intake to start tactical jets that do not have internal auxiliary power units (APUs).
- ICS: Intercommunications System. F-14 intercom system that allows the pilot and the RIO to speak to one another without anyone outside of the aircraft hearing their communications.
- IFF: Identification Friend or Foe. Transponder used to identify military aircraft.
- INS: Inertial Navigation System. Computer navigation system that pre-dated GPS (Global Positioning Satellites).
- JAGMAN: Judge Advocate General Manual. The military's preliminary legal investigation.
- JP-5: Jet fuel utilized by the US Navy with a higher flash point than JP-4 utilized by the US Air Force.
- JTF-EX: Joint Task Force Exercise. One of several exercises that a carrier battle group participates in as part of its workup cycle.
- LSO: Landing Signal Officer.
- METOC: meteorological conditions aka "the weather."
- MFD: Multi-Function Display. Cockpit digital display.

- MO: Maintenance Officer.
- Mother: Colloquial term for the aircraft carrier.
- MWR: Morale, Welfare, and Recreation.
- NAS: North Arabian Sea.
- NFO: Naval Flight Officer. Officer who flies in a multi-seat navy aircraft.
- Nugget: Less derogatory term than FNG to describe a brand new member of a squadron, primarily used in the aviation community to describe new aircrew.
- NATOPS: Naval Aviation Training and Operational Procedures Standardization. Comprehensive program to standardize training and operating procedures to minimize mishaps. May colloquially refer to multi-volume aircraft operating manual and emergency procedures checklist.
- nm: Nautical miles.
- NORDO: No Radio.
- OBE: Overcome By Events. No longer needed or necessary.
- OPSEC: Operational Security. Maintaining military operational information as classified.
- Pinkie Recovery: Night carrier landing scheduled for sunset, thus allowing for radiant sunlight.
- PLAAF: People's Liberation Army Air Force.
- PLAT: Pilot Landing Aid Television. Television camera embedded within the carrier deck that shows the final segment of an aircraft's landing aboard ship.
- PLEAD: Pacific missile range's primary frequency.
- Pollywog: Derogatory term to describe an uninitiated sailor, one who has not completed Wog Day, or Crossing the Line (equator) ceremony.
- Popeye: Flight in instrument meteorological conditions (IMC).
- POM: Pre-Overseas Movement. Acronym used to describe a navy ship leaving port to commence transit.
- P-way: Passageway.
- Q: Abbreviation for BOQ, or Bachelor Officers Quarters. Changed to Combined Bachelor Housing due to budget cuts and consolidation of military berthing facilities.
- RAG: Replacement Air Group. Former name for the generalized squadron that trained new aircrew on a specific type of aircraft. Currently called FRS, or Fleet

Replacement Squadron.

- Red Flag: Annual large-scale, comprehensive US Air Force joint exercise held at Nellis AFB outside of Las Vegas, NV.
- Reefer: Refrigerator.
- RIO: Radar Intercept Officer; NFO crewman in an F-14 Tomcat.
- ROE: Rules of Engagement.
- Roll'em: Nightly movie shown by a squadron in the ready room while on cruise. Origins date back to 16 mm reel projector.
- RON: Remain Over Night. A flight or mission that has a night layover at an airbase or carrier.
- RTB: Return to Base.
- SAM: Surface-to-air missile.
- SDO: Squadron Duty Officer.
- Shellback: Term used for a sailor who has completed Wog Day, or Crossing the Line (equator) ceremony.
- Small Boy: Colloquial term for navy ship such as frigate, destroyer, or cruiser.
- SNAFU: Situation Normal All Fucked Up.
- SWO: Surface Warfare Officer, or Blackshoe; alternatively, Senior Watch Officer.
- Splash: Shoot down a bogey or bandit, as in "Splash two bandits."
- SSC: Surface Surveillance & Control. Flight missions to identify and track unknown or hostile ships and other surface contacts.
- TACAIR: Navy tactical air, or another word for fighter or attack aircraft.
- TACAN: Tactical Air Navigation. A navigation aid utilized by military aircraft.
- TCS: Television Camera System installed on the nose of an F-14 that provides aircrew with magnified target identification capability.
- TOT: Time on target.
- Vampire: Inbound enemy missile.
- Wog: Short for Pollywog.
- Zappers: Squadron stickers.
- Zorching: Fighter pilot term for flying fast—cross between "zooming" and "scorching."

Made in the USA
Middletown, DE
22 May 2017